CHASING KASSIE

THE SERENITY MOUNTAIN SERIES

Cassie Colton

Mystic Marigold
PUBLISHING

Published by Mystic Marigold Publishing, LLC
Williamsburg, VA
Cassiecoltonbooks.com

Cover by Scott Carpenter
Edited by Rebecca Hodgkins

ISBN 979-8-9886007-3-2
ISBN 979-8-9886007-2-5 (epub)

To Mr. C,
Without your encouragement and unwavering support, this book would not have been possible. Thank you for enduring the late nights, the traveling, and the chatter sessions on the people that live in my head.

I love you.

Chapter One

Kaitlyn Reynolds anxiously waited for the plane to land. Matthew Cartwright expertly piloted the private jet on the last leg of the four-and-a-half-hour flight from Seattle to Corpus Christi. He assured her that the freak snowstorm wouldn't be a problem and that she should get some sleep, but that hadn't happened. With every bump from turbulence, her anxiety ratcheted up another level. Since it was a private aircraft, she didn't have to contend with crying babies, but at least that would have been a distraction. Alone, all she could think about was her little girl that she had been separated from when they escaped from dirty FBI agents at the hospital where she worked. Kaitlyn worried about Emma's safety and if running away without telling the retired SEAL team that had helped her for the last four months was the right call.

Kaitlyn's mind wandered to Chase. The ex-Navy doctor that had provided her a safe haven on Serenity Mountain. If she were truly honest, it was the man she had unexpectedly fallen completely in love with. Swallowing the lump in her throat, she wondered if Chase had found the note she left explaining why she had to leave the mountain.

The landing had been smooth and easy as she looked out the window for any sign of her daughter. When it rolled to a stop on the tarmac, Kaitlyn could see a tall Latino man holding Emma. The jet-black hair cut high and tight, and the black sunglasses made him look ominous. His muscular arms bulged from the blue short-sleeved T-shirt that stretched across his chest, making her four-year-old daughter appear like a tiny doll in his arms. Stepping off the plane steps and seeing a smiling Emma frantically waving her hands, Kaitlyn dropped her bags and took off at a run.

"Emma!" Kassie cried as the little girl jumped into her arms, and they clung to each other. Relief flooded her at finally being able to hold her daughter again after being separated for months to keep James Stanton from finding them. She turned her attention to the man patiently waiting while she reunited with her child.

"Good afternoon, Kaitlyn. From here on out, you're only known as Kassie for your protection. The less people who know that you're using your sister's identity the better. I'm Agent Julio Hernandez. Your sister and I worked very closely together, and we'll do everything possible to keep you safe."

Swallowing the lump in her throat, all she could do was nod her head. Still doubting whether she had made the right decision, she smiled warily.

Matthew Cartwright, a coworker of Julio's and former lover of her deceased sister, caught up with their bags as they walked to an awaiting car and headed to a secure location. Emma refused to let go of her mama. It wasn't until Kassie coaxed her with dinner and a warm bath that she relaxed. Within moments of her mama softly singing "Somewhere Out There", the child's eyes grew heavy and finally closed. Sighing, she tucked Em in and cracked the door as she went to find Agent Hernandez.

"Your sister left us a ton of evidence in the head of Em's doll. I found the location of the USB after going through a packet of information we found at one of the warehouses we raided from an anonymous tip. We can use it to shut the bastard down, and he'll go to jail. Our sources say that he's the one that ordered the hit on you. We still don't know why. Matthew's combing through the encrypted files. James plans to have you declared dead on Monday, along with Emma. Your parents left the shares of their company to you and your sister. Upon Kaitlyn's death, her shares went to Kassie. If Kassie is declared dead, he'll get your shares and your sister's. Kassie's will left everything to Phillip and Phillip's assets were left to his father. I'm sure they had no intention of letting Kassie live after they got what they wanted from her. It'll give him enough shares in the company for a takeover. He can use it as a cover to do anything from exporting drugs to sex trafficking."

Knowing her sister didn't have a choice because her husband had threatened her life and Emma's if she didn't cooperate, Kassie's stomach still dropped at the thought that James and Phillip Stanton had targeted her family by committing such horrible crimes. The fact that her twin had kept this knowledge to herself for so long when they had shared everything, made her feel like sometimes she hadn't known her sister at all. At least Derrick "Leo" Strong's retired SEAL team had started working behind the scenes and were able to save some of the victims they discovered while investigating Stanton. She vowed when this was finished, she would continue to try and find the people that had been hurt by the Stantons.

"What about Leo's team? Did you find out anything about them?" Her voice was strained as she waited for his response. Doubt was creeping in. The team had kept them safe, including getting Emma the medical care she needed. She started having second thoughts about not confronting Chase and Leo after overhearing their phone conversation. No. It wouldn't have mattered; Agent Hernandez already had a team en route to remove Emma, and she was her first priority.

"No, they're decorated Navy SEALs, except for two. Dr. Chase Winters and Dr. Michael Harris. The team rescued both doctors during a medical Goodwill expedition. I don't know their interest in you, so we'll err on the side of caution."

"My best friend, Catherine. Her husband was on the team but was killed in action. She called in a favor to the team. I overheard a conversation with their leader, Leo. He said I was a mission."

"All I can say is that I learned a mission went bad, and the team's op is completely blacked out. I'm unwilling to take any chances when dealing with dirty FBI agents and blank records."

He shifted sideways so he faced Kassie. His voice deepened. "You're going to have to continue to stay as Kassie to put this man behind bars and keep custody of Emma. Even if he goes to jail, he has enough dirty judges in his pocket to get custody. Are you willing to continue with this? If not, I'll ensure you and Emma disappear forever, and Matthew and I'll be the only ones that know where you are."

Surprised that an FBI agent would go to such lengths and was willing to break the law for her, she tried to calm the butterflies in her stomach. Something didn't feel right. Kassie shook her head. "Why would you do this? It's a lie. I know why I'm doing this. My parents and sister died because of this man. Kassie entrusted Emma to me, the outside world may see her as my niece, but in all the ways that counts, she's mine. I'm not losing my daughter. If anyone found out, you could lose your job, and go to jail."

Shifting uncomfortably on the couch, he hung his head. "I spent a lot of time with your sister. We grew close." Glancing back to the room where Matthew was working and back to her, his voice lowered. "When everything went down, Matthew and I were in shock. When you became Kassie, we weren't sure. You were assigned to a different team for protection while I was gathering evidence. Matthew took it hard. He loved your sister very much. He supplied the identities to the agent assigned to protect you so that you couldn't be tracked when Agent Thompson suspected the other two agents were dirty. Matthew hoped you'd reach out to him. He's been desperately searching for you, and wishing you were your sister."

She leaned in and softly whispered, "You were in love with my sister. That's why you're willing to do this. Does Matthew know?"

A slight smile appeared as he shook his head. "She only had eyes for him. I was like a brother to her. There's no need to dredge it all up. Kassie didn't deserve this. Neither do you. I can't change what happened, but I can damn well make sure you and Emma stay alive."

Patting her hand, he vowed, "Come Monday morning, you're going to shock the world as Kassie Stanton. Finally, there will be enough evidence to put that bastard behind bars. Besides operating a drug ring and being involved in sex trafficking, we have evidence that he orchestrated your parent's fatal car accident. With your help, we'll also be able to prosecute him for raping your sister. Then you can have your life back."

She closed her eyes, blinking back the tears that threatened to fall. She remembered Chase's arms wrapped around her as they sat in the window seat in his bedroom and watched the sun rise above the mountains. Longing assailed her when she thought about the first time he made love to her. The last few weeks before she ran, he had made her happy, and for the first time, she could imagine a life without being on the run. A life with him on the mountain. But most of all, he made her feel safe and loved. She squeezed her eyes shut, trying to wipe the memory from her brain.

It's not like he'd be coming to Texas…

Julio was determined that Kassie and Emma would be reunited with the only family they had left. The following day, he planned a short surprise. Joe and Maddie, Kassie's godparents, had helped her parents raise her and her twin. When her parents were killed in an automobile accident, Joe and

Maddie loved the girls as if they were their own. They had a long-standing pizza date every Thursday night. Still trying to determine if they were being watched, Julio thought it would be best to stick to the same routine. Since they were good friends of the owner, it wouldn't be unusual if the two of them followed him into the kitchen to sample a new menu.

When they opened the door to the cramped little office and saw Kassie holding Emma, they couldn't contain their joy. They held on to their girls for dear life. An hour flew by quickly, but Julio assured the family they would see each other again after Kassie made her appearance at the courthouse. The couple agreed to meet them there the following Monday.

Chapter Two

On the opposite end of town, Chase threw back the scotch Leo handed him in one gulp. The whole team had all assembled. Saint, Michael, Taco, and Shadow wasted no time coming to help him find Kassie.

Saint started the meeting. "I've gone through Stanton's emails, bank statements, and texts, and there's nothing concerning Kassie or Emma. His focus seems to be on Monday."

"Maybe we're looking at this the wrong way. We've spent months with absolutely nothing happening. You talk to her sister's ex-lover, and the next thing you know, Kassie disappears." Michael glanced at his phone as a text came through, and his facial expression was grim as he angrily sent a text back.

Leo sat up. "He couldn't be in two places at once. There had to be two teams. One for Kassie and one for Emma. How'd they know where either of them were?"

Saint stood, went to his computer, and started typing on the keyboard. "Son of a bitch!"

All conversation stopped as they waited for him to continue. "Matthew Cartwright flew for the Navy. He was shot down on a mission, injured his leg, and got a medical discharge. He returned home and went back to school. He's a highly sought-after hacker. The military uses him, but he's been helping Hernandez find Kassie. He sent a code through our encrypted video call. I also spoke with Julio Hernandez from the FBI. Both calls were traced. That's how they found them. I can only assume once he found out who we were, he waited for a call from Leo and found Em. I'm impressed with his skills but pissed that after finding out who we were, he still took those girls. I don't like helping and working with sneaky bastards."

Leo ignored his friend's rant. "She disappeared the next day. How would he know when she wasn't at the cabin?"

"There had to be a message. Did she tell him where she was at?" Saint asked his teammate, still clicking the keys.

Chase shook his head. "No, I sat through the entire call."

Leo sat forward in his chair. "Tell us everything that was said."

Scratching the overgrown scruff along his jaw, Chase recalled the phone call. "As soon as Kassie appeared on the screen, he told her he knew she was really Kaitlyn. She admitted it and told him she had good reason to pretend to be her sister. Admitting he knew it was because of Emma, he asked if she was okay. Toward the end of the conversation, he told her to be ready. Even Kaitlyn—Kassie—was confused by the comment, but we now know that's because he was tracking the call."

Saint continued to click away on his keyboard. "What did you say to Hernandez when you spoke with him?"

"I never spoke with him. He didn't call the next day, or we left to go into town before he called." Taking another sip of his drink, he wracked his brain, going over every detail.

"He did, Doc. There was a phone call, and the conversation lasted seven minutes."

Chase's mouth firmed in a straight line. "When?"

"The next morning after Kassie spoke with Cartwright. Someone answered the call at the cabin. If it wasn't you, it had to be Kassie."

"No." He shook his head. "I don't think she would talk to Hernandez alone. She doesn't know who to trust in the FBI."

Derek interrupted him. "If she thought it was Catherine or Emma calling, she's seen you pick up the calls enough, she'd know how."

Chase stood. "Where do we find Cartwright or Hernandez?"

"Coordinates sent to your phones now. How do we want to do this?" Saint was already packing his computer, ready to move as soon as Leo gave the orders.

"Saint, Taco, and Michael, head to Cartwright. Watch him. Something tells me that he and Hernandez coordinated their efforts. This was a military tactic. They were trained and organized. Doc, Shadow, and I will have a chat with Hernandez. Let's go, gentlemen. We've got two ladies waiting on us."

Julio assigned the team to the safe house four miles away and stopped at the deli by his condo for a sandwich, unaware that Leo, Shadow, and Chase had already broken into his home and were going through files they found in a locked box. There were financial sheets, names, dates, and logs of women, men, and children sold by Stanton. There were also pictures of drug drops and a list of dates when Phillip Jr. had used his wife to cement deals. Kassie amassed more information than she had let on. The amount of information was staggering and detailed.

The only thing Julio couldn't figure out, according to his notes, was why Stanton would want her dead. He had previously controlled Kassie through his son, Phillip. There was also a complete accounting from Kassie of the Stanton men raping her to get her pregnant. The abuse she suffered from her husband, the attack on her sister, and the evidence that James Stanton had killed her parents.

Opening the door while balancing his sandwich in his mouth and the cup of coffee in his hand, Julio heard the gun click just before he felt the metal touch the side of his head.

"Okay, you bastard. You've got two seconds to tell me where Kassie Stanton and her daughter are," Leo growled.

"Then you'd never find her, would you?" He dropped the deli bag to the floor and held out his arms. Saint approached from the front with his gun aimed directly at him. Chase followed behind, ready to confront the man who had Kassie.

The gun pressed harder. "Back off," Leo ordered Chase as he came toward Julio.

"Fuck that. She must be scared out of her mind! I promised her she was safe. He's going to tell me where they are!"

"Whoa, gentleman. You're Chase Winters and Derrick "Leo" Strong?"

"It doesn't matter. We just want to know where Kassie and her daughter are." Leo motioned for Chase to stand down.

"Listen, we're on the same team here. I probably could've communicated more, but we had to act fast. If you'll allow me to sit down and eat my sandwich, I got a couple of beers in the fridge. We can discuss this."

"He doesn't even know who we are and is already willing to give up information. He's going to get her killed!"

"Good plan, Doc. Get yourself thrown in prison for assaulting a Federal Agent when you know someone much worse is out there hunting for the same woman and her kid that you are. While I'll admit my agency isn't great at sharing information, I'm willing to read you in a bit if your friend removes his goddamn gun and you let me eat my sandwich before it gets soggy. It's been a long damn day."

Saint lowered his gun, and Chase responded. "I don't care if you know who I am. I want to know where Kass and Emma are."

"I know exactly who you are, and you're the one who will get her killed at this rate. From what I can tell, we have the same goal. And, if Kassie wants to see you, we'll find a way for that to happen. Little Emma wasn't happy about being taken from her uncle Derrick. She kicked one of my men in the nuts and poked the eyes of another. He just returned home from getting stitches earlier this morning. The third guy has sore ears."

Nodding to Leo, Chase indicated he would give the man a chance to talk. Both men relaxed, and Chase asked, "You teach her that?"

"No. Her mama did." Pride in the little girl was evident in Leo's voice as he lowered his weapon.

Chase's grin widened. "That's my girl."

Two hours later, Hernandez, Doc, and Leo sat sifting through all the evidence against Stanton. Chase had fidgeted through the explanation of why Stanton needed Kassie and Emma declared dead. Now that he had it, he was ready to get his girls.

"I'm telling you, it's not safe for me to take you there, and my team isn't going to open the door just because you tell them I said so." Picking up the documents, the agent placed them back into a folder and laid them on the table. "Plus, I don't know if Kassie wants to see you. She seems pretty shaken up and is under the impression that she was a mission. It seems she's a hell of a lot more than that."

"Just give me the coordinates, and we'll get in." Leo insisted. "We need to speak with Kassie. I think there's been a misunderstanding, and if we work together, we can accomplish more. The team can provide extra security since you can't guarantee that all the dirty agents have been ferreted out. If Kassie has an objection, I'd like to hear it from her."

"No, Emma and Kassie would be put at risk. I don't want bullets flying if my guys come across you," Julio insisted. "I'll relocate them tomorrow morning. Cartwright will be with her. I'll send you the coordinates as soon as they're settled."

"You can't be serious. You want her to testify against him as Kassie?" Irritated, Chase ran his hand through his hair.

Hernandez nodded. "Yes, we discussed it. It was her choice."

"Don't bank on that quite yet. I promised she could have her life back, not her sister's." His voice held an edge.

"When Kassie—both the real Kassie and her sister under the assumed identity—Agreed to help the FBI, certain arrangements were made. It's not up to me to discuss those. You'd have to ask her."

Determined, Chase was ready to do just that. "I plan on it."

Chapter Three

Kassie hadn't slept at all. Every floor creak or car horn woke her up. Emma was ensconced in her arms, and yet she felt empty inside. She relived every moment of her time with Chase on the mountain. A single tear fell down her cheek, and she quickly swiped it away. He had a job and he had done it. Now she needed to decide how she would start her life here.

Slipping out of bed, she headed to the bathroom. Leaving the door cracked in case Em woke, she took a hot shower. Running her head under the faucet, hoping it would help her rinse all the stress away, but her thoughts stayed on Chase. The last time she made love to him, she met him in the barn and gave him the excuse that she needed to go to town. Seeing him and knowing it was their last moment together, she'd kissed him. She didn't want to go, but fear for her child took precedence. She meant it to only be a kiss, but she was lost when he pulled her close and his mouth began to explore hers. When he picked her up and laid her down in the fresh hay, she was caught up in all the emotions and feelings only he could provoke.

Rummaging through the clothes Julio sent over, she finally found a pair of jeans and a light blue sweater. Emma began to stir and woke with a huge smile when she saw her mama sitting on the edge of the bed. Kassie quickly dressed and fed her. Finding a box of crayons and a coloring book, she distracted her long enough to braid her hair. Just as she was finishing, Matthew entered the room.

"Good morning. I've come to collect you and Emma. We're relocating." The tone of Matthew's voice concerned her immediately.

"Are we compromised?" The stress in her voice made him quickly reassure her that everything was fine.

Smiling a bit to put her more at ease, he reassured her. "We just had some changes in the plan, that's all. I'll explain more when we get to our next location. Can you be ready to leave in about fifteen minutes? Don't worry about packing everything. One of the men will do that. Bring what you need immediately for the two of you."

Waiting at the small rural farm, the team took positions along the buildings as Chase and Leo stayed inside the SUV.

"Okay, Doc, I know you're pissed. But Hernandez has kept his promises. We need to remain professional. Keep it together. You got that? You won't help Kassie by losing your shit right now."

Watching Cartwright's car, Chase lifted his chin to acknowledge his understanding. His body was stiff, and he kept flexing his hands to relieve the pent-up stress. "I got it, Leo."

Matthew turned down an old dirt road with cattle in the fields on both sides of the fence. "This is my grandparents' ranch. My brother runs it, but he's out of town for the month, and his foreman's in charge when he's gone. He stays on the property in a small cabin just down from the house. He thinks you two are family just staying with me for a visit. I think you're going to love it here, Emma. We've got cows, chickens, horses, and llamas."

The sullen child stayed quiet as she held Kassie's hand.

"I'm sorry. I think the last few days have been a bit much for her." Kassie pushed Em's bangs out of her face.

"Don't apologize. You both have been through a lot." The house appeared, and two large vehicles were sitting in the driveway. His hands tightened on the steering wheel. "I'm sorry, Kass. They arrived earlier than expected."

She focused on the SUVs as she braced herself for whoever was in the vehicles. The doors opened, and she momentarily panicked as she thought she had put her trust in the wrong team.

Leo and Chase walked to the back of the vehicle. The men wore dark clothing, and they both appeared armed. Their jaws were set in a hard line, but their arms hung loosely at their sides, like they expected to have to draw weapons at any moment. She imagined this was how they looked operating in the military—alert, dangerous, in control. Relief hit her at the sight of the two men at first, then it disappeared, and her anxiety took over.

Chase stepped out into the drive. His usual stubble on his face had grown, and his eyes tracked the car as it rolled to a stop. Leo took off his sunglasses as he watched.

"Uncle Derrick! Dr. Chase!" Emma squealed in delight at seeing both men. When two figures came to stand on the front porch, Emma pointed and bounced in her car seat. "Look, Mama! It's Auntie Cat and Melody!"

Kassie's stomach fell as she took in the grim faces of the men and Catherine's anxious face waiting for her to exit the car.

"This wasn't my call. Apparently, Julio changed the plan." Matthew couldn't hold back the annoyance in his voice. "I'm going back to check with the foreman, but I won't be too far if you need me."

Kassie didn't say anything as Chase came to Emma's side of the vehicle and opened it. She could feel the tension radiate from him from the opposite end of the car as she got out.

Holding his arms out for Emma, Chase caught the enthusiastic child as she jumped right into them. "It's good to see you, Ladybug! I hope ya don't mind, but little Miss Melody missed you so much I brought her. Can you play while I talk to your mama? I even brought you a friend."

Saint opened the door to the back of the other vehicle, and Rollo came bounding out of the car. "Rollo! Mama, look. Dr. Chase brought me Rollo!"

Kassie smiled nervously. "I see that." The dog bounded toward her, and she laughed at his affectionate greeting before he took off to smother Em in dog kisses, causing her to giggle with glee.

Catherine came up, and the two women embraced as Leo and Catherine's daughter, Melody, joined the little group. "I found a tire swing out back that will hold two little girls and a big backyard to play fetch with Rollo if anyone wants to play..."

The girls let out squeals and took off, running toward the house. Catherine squeezed Kassie's arm as she glanced between her and Chase. "We'll talk later."

Chase walked slowly toward her. She licked her lips nervously. Part of her wanted to run to him, but the tension in the air was thick. Not knowing what he was thinking, she looked around to see Matthew watching, and he stiffly nodded to her.

"Hi, Princess. Do you think we could talk for a bit?" Looking into his eyes, she noticed there were dark circles under them, and they were bloodshot. His clothes were rumpled as if he had slept in them.

Nodding her agreement, she walked beside him as he gently steered her to the fence along the barn.

Rubbing his hand over his face, he stared at her for a minute, ensuring she was okay. "Kassie, please help me to understand. Help me understand how we went from making love in the barn to you running away without talking to me."

She watched him, but her thoughts were still too chaotic to respond. After a minute, he sighed. Resting his foot on the bottom rail, he focused his gaze on the field of cows. Then he continued. "Why did you leave, Kass? If you wanted to go, why didn't you tell me about the call? We could've devised a plan together, ensured Cartwright and Hernandez were trustworthy, and worked with them. I thought Stanton had taken you and Em, and it tore me apart."

She looked out over the same field and gripped the fence railing. "Any more than I knew you or Derrick when you took me to the mountain? I didn't know Derrick or as you call him Leo, when you befriended me because I was a job."

"Is it the money?" he softly asked her. "Did you agree to this because of that? I know about the arrangement with the FBI."

She stiffened at his question. Surprised that he would still think she was motivated by money, and it hurt. She tried to explain that he couldn't guarantee Stanton, with all his money and lawyers, wouldn't take her daughter. She couldn't risk it. Emma's life hung in the balance. "It's never been about the money."

"I've had three days to question why you would deliberately leave the mountain and return here. You could be Kaitlyn Abigail Reynolds again if you'd only waited for Leo and the team. Yet you've known this guy for five minutes over two phone calls, and at the first opportunity to get back here, you took it."

Her cheeks flamed red, and her hands balled into fists. She took a step back from the fence and glared at him. "What difference does it make, Chase? We were a mission for your team! A favor owed to my best friend. You were *ordered* to sleep with me to discover what the widow knew! I have to do what is best for my daughter and family, and I seized the opportunity."

"The money was just a convenient benefit of being the widow. Were the last three years a small price to pay to have more money than you will ever need at your disposal?" His jaw ticked. His hand went to the bridge of his nose as if he was getting a headache.

She turned and headed toward the house at a furious pace. He reached out and gently grasped her wrist to stop her, and she jerked away.

"Don't you EVER sit in judgment of me! What about you? You have sex with women for missions! I made a promise to my sister! I intend to do whatever I must to protect my daughter!"

"But she's not your daughter," he countered. "She's the niece with a hefty bank account attached to her, and as her mother, you have access to a life of luxury."

His words took the wind out of her. He wasn't going to believe anything she had to say. "Since you're so concerned with the money, I'll ensure you're paid for your services. Should I include a tip for *stud* services? I'm not sure how this all works. Tell me what your services were worth, and I'll write the check."

He hadn't even been this mad at his ex-fiancé Rachel when she had tried to marry him, pregnant with another man's child. The days of worrying if she was okay and the stress of not knowing where she was, had finally taken their toll. His pride was bruised that she hadn't trusted him. Now, she had locked herself into always being in her sister's life. He didn't know what to believe. Now she was offering to write a check. That was the last straw.

She turned toward the vehicles, and he made one desperate attempt to stop her. He took her hand as she angrily swatted him away.

"Get your hands off her," Matthew's steely voice commanded, and his eyes narrowed at Chase.

He had been so focused on Kassie, he hadn't noticed Cartwright coming up. It was because of this asshole that he was standing here in Texas instead of having her safe on the mountain.

Chase dropped his hand from Kassie's, pulled back, and slugged Matthew on his jaw. Matthew raised back and swiped Chase's feet from under him. The two men exchanged punches. Chase fell to the ground and immediately rolled back to his feet. Matthew was ready with a hit to the jaw. Chase returned with a fist to the nose. Both men fell to the ground exchanging blows, refusing to yield.

"Stop!" Kassie yelled, but the men moved away from her to keep her from intervening. Her shouts brought Julio and Leo running.

"Damn it, Doc! You're completely FUBAR right now. Stop!"

Julio held Cartwright while Leo got Chase under control. "Lock it down! We gotta job to do."

Shaking, Kassie stood facing the men. Her hair had loosened from her braid and the wind whipped it in her face. Her face was flushed, and her eyes shot daggers. "No. You don't have a job to do. I'm no longer a *mission*, Leo. Julio said your records were redacted. He didn't know if you could be trusted and sent a team in to get Emma. I had to make a choice, just as I do now. You're fired!"

Leo's gaze fell on Julio as he let go of Chase. "Did you tell her that?"

Julio let go of Matthew and smirked. "Yes, I did. I didn't trust you until Cartwright dug up the rest of the files. I knew she'd willingly come if I had Emma, plus her sister hid the USB in Emma's doll. We needed to retrieve it. We were on a time limit and needed to get her here."

"At the expense of kidnapping her child and traumatizing her friend and both girls? You knew who we were. You could've let us in on this so we could have protected her and brought them in safely." Leo's voice was deadly. "You're having her impersonate her sister, which, last time I checked, was illegal and makes me want to question what side you stand on."

"Don't get all high and mighty with me. I've seen your records, Leo. I know about the mission gone bad. Do you want to tell me you've always made the best decisions for your team? I failed her sister, but I'll do whatever it takes to keep her safe. Can you say you did that for your men?"

A fist flew and connected with Julio's nose as Leo advanced. Then it was Chase and Matthew's turn to hold their bosses back.

Walking toward the SUV, Saint climbed into the driver's side while Chase slid into the passenger seat. Leo leaned into the driver's window. "Take our brother and get him a drink until he cools down. I'll work on straightening out this mess." Saint started the vehicle.

Chase threw Leo a quelling look. "Good thing we all stayed professional." He swiped the blood from his head.

Wiping off the blood seeping from his split lip, Leo grinned. "He had it coming. He lied to her to get her here and had Emma. You know as well as I do as soon as he took the kid, he had her. I imagine years of guessing whom to trust played havoc with her mind, brother. We're here now. Let's work with what we got."

Catherine held onto Kassie as she visibly shook. Leo walked into the kitchen and took in the women. Catherine's eyes held a condemning stare as she murmured reassurances to her friend.

"Kassie, we need to talk."

She shook her head. "No, we don't, Mr. Strong." The formality in her tone provided the distance she needed between them. "Am I to assume that your client's privacy is bound by confidentiality?"

Frowning at her tone, he replied, "Call me Leo, Kassie. We're friends." Leo tried to diffuse the situation. "Yes, anything discovered will be kept between the team and you."

"Good." Keeping her face and voice expressionless, Kassie stepped back from her friend. "Catherine, I know you meant well by calling in a favor for me. I appreciate your intent."

Kassie pulled Catherine in for a quick hug, and she stood in front of Leo. "Mr. Strong, invoice me, and I'll have a check sent to you. I'm not sure what your going rate is, but I'm sure you and Joe can come up with an agreement. I want you and your team to leave immediately."

Catherine let out a gasp. "Kassie. Don't do this."

"I'm sorry, Cat. I truly am. I need you and Melody to leave too. I don't want you in any danger. I love you."

"Kassie, you don't want to do this," Leo said. "I know Chase lost his head, but he's…" He paused while attempting to explain the hell his brother had gone through.

Kassie stopped him. "No, *Leo*. Chase made it clear what he thought. I don't want the team here. Any communication can go through Joe. I need you to leave. Please."

She walked out the kitchen door and felt his eyes follow her as she hugged Melody. Picking up Emma, she walked the fence line and pointed out the llamas and horses.

She kept Emma distracted until Leo rounded up Rollo, and he and Catherine left.

For Emma and her sister, she'd find the strength to see this through. But worry churned in her stomach, leaving her nauseated and shaky. Everything seemed to be coming apart.

Chapter Four

The team sat around their suite's living area early Friday evening to discuss their next step. Chase sat in a leather chair in the corner while Saint and Leo took up the couch, going through the farm layout where Kassie and Emma were staying. Shadow and Taco were taking out cartons of Chinese takeout and sat them on the coffee table with a stack of paper plates and silverware. Michael handed Chase a bottle of water and sat across from him.

"Hernandez and Cartwright have the farmhouse locked down. Saint found some motion sensors and cameras, so we can assume they'll see anyone coming or going. Shadow, Saint, and Taco, head back, and get an eye on the three roads leading onto the property. Tomorrow, Chase, Michael, and I will relieve you." Grabbing a plate, Leo doled out the orders as the men shoveled food into their mouths.

"You need to eat, Doc. Then clean up. We've got someone to meet."

Raising his brow, Chase stood and headed to the room he shared with Michael.

He couldn't eat. All he could do was replay his conversation with Kassie in his head. Still questioning why she trusted Hernandez and Cartwright over him, it stung. Obviously, she overheard his conversation with Leo. But then, why was she so upset? He thought back to the phone conversation.

"Listen, I know I told you to sleep with her and it's obvious that you took your job seriously, but you have to let her go." Leo's eyes narrowed as he took in Chase's body language. His hands were clenched, and his jaw was locked. His nostrils flared.

"Yeah, she's nothing but the mission. Just about as much of a job as Ash's widow is to you. Tell me, Leo, would you place Catherine in danger if the positions were reversed?"

Leo sat back in the chair. He shook his head and ran his hand across his jaw. "Winters, I'm sorry. Years of military training have kept me from adding emotions into factors. It's obvious you two have grown close. I sincerely apologize…

If she overheard the conversation, then she would have known how much she meant to him. He had to be missing something. Regretting how he handled the situation and the fact she shut down and refused to talk to him or Leo made him ill at ease.

Finishing with his shower and freshly shaved, he met Leo back in the living area. His friend slapped a plate in front of him.

"Eat. That's an order. You're not going to help her if you fall over."

Sitting, he dug into the food, not caring what he was eating since everything seemed to taste like sandpaper. "Who are we going to meet?" He questioned Leo between mouthfuls.

"I think we need to offer our services to the people Kassie trusts the most. Joe Richardson is Kassie's godfather, and if anyone would be willing to listen to us about her safety, he would. Hernandez isn't going to give us access to Kassie again without a fight and at this point, it would be detrimental to our goal of protecting her and Em."

"Will she talk to Catherine?"

Leo shook his head as his mouth firmed in a grim line.

"She asked Catherine and Melody to leave because she didn't want them in danger. I asked Catherine to return to Seattle, and she refused. I have them in a suite down the hall. She promised to stay in the suites until we can talk to Kassie. So, we need to succeed in getting Joe and Maddie on our side."

Throwing the plate in the trash, Chase wasted no time in heading for the door.

Dialing the number written on a piece of paper, Leo waited for Joe to answer.

"Joe Richardson speaking." Leo glanced at Chase.

"Good evening Mr. Richardson. My name is Leo Armstrong. Your name was given to me in hopes of helping me export some new merchandise. I'm sorry to bother you so late on a Saturday, but I unexpectedly ended up in Corpus Christi. Could you give me a few moments of your time?"

After a slight hesitation, Joe said, "I'm sorry. I don't do business on weekends, but if you call my office on Monday, we can make an appointment to meet."

"I wouldn't bother you, but I'm afraid my client insists I get this handled tonight. I would be willing to meet you over dinner with Mrs. Richardson." Hoping Joe would take the bait, Leo waited for him to respond.

"I'm sorry, this weekend doesn't work for me. Please call my office on Monday." The line disconnected.

"Shit. Now what are we going to do?" Raking his hand through his hair for the millionth time, Chase leaned back into the SUV seat.

Leo redialed the number, and Joe answered. "I'm so sorry to inconvenience you, sir. I must speak with you before I leave. Could I have thirty minutes of your time?"

They heard a sigh on the other end of the line. "I'll give you thirty minutes. My wife and I are just finishing dinner. Could you be here within the hour?"

Leo grinned at Chase. "Yes, sir. I can be there within a half hour if that works for you?"

A slightly disgruntled-sounding Joe gave an affirmative grunt before he hung up the call.

"Okay, Doc, we only have one shot at this. I'm counting on you not to blow it."

Chase sat up in his seat. His eyes held a determined glint as he resolved that he would do anything to plead his case to Joe and Maddie so Kassie would let the team protect her and Emma.

Precisely thirty minutes later, Joe answered the door. Holding out his hand, Leo offered a greeting and introduced Chase. The men shook hands, and Joe ushered them into his office. Chase smiled when he noticed all the pictures of the twins and baby pictures of Em displayed in the room.

"So, what can I do for you, gentleman?" Joe was direct and to the point. Leo smiled as he took out a piece of paper from his pocket.

Your office is bugged. We are friends of Kassie/ Kaitlyn. We need to speak with you and your wife about her safety. Go along with what we say. Don't speak until we are alone.

"I work for a manufacturer, Sherwood Textiles," Leo said. "We handle a variety of clothing and accessories from around the world. My boss recently ended his relationship with his distribution company and is shopping for another. We understand that you are well known in the industry, and we're prepared to offer you a contract." Leo slipped the paper to Joe.

His eyes widened as he read the note. Then looking at both men, his eyes narrowed. "How can I be sure that the numbers on this contract are correct? Something this big seems priceless."

Chase removed his phone, showing a picture he had taken of Kassie in the window seat of his bedroom, her face soaking up the first rays of the sun. She looked like an angel, which had prompted him to snap the photo.

"I'm sorry, it probably seems sudden, but my employer just brokered a significant deal and is anxious to settle everything quickly. I was wondering if we could convince you and your wife to have some dessert with us while we work on the numbers, and I can give you time to let your lawyers look over the contracts. I heard there was a great German bakery that I must visit in the area. Could I interest you and your wife in joining us?"

Joe briefly eyed the two men across from him before he spoke. "I know the exact place. Let me fetch my wife, and we'll meet you there. I'm afraid I only have about an hour to give you, as my wife and I have a strict agreement about business on the weekends, but I'm sure she'll make the exception for apple strudel."

Leo leaned over the desk and wrote on the piece of paper.

Car may be bugged.

Nodding in understanding, he ushered them to the door while calling for his wife. Chase waited until they were in their car before he said anything.

"Do you think he's going to believe us?"

"I'm leaving it up to you to convince him. You'll figure it out." Pulling out of the drive, they followed Joe and Maddie to the bakery, and Chase prayed they would allow him to explain. With only an hour, he couldn't waste any time convincing them.

At the bakery, they ordered desserts and sat at one of the tables. Sitting across from Joe, Chase looked directly at him.

"My name is Chase Winters. I've known Kaitlyn as Kassie Smith in Seattle for several months. I helped her when she was hospitalized and took her to my home to keep her safe from James Stanton. Leo," Chase nodded to his friend, "Derrick Strong is my boss. He's a retired Navy

SEAL that assigned me to Kassie. Until four weeks ago, your goddaughter kept us in the dark as to who she was. When she found out that Agent Hernandez and Matthew Cartwright had Emma, she fled the safety of our protection for that of Hernandez. I ask that you consider letting us act as her security until this trial ends. We believe there's still a hit on her and possibly Emma."

"You don't feel that Agent Hernandez is adequate to do the job, son?" His eyebrows went up in question. Maddie sipped her coffee and watched the young man talking.

"It's not that he isn't a professional, sir. Kassie made a hasty judgment call once she knew they had taken Em, and I want to ensure she's protected and right now, she's unwilling to talk to us concerning her safety." Chase took a sip of his coffee, knowing that Joe would be wondering why, and he refused to lie.

"Does my Little Bit have reason to doubt your sincerity in protecting her?" Joe's voice sounded calm, but his eyes bored into Chase's.

"Yes, sir. We've had a disagreement of sorts. She misunderstood a conversation that she overheard, and I believe that's why she doesn't want our involvement." Chase swallowed the lump in his throat but refused to break eye contact with Joe.

"I'm sorry, son. Right now, her safety's on the line. She's made it three years on the run by trusting her gut. If she doesn't want you to be part of their security, then I have to believe she's doing so for a good reason. I've no intention of questioning her choices." Starting to rise from the chair, he stopped when Maddie's hand covered his.

"You're in love with her, aren't you?" A soft smile played on Maddie's lips as she focused her attention on Chase.

"Yes, Ma'am." Chase admitted unabashedly. "These two are my whole world. I'm afraid we're having a bit of a disagreement, and if you remember anything about your goddaughter, you know she can be the most stubborn person on the face of this earth. I mean no disrespect." Grimacing, he hoped he hadn't blown it by saying that, but he had nothing to lose.

Laughing softly, Maddie's eyes danced as if she knew a secret. "Yes, Sugar. I know exactly what you mean." Turning her attention to Joe, she took his hand and gave it a light squeeze. "*Cher*, I don't think it would hurt to have the two teams working together, especially if they prioritize Kassie and Emma's safety. Although we've been a bit blindsided by everything over the last few days, I think Joe should make sure you are who you say you are. Give us some time to discuss it and make some calls. Where can we reach you?"

Leo wrote on the back of a business card then slid it across the table. "This was my commander, and he can confirm we're legitimate. I'm afraid I'm the one that caused the miscommunication between these two. Kassie and Emma are my team's priority. All I ask is that you remember she wasn't running from just James but from corrupt FBI agents. I request that you insist that Kassie let us team up. Chase will be with her while I guard Emma. The rest of my team will follow or be dispersed through the crowd of reporters her return will garner. Please don't discuss this in your house, car, or office. Your phones and computers are likely monitored as well."

The couple stood and shook hands. Opening the door, Joe led Maddie to their car and helped her in. Leo strolled to the door and watched them drive down the street. The two men pretended to be loitering around the bakery long enough to see if the Richardsons were being followed. Satisfied they weren't, the two men headed back to the hotel.

Wanting to check in on Catherine and Melody, Leo headed toward their suite while Chase headed to theirs. Worried that Joe wouldn't call, his thoughts turned to Kassie, and he wondered what she was doing on the farm. Glancing at the clock by his bed, he imagined she had gotten Emma to bed and was probably spending time with Matthew and Julio going over Monday's court date. He sighed, knowing he needed to wait for the Richardsons to contact him, but he already knew that regardless of their decision, he'd be watching over his girl.

Sunday evening, Joe called Leo from a burner phone in the park.

"All right, son, I got confirmation that you are the best of the best. I'll allow your team to help. I want to meet your team and I want assurances from Chase he'll do anything to protect our Little Bit and Em."

Leo placed the call on speaker. Chase leaned into the phone, "Yes, sir. You have my word. I'll protect them with my life."

"Good enough, son. We'll see you at the courthouse at eight in the morning. Proceedings are supposed to start at nine-thirty, but I am going to have to chat with Little Bit to get her to agree with you being there. And son?"

"Yes, sir?"

"I'd be negligent in my duty as her godfather, if I didn't tell you that I'll be watching. Make sure you don't hurt our girl. You clear this misunderstanding up as soon as possible."

Chase agreed. "Yes, sir, I intend to do just that as soon as she's willing to listen to me."

He heard a chuckle on the other end of the phone before it disconnected.

Chapter Five

Matthew hadn't given her time over the weekend to dwell on what had happened. Making her dress every day in high fashion, even though they were on the small farm, he quizzed, questioned, and even corrected how she walked.

"You must be exactly like your sister. There's no room for mistakes. Kassie Stanton wouldn't be caught dead in a pair of jeans and a T-shirt. You have to look and play the part."

She detested it. She loathed the excessive make-up, the stickiness of the hairspray, and the spiked heels. The earrings were bigger than she usually wore and weighed down on her ear lobes. She drew the line at six in the evening so she would have time to eat dinner with her daughter and get her ready for bed. Julio took Emma for horseback rides and purchased paints and craft clay to keep her occupied while Kassie was with Matthew. Kassie could tell her daughter wasn't any happier with the arrangement than she was.

Sunday came quickly. They finally chose the outfit she'd wear to the courthouse and all the accessories. Her designer bag and shoes sat by the door. Looking away in disgust at the weapons of torture someone called high heels, she made her way to the bathroom to wash her face. Knowing what Matthew was like, she looked into the mirror and couldn't help but think if Kassie were alive today, if she would have been so concerned with her appearance.

Sighing, she put everything away and took out her little notebook. She started making her lists. First, she wanted to make sure the stylist who had befriended her in Serenity was paid for all the products she had sent Kassie along with the clothing. Samantha had become such a wonderful friend and she missed her. In fact, she missed everything about

Serenity. Jake, Chase's godfather, always made her laugh. Rollo, Chase's dog, had turned traitor and followed Kassie around the cabin. He also saved her life. Bear's honey was really the best she'd ever had. Her time in Serenity had passed so quickly. If things had been different, she would have considered living there.

She got back to her list.

José was a former patient of hers. She wanted to set up a fund for him while he finished school and pursued his military career. Carol Reese, Catherine's mom, had taken her and Emma in and given her a semblance of a family. Because of Kassie, Carol's house had burned down and if it hadn't been for Leo's team, Carol, Melody, and Emma would have been inside. She needed to replace the house and her belongings. She also wanted to visit the widow of Agent Mike Thompson. He had given his life to save her from the dirty FBI agents and Kassie would make sure his family was well provided for…

Before she knew it, Kassie had filled over half the pages.

Yawning, she put the list in her designer bag and pulled the blankets down on the bed.

This was the part that she hated the most. Every night, her thoughts would drift to Chase and how her interpretation of things could have been so wrong. She had spent the last three years running on instinct alone. Now for the first time, her gut had failed her. It let her have feelings for a man who only thought of her as a mission. She squeezed her eyes shut and willed the tears away as she'd done every night since their confrontation at the farm. She couldn't get distracted by what could have been now. She needed to focus on protecting Emma. Because she already failed at protecting her heart.

Arriving early at the courthouse, Kassie and Emma were ushered into a secure room before the proceedings. Joe and Maddie were already there. Joe swung Emma into his arms while Maddie embraced Kassie. She smelled of cookies and home. After today, she and Emma could see them as much as they wanted.

Joe set Emma down so she could enjoy all the magical things Maddie pulled from her bag. "*Cher*, we've been on pins and needles all weekend. Are you sure about this?" he asked Kassie.

She didn't want to have this argument again. "Mama, Daddy, and Kass deserve justice. This is the only way to give them that and protect Em. We can't get them back, but I'm not going to let that man walk. He robbed us of years together, he took away the people we loved the most. I've made up my mind. Mama always said, love doesn't run." Her determined voice lowered to almost a whisper. "There's no turning back."

Joe made no effort in disguising his frustration. "After this morn'n, this whole *gris-gris* will be lifted. Then we're gonna go home and all you two need to worry about is how y'all want that po'boy dressed."

Kassie smiled. She knew Joe would make sure they were okay. It felt good to be home. She had missed them terribly and longed to call them. Especially on birthdays and holidays when she had felt the separation the most. Maddie pulled out two cookies and a carton of milk from her bag and busied Em with coloring books and a snack. Watching her daughter react to Maddie's mothering just as she and her sister always had, Kassie couldn't help but smile.

Joe gently pulled Kassie to the side. "Maddie will keep Em in here while we go into the courtroom. But I need you to do me a favor, *Cher*."

"Of course, anything."

"I got a team of men outside that say you up and fired 'em. I hired 'em back. I've made some calls. These men are good men. I don't think we can have too much protection at this point." Seeing she was going to argue, he made a bargain. "Just until this is over with. So, indulge an ole man, Little Bit."

Kassie huffed. "Couldn't you have Julio assign more men from his team?" She shook her head; she didn't need this sprung on her at the last minute. "Joe..."

"Listen, there's a determined young man out there that insists he's taking care of my girls no matter what. I don't see why I would bother with extra work for anyone else since they've been watching over you all weekend, even after you sent them on their way."

Her eyes widened as she realized they hadn't left. Sighing, she begrudgingly agreed. "Fine, but as soon as this is over, I don't want anything to do with them. Let them get back to their jobs. And Joe? I don't want Chase near me."

"Sorry, Little Bit, Leo already assigned him to escort you in and out of here. But I'll be right next to you, and I can still wallop that boy if he takes a step outta line."

Kassie let out a laugh. "Okay, but after this make it clear, I don't want Chase to escort me. Send someone else."

"We can talk about that later. Now, let's go set Stanton on his ass." He kissed her forehead just as the door opened.

Matthew and Chase entered at the same time. Chase's face was turned up in a scowl, Matthew's face remained blank as he addressed Kassie. "It's time."

She kissed Emma and Maddie and then took a moment to breathe. Maddie hugged her and whispered in her ear, "It's going to be just fine, Sugar. Your parents would be so proud of you. You got your family behind you. We aren't going to let James Stanton take anything else away from us."

Checking to make sure her hair and make-up was perfectly in place, she walked out of the room with her head held up high. The doors to the courtroom opened and audible gasps sounded as she walked right up to the front and stood at the opposite side of the aisle from the man she hadn't set eyes on in three long years.

The judge banged his gavel at the sudden disruption of his proceedings. Once the courtroom had settled the judge turned his attention to the young woman who had caused such a stir. "Ma'am, could you please state your name for the court?"

Her hand trembled slightly.

Matthew took it and gave her an encouraging smile. For a moment, she thought she heard a low growl coming from the other side of her.

"My name is Kassie Marie Stanton. I'm the widow of Phillip Stanton and the daughter-in-law to James Stanton." Kassie's gaze roamed to meet the heated stare of James Stanton. Outwardly he appeared calm, but she noticed how his hands clenched as he nonchalantly put them in his pockets. Leaning over to whisper something to one of his lawyers, he never broke eye contact with her.

The crowd grew louder. Cameras flashed as Julio explained how Kassie had been in protective custody under the care of a retired Navy SEAL security team at an undisclosed location.

The courtroom settled as the judge dismissed the case and recognized Kassie and her daughter as alive and well.

Joe hugged Kassie. "Welcome home, *Cher*. We sure have missed you, Little Bit, and that youngin'."

Pandemonium erupted when a team of FBI and DEA agents entered and began reading James Stanton his rights. He continued to stare down the young woman before him but wisely didn't speak. His lawyer was already on the phone making arrangements for his bail. As he was escorted from his seat, he stopped in front of where Kassie and the team stood. Chase immediately placed his body in front of hers.

"Welcome home, Kassie. I'm so thrilled to find you alive and well. I'll contact you so we can set up a time to for me to meet my… granddaughter." James smirked as the agent behind him prodded him to keep moving forward.

As expected, a podium had been placed outside. A crowd of reporters swarmed around the group as soon as they exited the courthouse. From the stiff body language and the way the men carried themselves, Kassie could tell they weren't happy. Cameras flashed as the crowd pressed closer to the long-missing heiress and her daughter. The men were on high alert. Shadow disappeared into the crowd while Saint and Taco took the perimeter. Chase pushed past Matthew and flanked Kassie on her left, leaving him to follow and protect her back. Leo had taken up her right side. Joe held Emma next to Leo with Maddie on his arm. Julio took up Maddie's other side.

Kassie's anxiety rose as she watched the crowd pushing against the police barrier. She had to blink a few times from the flash of the cameras and bright lights from the television crews. She perfected her "Kassie" smile and clutched her purse tightly to keep her hands from shaking. She was supposed to appear confident. All she wanted to do was go back to the mountain and curl up in the window seat in Chase's bedroom.

Julio approached the podium.

"Thank you for being here. I'm sure everyone has questions, but due to the legal implications of this case, Mrs. Stanton will read a brief statement and will not be answering any questions at this time. We ask that you respect Mrs. Stanton and her daughter's privacy as they work through their transition of returning to their lovely home state of Texas."

Julio returned to Maddie's side so she could step up to the podium. Gripping the wooden edge, she started to speak, "Thank you."

A small red dot appeared on her chest against her dark-blue designer coat.

Chase shoved her to the ground as shots fired. Chaos ensued as people began running and screaming. Chase covered her entire body despite the fact she wore a bulletproof vest.

Kassie beat Chase's chest to get him to loosen his hold so she could get to Emma. Taco returned fire and a gunman went down. Matthew threw himself over Maddie, while Leo covered Emma and Joe. Saint was securing an exit. She could hear Shadow speaking through the coms attached to Chase's ear, telling them to stay down. Another shooter was on the roof, and Shadow was intercepting him with Julio's team.

The ringing and buzzing sound in Kassie's ears wouldn't stop. Chase finally lifted his weight up off her as the crowd was dispersed by police and other agents arrived on the scene. That's when Kassie noticed the blood. She followed the river of red with her eyes until she found where it had started. Blood blossomed from Joe's chest.

"Joe! Joe!" she screamed as she removed her coat to staunch the blood. Leo grabbed her from behind and Chase stepped in, ripping the bloody shirt in half. Michael dropped a bag next to him. Kassie's medical training kicked in. She pushed Leo away, grabbing the IV bag, tubing, and a start kit, located a vein, and began to push fluids. Saint and a couple of agents rushed in and whisked Maddie and Emma to a contained area as Kassie continued to talk to Joe.

"Hold on, Joe. Chase is the best trauma surgeon you're ever going to find. Don't you dare give up! I just got you back." She continued to keep calm as she helped staunch the blood and held on to Joe's limp hand while Leo and Matthew covered her.

"Oh, *Cher*, I'm always gonna be with you. You, your sister, and now Em have been my life. The best day of my life was the day I stopped and helped your Mama. Y'all saved my Maddie. Take care of her, Little Bit. Tell her I love her. I love you, Little Bit."

"No! Joe, please don't leave me!" she pleaded. "I can't do this again! Noooo!" Sobbing, she grabbed his hand tighter, afraid to let him go.

Joe placed his hand on Kassie's cheek. "Shhhh, baby girl. It's up to God, not me, not you. Promise me. Don't stop your life. You done all you could for your sister. Now you go be happy." His breathing turned harsher.

"I can't if you leave me. I need you, Joe. Maddie does too. You haven't even got to know Em yet. Stay with me! Now stop all that jabbering and save your energy. Chase is trying to work, and an ambulance is on the way. Take shallow breaths."

Joe turned his head and watched the young man working diligently to cut off the source of all the blood. "You take care of my girls. You make her live *her* life. She's special, my Little Bit." Joe closed his eyes.

Chapter Six

The night was a long one. Kassie and Maddie watched the hospital staff come and go. Joe had made it through surgery, the bullet had barely missed his heart. Preparing for the worst, Maddie prayed as Kassie sat numbly in a chair, clinging to Joe's hand. Taco and Shadow took shifts guarding the door. Saint and Rollo went with Julio's team to watch over Emma, who was with Catherine, and Melody. Julio and Leo worked on security to get the Stanton estate locked down. Michael flew home to Seattle and would return in a few days. Chase booked a hotel suite across the street from the hospital.

When Chase returned, he stopped at the door and watched as Kassie continually glanced at all the settings and Joe's chest moving up and down. She quickly swiped fresh tears away from her drooping eyes. She refused to leave the older man. The blood on her clothes had started to turn brown, her hair was in disarray, and he could tell she carried all the blame for what happened.

"It's my fault," Kassie choked out as she glanced at Maddie. "I shouldn't have come back."

"Hush now," Maddie said. "My husband is one of the strongest men I know. He'll fight until God calls him home. But we've had a wonderful life, Sugar. If Joe passes, it's not because of you. It was whoever pulled that trigger's fault and I won't be hearing of you taking any blame for this. Do I make myself clear?" Maddie's voice was stern and brooked no argument from the distressed young woman across from her.

"Yes, ma'am." Kassie's acknowledgment came out as half sniffle and half whisper.

"You two need to eat and get some rest," Chase stated quietly. "Joe's not going to be happy to wake up and find you languishing at his bedside."

Kassie refused to look him in the eyes. She sat stiffly in the chair as if waiting for him to say I told you so. He knew she would refuse to accept any comfort from him with everything that had happened. Still, Chase was determined to make sure she didn't place the blame on herself.

Chase made a call and a few minutes later Leo appeared at the door with two trays of food. He set a meal in front of Kassie who promptly brushed it aside. He set the other tray in front of Maddie.

"I promised Joe I'd watch over you. You need to eat. I know you're going to be as sassy as that one over there." He nodded toward Kass holding Joe's hand. "One of you at a time, while the other rests. I've reserved a room in the hotel across the street. Shadow and Hernandez have a team sweeping the hotel room and getting it secured."

"Maddie, I'll take the first watch," Kassie said. "He's going to be sleeping for a while so you might as well get some rest."

"Thank you, Sugar. I'll rest for a little bit and then I'll come relieve you. Young man, who's going to be staying here with her?"

"I will, ma'am. When you return, I'll be able to give you a progress report. Joe's vitals have been stable for the last hour, but we don't know what the next forty-eight hours will bring. There's an excellent surgeon on staff here. He's in good hands."

Maddie picked at the food on her plate and sipped at her coffee. She watched the young woman taking in all the vitals and watching her husband's chest rise.

"You were his greatest pride, you know. His greatest gift was that he was able to hold you girls in his arms one more time. Joe was so happy to see you." A single tear ran down her face. "Don't you forget that. Our lives have never been the same since you left. This wasn't your fault. It was James Stanton. He took enough from us." Kassie's reddened eyes met Maddie's steely gaze. "You're a Reynolds. Abigail and Nathan gave you the strength to overcome anything. Don't let him take any more of our family, our happiness, and most importantly, don't let him take you. Joe wouldn't want that."

She pushed the tray away from her and indicated to Leo that she was ready to leave. Leaning down, she kissed her husband's forehead and whispered something in his ear as she brushed his hair to the side. She walked to Kassie and kissed the top of her head. "I'll be back soon, Sugar."

Chase quietly sat down beside Kassie, making no move to touch her.

She was on edge. He watched as her eyes took in the numbers on the machines and she counted Joe's breaths. Her hand slid to his wrist as she checked his pulse as if she didn't trust the monitor to tell the truth.

Finally, not able to take the tension any longer, Kassie addressed him as she refused to take her eyes off her godfather. "Why don't you say it, Chase? I know what you're thinking. If I would have stayed on the mountain, none of this would've happened." Her voice sounded choked with self-condemnation.

He gently pulled the stray hair that had fallen into her face and tucked it behind her ear. Then he softly spoke. "No, Princess. I wasn't thinking that. I'm worried about you."

A stray tear rolled down her cheek and she quickly swiped it away. "No need to worry about me. I'm all set with my big bags of money from my daughter, I'm sorry, my *niece*." Her voice wavered and he recognized the hurt in her voice.

His hand moved to the back of her head and kneaded the taut muscles in her neck to relax Kassie as she sat stiffly, waiting for him to attack.

"Princess, I know you're upset, and we got off on the wrong foot. We'll address this later after you've put some food in your stomach, gotten out of those soiled clothes, and had some sleep. Joe's vitals are holding steady. As soon as Maddie returns, you're headed to the hotel." He wasn't asking.

Watching her mouth form into a straight line as she refused to converse with him reminded Chase of how she had reacted when he'd first brought her to his mountain. Kassie had built a wall around herself to protect her and Emma, not allowing anyone to get close. Chase had broken through it before by removing one brick at a time. He knew she was rebuilding it as fast as she could, and he was determined to tear it right back down.

Six hours later, Kassie's head rested on the bars of the bed. She hadn't let go of Joe's hand except for the one time she'd pulled the blankets over him. Leo hadn't moved from his position at the door. He nodded as Chase came in with a tray of hot tea and toast.

"Maddie called. She's taking a shower and then you're headed to the hotel."

"I'm not leaving." Kassie blandly stated. The adrenaline rush had left her body drained and her voice didn't hold the conviction it had earlier. Chase wasn't taking no for an answer.

"Drink the tea at least. It should revive you. Dr. Abbott is going to be watching over Joe while you're at the hotel."

"I'm not leaving." She refused to look at him and watched the monitors recording every heartbeat, every breath.

Chase didn't bother replying. Watching her take a tentative sip of the tea, he could tell she was crashing. He had seen her do it with Emma. He'd bide his time until Maddie returned.

Dr. Abbott introduced himself to the women sitting next to Joe's bed. "His vitals stayed steady all night, so that's always a great sign. He's still not out of the woods, but it's encouraging. He's in great shape for a man of his age and that'll help. For now, it's just a waiting game."

Both ladies let out a sigh of relief. Chase walked in and directed his attention to the older woman who arrived just in time for the doctor's report.

"Maddie, I'm taking Kassie over to the hotel. We're going to get some sleep, but I've left instructions to be notified immediately if anything changes."

"I'm…not…leaving." Kassie's words were slurred, and her eyes were having a hard time staying open.

Chase crossed to the room and scooped her up into his arms. "You need to get out of those bloody clothes, then get some food and sleep. Just a few hours and I promise to bring you right back over. Joe put his trust in me and I'm not letting him down."

He heard her muffled protest but kept carrying her out of the hospital. Crossing the street, he inwardly grinned when he heard her sigh and wrapped her arms around his neck. Her breathing already slowing from the adrenaline crash, he adjusted her higher so Kassie could lay her head on his shoulder as she drifted off. His only regret was Cartwright was beside him as an extra set of eyes. Shadow opened the suite door and allowed them in. His eyebrows rose as he watched Matthew fuss over the bed as Chase laid Kassie down and removed her shoes.

"Do you mind? I'd like to get her a bit more comfortable," Chase bit out.

"Really? I could have sworn she told me she was your *job*?" Matthew snarked back.

Chase bristled. His mouth firmed in a straight line and his jaw ticked. "I'm afraid that was a misunderstanding, but I assure you. She is *mine*."

"I think the lady has a say in that and I don't think she's particularly interested in you. She's made it clear she wants you and this team gone."

"Okay, guys. Let's stop the pissing contest and let her get some rest. I'm sure there's a lot to discuss but the main concern right now is getting the family safe and Stanton behind bars. I just got word that he's made bail." Shadow stared down both men.

Matthew left the room long enough for Chase to assist the already half-asleep Kassie to take off the bloodied clothes. He washed her off and pulled a T-shirt over her. She could shower when she woke up and grab a bite to eat. He pulled the covers up over her, brushed the hair from her face, and lovingly caressed her cheek.

Shadow met him outside the door. "There's coffee and I thought you'd like a shower. How long do you think she'll be out?"

Chase snorted. "Probably four hours at the most. I'll grab a shower and sleep while she's out. She's going to be a bear when she wakes up."

"Sucks to be you, man." Shadow ran a hand across the dark stubble that lined his jaw, chuckling.

"I'll stay in here with her," Matthew declared as he reentered the room and made himself comfortable in the chair beside the bed.

"Like fuck you will. Shadow will be watching over her. You can get your ass back outside with Hernandez's team."

"I made a promise to her sister and I intend to keep it." Daring Chase to try to remove him.

Chase started to cross the room when Shadow grabbed his arm. "It isn't worth it, brother. Go get some rest while you can. I'll be here." They exchanged a look of understanding before Chase turned and went to find a hot shower.

Five hours later, Chase woke and dressed. The suite was quiet, and he headed toward Kassie's door, surprised that she would have slept that long, and that Shadow was nowhere to be seen. Her bed was empty and made. He quickly crossed the room as he glanced at his phone and saw the text from Shadow.

> Sorry, brother. Kass woke up and insisted on going back. Asshat is with her. No time to wake you but I'm tagging them.

Cartwright was getting on his last nerve. He put on his shoes and exited the suite. He found them in Joe's room. Cartwright's arm was around Kassie's waist as they looked down at Joe and conversed with Maddie in low tones.

When Kassie turned and noticed Chase, she excused herself from the group. She looked rested. "May I speak with you?"

She ushered him into the hallway out of earshot of the others. Kassie looked at the floor as she addressed him. "I want to thank you for everything that you did for Joe. I'm grateful to you. But Julio and Matthew seem to have security under control. I think you and the team can go back home now."

"Is that what you think, Kass?" Chase ran his hand through his hair, then placed a finger under her chin, lifting it until she begrudgingly met his eyes. "I think we need to sit down and clear up a few things. You do realize that Joe was the one that retained us? We answer to him."

She swallowed and stepped back from his hold. Kassie shook her head avoiding him. "I'm sure that Maddie will be happy to release you as she's his spouse."

A growl emitted from his throat. Kassie licked her lips nervously.

Maddie came out and interrupted them, embracing Chase. "I can't thank you enough for helping to save my husband. Dr. Abbott says he's slowly but steadily improving, and we've a bit of hope that he might pull through."

Still holding Kassie's gaze, Chase answered. "Maddie, I'm under the impression that you don't want the team for protection anymore."

"What? Good gracious, whatever gave you that idea?" Maddie exclaimed.

Both faced Kassie. She scrunched up her nose and had the decency to turn red from head to toe. "Matthew is with me all the time and assured me that Julio can bring in more security. It's just silly to ask them to be this far from their home. They have other jobs."

"Joe will make that decision, Sugar. Until then, unless Mr. Leo tells me otherwise, they're still on security detail. I don't trust Stanton to not try something while we're preoccupied elsewhere. If anything, after what happened, we need them now more than ever."

Kassie cringed when she heard the tone in Maddie's voice.

Leo came around the corner and joined the group. Chase and he exchanged looks.

"If you have to stay until Joe releases you, then I insist that Chase be assigned elsewhere. I think it's best if we keep some distance between us."

Maddie gasped at her rudeness, but she held her look of defiance. "I will be forever grateful for what you did for Joe. But Emma and I need time and space to figure things out from here on out. I don't want to confuse her."

Chase stepped toward Kassie. Leo placed his hand on his arm and shook his head slightly. Chase's jaw ticked. His chest expanded and he exhaled as if he was fighting off what he wanted to say. Kassie turned and left the men standing in the hallway.

Chapter Seven

That night, Leo and Matthew walked Kassie across the street to the hotel. Maddie had taken a long afternoon nap and Joe had woken up. It had only been for a moment, but it ignited hope in the women. Kassie made sure Maddie had eaten a good meal, checked in on Emma, and now she was ready for bed.

Leo opened the door to the hotel suite and blocked Cartwright from entering. Matthew started to protest but Leo gave him a quelling look. "We'll be outside if you need anything."

The suite was quiet as she made her way to her room. Kassie was tired. As she set her phone's alarm for four hours later, she jumped when a movement from the couch caught her attention.

"Good evening, Princess. I ordered dinner for you." Chase patted the seat beside him. On a coffee table in front of the couch sat a tray with a plate of food and a glass of tea. There was also a glass of whiskey she assumed was his.

"I'm not all that hungry and I'm ready for bed. I mean it, Chase. I think you've made it clear how you feel, and I don't want to keep arguing. I need to take care of Maddie, Joe, and Emma." She sighed tiredly.

"Sit." The tone in his voice conveyed that it wasn't a question. "Eat everything on that plate. You've barely eaten all day. And who's taking care of you, Princess?"

"How would…"

He raised his eyebrow, daring her to ask how he would know.

She sat beside him then picked up the fork and started eating the grilled chicken and veggies while he quietly sipped his whiskey. When she got halfway through, she played with the remaining veggies and began to fold the napkin. Chase hadn't said a word as he watched her eat. She imagined he didn't want to give her an opportunity to leave before she got something in her stomach. He swirled a glass of whiskey in his hand and waited. They still needed to clear the air.

"Why did you leave, Princess? Why didn't you trust me long enough to help you get completely out of this?" His voice was calm and quiet. "Did you come to the barn that day knowing you were leaving?"

She swallowed down the piece of chicken that seemed to have gotten lodged in her throat. She took a sip of tea. Avoiding looking at him directly, she softly answered, "Yes. I knew when I came to the barn. Julio was bringing a team up the mountain. He'd already dispatched them to get Em. I was going to tell you, but you wouldn't listen." Picking up the fork and moving the food around her plate to avoid looking at him, her last words came out as a whisper. "If he would've come up that mountain, you could've been hurt. There wasn't any choice."

"So, you felt your only option was to run with two agents that you barely knew because they said they had Emma? Why didn't you just tell me that?" His confusion was evident in his voice.

"When I talked to Julio, he said that Leo's team had something called a sleeper. Then I overheard you and Leo talking on the phone. You said I was a mission." Her voice faltered. "I heard Leo say you needed to finish this to get the girl. Now I guess you can say you told me so. Joe's lying in that bed because I jumped to conclusions. What about you? When were you going to tell me that your boss ordered you to sleep with me?" She closed her eyes and sighed as she tried to keep her emotions under control so he wouldn't see the hurt and betrayal she felt.

Chase's hand reached for her, and Kassie sprung from the couch, not able to bear his touch yet craving it at the same time. "I'm not sure why you're even here now. You've done your job. Julio has everything covered."

"Is that what you think? You haven't been a job to me since the moment you landed in my lap at Sharkey's. I think you heard part of the conversation with Leo, not all of it. I'm not going to lie, I thought you trusted me. You're going to step into your sister's life and everything's going to be sunshine and roses? Have you even thought there could be more than one hit on you or Em? You'll constantly be on guard. Is that the kind of life you want?" He leaned closer to Kassie as she blanched at his words.

"No. Julio has shown me the agreements between the FBI and my sister. As Kassie, I'll have enough funds to keep security at all times. I haven't given it much thought from there. Right now, I just want to get through this so we can start our lives."

"Princess," Chase sighed. "I wish you would've waited for the team."

"I couldn't wait, Julio had Emma. I'll always choose Emma. I'm sorry, Chase." Kassie's sadly replied.

Intending to go to her room, she stopped short when Chase appeared in front of her. Pulling her to his chest, he lightly tugged on her hair and kissed her gently on the mouth. Tasting the whiskey on his tongue, her hands dug into his shirt as he continued his assault on her mouth. She melted into his body. A whimper escaped when she realized she needed him to hold her and make her feel safe.

Her fingers gripped the back of his head as he made his way down her neck, leaving punishing little nips in his wake. She leaned to the side giving him more access to her.

"I was so scared." Letting go of the tight grip on his shirt, she placed her arms around his neck. "I never thought you'd come here."

Placing a finger over her lips, Chase gently shushed her. "I'll always go where you go, never doubt that, Princess." Sliding his hand through her thick mass of red curls, Chase cradled her head. His lips sealed his promise as he met hers. Kassie's tongue melded with his.

Sighing, Kassie let out all the pent-up stress of the last few days, the fear, and the anxiety. Being in Chase's arms made her feel safe. An ache of longing unfurled in her belly. She missed him. As if reading her thoughts, Chase picked her up and carried her to her room.

As he sat her on the bed, she promptly sat up onto her knees and hastily began undoing the buttons on his shirt. She needed to feel him. When she finished, she pushed the offending shirt down his arms. Chase tenderly caressed her arms and the sides of her breasts until she removed the shirt. Stepping away, he slid his shoes off and unbuttoned his jeans, removing everything. Chase's cock strained upward and a tiny pearl of precum sat on the tip.

Brushing her hands away, he took his time undressing her as if he was memorizing each piece of her in his mind. Yanking the blankets down, he gestured for her to get under them. A giggle escaped as she thought of how he always ensured her comfort even when the evidence of his desire was clearly standing at attention.

"Ah, I see you have the giggles, I think I prefer you panting and wailing my name."

Boldly, Kassie looked him in the eyes. "Make me."

"Trust me, Princess, you'll be doing both before I'm through with you."

Opening the blankets wide so he could slide in beside her, Kassie let out a surprised gasp as he quickly grabbed her and settled her beneath him. Cupping her face, he lightly kissed her lips. Chase's hands caught hers and he held them firmly while he explored downward to her chest. Using both of their hands he pushed her breast forward into his mouth and captured her nipple in his mouth. Kassie closed her eyes relishing the feel of him and how he smelled of trees and the mountain.

"I've missed you." He whispered as he gave her other nipple his undivided attention. Kassie squirmed underneath him. The heat from her belly traveled downward and the ache between her legs wouldn't be satisfied until he filled her. Trying to remove her hands from his, she tugged to bring him toward her, wanting to feel his full weight over her.

"No, Princess. I thought I lost you, I'm not letting you go" Chase's voice deepened, and she opened her eyes and watched him as he kissed his way down her stomach. Nipping her hip bone and then lathing it with his tongue. Kissing just above the top of the mound of strawberry curls, he glanced up toward her.

"Lift your legs, darlin' and hold on." His eyes darkened as he positioned himself and waited as she unabashedly opened herself up to him. With him, she had nothing to hide, and her body responded to his command without hesitation. Still clasping her hands, his head dipped down and licked her like an ice cream cone. Kassie moaned as her hips moved of their own accord.

"I want to touch you." Kassie whined as Chase sucked her nub between his teeth.

"No."

"No?"

Pulling her hands to her stomach, his one hand held both of hers as the other slid between the delicate folds. Kassie's head flew back as her body clenched around his fingers as he drove inside her. The pressure built. His fingers curled upward as he held her hands easily. He was determined. The pent-up anxiety melted away to something more delicious. His mouth covered her, and she felt his tongue glide up and down her like he was licking an ice cream cone at a lingering pace. His fingers moved in rhythm with his tongue. The achy need for him was growing stronger by the minute.

"Chase!" Her eyes closed as the first orgasm threatened to take her over the edge.

"Not yet, Princess. I want to feel you around me." Briefly letting go of her, he pulled a condom from his wallet and slid it over the head of his cock. Adjusting himself to her entrance, he leisurely slid up her body, clasped her hands and held them on each side of her head. It was as if time stood still. Kassie closed her eyes wishing she could stay right in that moment.

"Open your eyes, Princess. I want to watch you come. I want you to watch me make you mine, so you'll never forget again."

Her blue eyes met his dark green ones as his cock slid deeper into her. Kassie tried moving her hips, desperate to feel the orgasm she knew was coming.

"Chase, please." She half begged half pleaded for him to go faster, harder.

Chase didn't respond. His pace stayed steadily slow as he rocked his hips in one with hers. The strokes deepened by degrees as he looked into her eyes. Her hands gripped his tighter and tighter as she mewled. His breath became faster. The pace was excruciatingly slow as he filled her deeply. Chase held their bodies so tightly together, even the slapping of their skin meeting was nonexistent.

Kassie's frustration started to increase at first but the longer he kept the rhythm, her body began to float as he controlled their lovemaking and refused to let go of her hands. A warmth spread through her as he held her gaze. Chase was taking no prisoners. His face told her he meant it, she wouldn't come until she knew she was his. Just the thought made her slick as her body met his thrusts as if surrendering to his command.

"Say it, Princess. Say your mine."

"I'm yours, only yours." At the admission, her body convulsed around his cock sending them both over the precipice at the same time.

Kissing her lips, he thrust upward one more time before sliding out of her. "I'll be right back, sweetheart."

Kassie's eyes closed of their own accord. She felt him slide back into bed after discarding the condom and pulled her into his embrace. Settling into his shoulder, Kassie slept all night since leaving the mountain.

Waking up the next morning, Kassie stretched. Her body was completely sated as a smile slowly spread across her face. Her stomach growled, letting her know that she must have overslept past the time she planned, and she rushed to shower and dress to relieve Maddie. Chase wasn't in bed with her, but she knew he wouldn't leave without waking her if something had changed concerning Joe.

Opening the door, she heard Shadow and Chase talking in the kitchen.

"What about the money? Do you think she wants to keep the money the FBI has promised?" Shadow questioned Chase.

Leaning against the wall, Kassie waited to hear what Chase would say. "I'm not sure about the money, honestly. Kassie isn't a gold digger. I'm more concerned that she wants to stay Kassie. Slipping into her sister's shoes is going to invite even more issues and I don't think she's thought this through."

"What if she can't give it up?" Shadow's concern was evident in his tone of voice.

Kassie could hear Chase sigh in resignation. "I don't know. I don't want this for her. I don't know why she wants it so badly. Damn it, if she only would've waited for Leo and the team, we could've avoided all this. She could have had *her* life back."

Kassie's heart cracked in two. He still didn't understand. She would always choose Emma. It was about a promise made long ago. Walking into the kitchen, Kassie grabbed hot water from the Keurig into a plastic cup and added a tea bag.

"Shadow, if you could walk me back over to the hospital in five minutes, I'd appreciate it. I'm already late." Kassie pointedly ignored Chase as she exited the room.

Making it back to her bedroom, she grabbed her shoes as the soft click of the door let her know Chase had followed her inside.

She could smell oak and mint as he stepped behind her. "Kassie, let me explain."

Looking at the messed bed where they had spent the night making love, her head shook in denial. She fell for the illusion of safety, of comfort. Trying to hide her humiliation, she tilted her chin up.

"No. I think I've heard enough. You'll never understand that the choices I've made are because I have had no other option. You'll never understand that Kassie was a huge part of me, and I made a promise. Emma's best interests will always be my priority. I never asked for the money, but it comes as part and parcel of this arrangement. Do you think that I haven't tried to think of a way to get out of this without losing Em and keeping my own identity? As good as your team seems to be, I doubt they could've come up with a solution that I haven't already thought about in the last three years. I think it's best if we steer clear of one another until your team leaves. Goodbye, Chase."

Chase reached out to her, and Kassie stepped back and shook her head. Stiffly passing him, she followed Shadow out of the suite. Stepping into the elevator, she leaned against the wall as it made its way down to the first floor. Kassie closed her eyes and swallowed down all the turmoil she felt inside. It was like he didn't know her at all. The gap between them seemed wider than Serenity Mountain.

Chapter Eight

Four weeks had flown by. Joe was coming home, and it was decided they would stay at the Stanton mansion as it was closer to the hospital in case Joe needed to go back while recovering. Catherine, Kassie, and the girls finished setting up Joe's and Maddie's room with the hospital equipment and all the comforts of home. Catherine and Melody moved in as her friend refused to leave.

As soon as Joe's health had improved, Kassie insisted that the team be dismissed. Joe refused. Now, more adamant than ever that the team stay as they had played a key part in saving his family. Frustrated, Kassie was determined that Chase not be a constant reminder of her time on the mountain and requested that Leo assign Chase elsewhere. She assumed he went back to the mountain as she hadn't seen or heard from him since the day at the hotel.

The media frenzy had not died down and James Stanton would be standing trial in two weeks. The DA running for reelection was hot to prosecute the case knowing it would help him win votes. Kassie would be called to testify. There had been some security issues, but Julio and Leo's team had handled everything perfectly. They placed more security cameras and assigned teams around the perimeter.

Kassie started making decisions concerning her and Emma's lives. As soon as Joe was able to move home, she was placing the house up for sale. Joe and Maddie insisted that Emma and her come live with them, but Kassie refused. They made the offer out of love and technically her childhood home was hers, but the thought of returning to it reminded her of everything she had lost. It was hard enough walking by the study where her sister was fatally shot. She immediately requested that the door be locked upon their arrival. Luckily, the office was off the path of her rooms and the main living areas in the house so she could avoid it easily enough.

Her thoughts would drift to Chase and what he was doing on the mountain. Every now and then she caught herself looking for property in the small town that captured her heart, before she would shake her head back to reality. She couldn't be that close to him. Her stomach dropped just thinking about him starting his life with someone else. She couldn't watch him do that.

While waiting for Joe to arrive in the ambulance, she was putting the last-minute touches in his room when she was asked to come to the foyer. She hadn't even gotten halfway down the stairs when she heard a squeal and Samantha, her friend from Serenity, ran toward the staircase. Running down the rest of the staircase, she let out a happy sound of surprise and the two women embraced.

"What are you doing here?" Kassie ecstatically exclaimed.

"Oh honey, I needed to see if you were okay! I hope you don't mind. I saw the news and the papers, and you looked so stressed, I needed to come take care of you for a bit." Samantha looked around her at the massive house.

"Oh Samantha! You didn't need to come all this way! What about LJ and your Mama?" Worried that her friend had dropped everything to come to her, she frowned.

"LJ is with Liam's parents and having a blast on their ranch. Mama's visiting family and I came to see you. Plus, Leo thought with the trial coming up, you needed to look your best and who would be better than me to make you look all glamorous?" Her arms went around her friend.

Kassie laughed and squeezed her friend harder. "Thank you. I'm glad you're here, but the trial doesn't start for a couple of weeks. Joe's going to be here any minute and he'll know all sorts of contacts for you to get your products out! Lord knows he's driving Maddie crazy. He's so bored and she won't let him do anything with the company. It's being perfectly managed by the vice president and Joe needs a diversion. Perfect timing." She smiled, trying to make everything appear light for her friend. The stern gaze Samantha gave her let her know that she hadn't succeeded in fooling her.

"Catherine is here! I can't wait for you two to meet!" She changed the subject because she couldn't stop the urge to ask if Samantha had seen Chase. "Let's get you settled into your room. Melody and Emma are playing with Rollo in the backyard with Saint and Taco."

Samantha smiled and followed her friend.

The week before the trial, Matthew quizzed Kassie on all the small details. They went over the testimony and back again. It was like reliving a nightmare. Tossing back two acetaminophens to stave off another throbbing headache, she stifled a yawn, practically falling asleep in the chair. Her exhaustion was starting to show. She was using more makeup to hide the dark bags under her eyes and trying to push through the endless questions and prep work.

After the third day, Samantha advocated for her friend. "You're pushing her too hard!"

"They're going to look for the slightest slip from her and they'll pounce, and this'll all be for nothing." Matthew turned the page to the next grouping of evidence they needed to go over.

"She's so tired she can't even hold her eyes open. It's eleven at night and you've had her in here for hours and she missed Emma's bedtime!"

Helping her to stand up, Matthew said, "Sorry, sweetheart, I'm just trying to make sure everything is covered." He kissed her forehead as she yawned.

"I'm sorry, Matthew. I'm just so tired. I promise I'll do better tomorrow."

"No!" Samantha said. "Tomorrow, I'm cutting your hair and you're going to relax." She held her hand in Matthew's face. "Nope, don't even start. Kassie's taking the day off. If she's tired and stressed, she isn't going to be any good to you either."

"I'm going to bed," Kassie announced. "Samantha, you can have me tomorrow after ten. I know Matthew will want to do a morning drill. I'll meet you here at eight and then Samantha gets the rest of the day. I promise, I won't let you down." Placing a hand over her mouth to hide yet another yawn, Kassie tried to placate her two friends.

Matthew brushed her hand away. "You can never let me down Kassie."

Samantha rolled her eyes and grabbed her friend. "Okay, let's go before you fall flat on your face."

The next morning, Kassie sipped her tea and watched Rollo out of the massive window playing ball with a member of the security team. She wasn't sure why Chase had left him behind, but every night he'd follow her upstairs to tuck Em in, then to her room where he slept at the end of her massive bed. She left her door cracked in case Emma woke during the night, and Rollo would be gone by early morning for his morning run.

"Hi, gorgeous! You sure look beautiful this morning." Matthew walked in holding a cup of coffee and a bundle of files. At the sight of the files in his hand, she inwardly groaned. She knew it was a necessary evil, but her stomach churned at the thought of going back over the evidence. Looking at the pictures of her sister half-dressed or naked with complete strangers was more than she could bear. After the trial, everyone would know what her sister had done. Because she'd assumed her identity, everything in those pictures would be associated with her. It wasn't that she was embarrassed, she was mortified by all her sister was forced to do. One day, she'd have to explain all this to Emma.

"Thanks. Catherine and Samantha are going through the closet and planning my outfits for the trial."

"Well, they did an excellent job, you look just like her." He placed an arm around her and gave her a slight hug.

She smiled and watched Shadow and another person she didn't recognize doing a sweep of the yard and checking everything. "Can I talk to you?"

"I always have time for you." Refilling her cup of tea and adding honey, he handed it back to her and took a seat on the couch.

"I just want to tell you that I appreciate everything you did for my sister and for us. You've been a very good friend."

Matthew shifted in his seat. "Why do I feel like there's a but in there?" Sipping his coffee, he waited for her to continue.

"And as a friend, I'm going to tell you, you can't stay in the past. Kassie would want you to go on with your life. My sister made mistakes, but you were never one of them. She was in love, I think for the first time. I'm sure she would've walked completely away from this life to be with you. But now, you need to let her go. So do I. Once this trial is over, Emma and I are going to start living our lives. I want that for you."

Matthew stood and walked back to Kassie and embraced her, quietly whispering in her ear, "I know she'd want both of us to be happy."

Samantha walked in and scowled at Kassie hugging Matthew. As if she had tasted something sour, she informed Kassie, "Derek wants to see you. He needs to go over security and Joe is insisting he's going with you." Grabbing a cup of coffee and a scone, Samantha waited for Kassie to follow her out of the room.

Pulling back from Matthew's hold, Kassie set her cup down. "Okay, let me run up to see Joe and then I'll head to Leo. Is he in the library again?"

"That's the last place I heard him and Catherine arguing." Sam checked Kassie's nails and led her from the room. "Girl, these are acrylics. How the hell do you chew on them? Ugh. We'll fix them the day of the trial because it's the second time I've fixed them!"

Kassie found Joe sitting up in a chair with his e-reader in his hand. He took off his glasses and motioned for her to have a seat in the chair across from him. "Maddie just left to go make cookies. She says you're losing weight and not sleeping."

"I'll be better once this trial is over." She kissed his cheek and sat down next to him.

"Hmmph. You know this could last for weeks." He closed the cover of his e-reader and gave her his full attention.

She sighed, "Yeah, I know. I want to talk to you. I don't want you at the trial."

"I'm going, Little Bit." Joe's voice held an overprotective parental tone.

"No. You can't. I have to be my twin. I can't sit in that stand and say the things I need to say with you and Maddie there. It's bad enough we lived it, but all of us don't need to hear the ugly parts. Please. I'd feel better if you stayed here."

Joe regarded her for a moment before speaking. "Okay, Little Bit, but if we're compromising, I want you to give me something in return."

"What?" Knowing by the way Joe was focused on her she wasn't going to like what he had to say. She adjusted the blanket on his legs and checked his water pitcher.

"You have Leo call Chase back here. I'll feel better knowing he's there with you." Joe's voice had taken on a firm, fatherly tone and she knew that he wasn't going to relent.

Kassie frowned at him. "Julio's team's doing an amazing job. I don't see why we need both. He's vetted everyone here and Saint's been doing deep background checks on everyone. There's no need to have Chase come all the way back. He has his own life to live. Leo's here because you won't release them."

"That man saved your life and his team saved the rest of ours. Julio's team is fine, yet Leo's team seems pretty protective of you. I can't help wondering if that's because of Chase. Leo would defend you and I've no doubt he'd do it with his life. But he's not in love with you, Little Bit, and I think you need Chase there as much as he needs to be." Confusion showed on her face and her nose scrunched.

"Protecting me doesn't involve love. I'm a job they're working. When this is over, they'll collect their paychecks and go home. This isn't about love." She waved her hand in the air to dismiss his excuses. The ache in her heart melted into her voice.

"I want Chase with you. That man loves you, Kassie. Truth be told, I think you have feelings for that boy as well by the way you've been since he left. I was hoping you would catch on after a few days or a couple of weeks apart, but you two are both stubborn mules. Talk to him. You'll figure out the rest."

"I asked for him to be reassigned and he hasn't even called." Her head hung dejectedly. "He doesn't love me, Joe. By staying Kassie, Chase thinks I'm giving up my life. I should've waited for the team. He keeps saying I didn't trust him. Where was his trust in me? I'm grateful for everything he's done, but I can't..."

"Love isn't easy, Little Bit. If I waited until Maddie came to me every time we had an argument, girl, I'd die of old age waiting for her. Sometimes, ya just swallow your pride, put your big girl panties on and get it done. He's wrong too. You have to remember that he never met your sister and I imagine his feelings for you have clouded his judgement. He'll always take your side. Even I disagree with you on this, I also have the advantage of watching you and your sister grow up and have some understanding of why you're doing it. Chase sees it from what this has done to you. I know that you've downplayed whatever you went through to protect me and Maddie. You didn't fool me though and I know a lot more went down than what you've mentioned. I don't think your relationship with this Cartwright fellow is helping your situation."

Kassie stood and smoothed out the invisible lines in her pantsuit. "We're just friends. There isn't any *situation*. Matthew's been filling in the blank spots about my sister. I don't understand why she didn't come to us. Toward the end before she died, we were drifting apart because I didn't understand her. Now I do. Most importantly, I'm glad she got to experience love."

Joe patted her hand. "I know. I'm happy about that too. The truth is Kassie's choices affected your life. That man downstairs, he may be a good friend, but I think Matthew's got his own demons, and I don't want him to replace Kassie's memory with you. Just make sure to keep a firm line on your friendship. And, *Cher*, either I go, or Chase accompanies you, it's your choice."

Huffing deeply and showing her displeasure, she leaned over and kissed him again. "Fine. Now I have to go find Leo. I'm only doing this cause I'm compromising." She grumped and exited the room just as Joe chuckled.

"Whatever you have to tell yourself, *Cher*." She glanced back and narrowed her eyes at her godfather at the doorway before she blew out her breath and went in search of Leo.

Chase was patrolling the perimeter when his phone rang.

"Doc, I need you to escort Kassie to the trial."

"Did you run it by *Mrs. Stanton*?" He was still salty from seeing Matthew deliberately hug Kassie through the window, knowing Chase was outside. He'd been sleeping in the staff quarters and giving Kassie some space. The only time he entered the house was to retrieve Rollo from Kassie's room for a nightly walk after she fell asleep and, in the mornings, before she woke. With each day that passed, Matthew had taken full advantage of the strained relationship. He always seemed to be laughing with her and showing up everywhere she was.

"Don't be an ass. She thinks you left, so make sure you're shaved, cleaned up, and at the house in the morning. That's an order." Leo admonished his friend.

Chase ran his hand through his beard. It was definitely time to shave. "I'm sorry. I'm sick of seeing Cartwright with his hands all over her. Every time, I try to find her alone, Matthew's conveniently in the room. By the time he's done prepping her for the trial all day, she's exhausted and I don't want to add to her stress right now. Kassie's scared, Leo. When she's overwhelmed, she runs. She can't do that this time, once she's committed to this, she'll have to see it through. It doesn't help that Cartwright and Hernandez are encouraging her that this will put the man that hurt her sister away. I want to see Stanton in jail too, but not at the expense of her losing herself. She's shutting me out and he's doing everything to get closer to her."

Leo assured him. "From what I've seen, Kassie's never given any indication that she's into Cartwright. Be patient, brother. Let's get through this trial. Then you'll have time to talk to her and straighten this all out."

Frowning, Chase headed out to find Rollo before going to get cleaned up. The dog had latched on to Kassie and never left her side. The only time he did was to go outside since Kassie wasn't allowed to be outdoors. He had to hand it to the mutt, he was one slick dog. "I hope so, Leo. I don't have a good feeling about any of this."

Leo agreed. "Whatever happens, we're here."

Chase made his way to Kassie's room knowing that Rollo would appear as soon as he heard Chase at the top of the stairs. When Rollo didn't come, Chase headed down the hall, giving out a low whistle. It was then he noticed Kassie's door was completely closed. The handle turned and he moved around the corner behind the enormous potted plant, not wanting Kassie to see him. The door opened and Rollo ran out. It opened wider as Matthew slipped out leaving the door cracked. Upon seeing Rollo run up to his master, Matthew smugly grinned as he tipped his hat and turned in the opposite direction.

Chase's stomach dropped. The pain in his chest was heavy. Rollo whined as he watched his master and Chase absently rubbed him behind his ears. "Come on, boy. It looks like she's made her choice, so don't get too comfortable. We're heading home as soon as this is done."

Chapter Nine

Kassie's morning had turned to hell. She hadn't slept and Chase was supposed to arrive at any time. The trial started tomorrow. Just the thought of it made her sick. Nauseated, she sat up and ran for the bathroom.

A slight sweat covered her forehead. She grabbed a washcloth and washed her face and brushed her teeth. Leo wanted to go over the security details again at breakfast. The thought of food sent her into another round of vomiting what little she had eaten the night before.

She asked the server to bring her toast and tea while Leo sipped coffee and went over everything. Kassie pretended to listen while she glanced at the clock.

Leo suddenly stood. "Good to see ya, brother." He shook Chase's hand.

"Thanks." He nodded at Kassie. "Hello, Kassie." His voice was polite and professional.

She hesitantly smiled, unsure of his greeting and cool manner. "Hello Chase. It's good to see you."

"Leo has briefed me on the plan, and everything looks good. We shouldn't have any problems." His voice was cold and professional. Not that she expected him to be thrilled with her, but he was always the calm in her storm. She was confused by the need to want him with her and the stark reminder that staying as Kassie could destroy any hope of working it out.

She couldn't hold the smile any longer. Looking down to let her hair cover her face, she grabbed her phone. "Thanks." She got up from the table. "If you don't need me, I'm going to find Emma."

"We don't know how long this is going to last, so your time with

Em might be limited. Go spend as much time as you can with her," Leo reminded her. Kassie nodded and glanced one more time in Chase's direction before going to find her daughter.

Kassie shut the door to her bedroom and slid down the wall. She needed to get her emotions under control before she saw Catherine and the girls. It wasn't that she was surprised by his attitude toward her, it was just the hollow feeling of being completely alone again that haunted her.

She shook her head. She wasn't alone. She finally had her family with her. She had friends. Walking into the bathroom, Kassie splashed cold water on her face. If her sister could survive all she had, then certainly she could survive something so small as a broken heart.

The trial started at ten and she had been up since five. Her stomach wouldn't settle. She brushed her teeth for the second time. She threw herself on the bed and tried to breathe deeply. Nausea rose again. She barely made it to the bathroom before spilling what was left of the contents of her stomach. She lay on the cold tile floor praying to die.

How am I going to get through today?

A knock on her door woke her up. She had fallen asleep on the floor. Three women stood in the doorway looking at her like she had been caught on an all-night bender.

"Oh honey, you look like death walking!" Catherine leaned down to help her friend up and placed her on the toilet. Samantha got a cloth and wiped her face.

Maddie sat on the edge of the tub watching Kassie with a critical eye.

"I'm going to find Chase. Maybe he has something in his bag to help calm her nerves." Samantha pulled her hair back and flipped it into a ponytail on top of her head.

"That's a good idea, but nothing really strong. She has to make it through today." Catherine held her friend's hand. "We gotcha, girl."

"Ladies, nothing is wrong with my baby that a couple of crackers and ginger ale won't cure. Catherine, could you go down to the kitchen and grab some?" Maddie asked as she knelt next to Kassie and tucked a piece of hair behind Kassie's ear.

Catherine and Samantha stared at the older woman as Kassie responded, "Maddie, I don't think I can hold anything down. I'm just stressed about today."

"No, baby. You're pregnant. Joe and I are gonna be a Gran and Papa again." She smiled wider. "I was hoping you'd figure it out on your own or I was planning to tell you after today. First things first. Samantha, if you'll go get my purse in my room, you'll find a pregnancy test."

"I can't be pregnant." Heat rose to her cheeks. Speaking of her sex life in front of her godmother was embarrassing.

Maddie laughed. "Sugar, I assure you, I'm well aware how babies are made."

"But we used protection…"

"They aren't always effective you know." Samantha started to laugh. "How far along do you think you could be?"

It hit Kassie like a freight train. "Eight weeks ago." She turned red at admitting such personal details in front of Maddie. "The day I left, we… ugh, forgot to use protection."

Samantha began to cackle with glee. "I can't wait to see his face. He loves kids!"

Handing her the test, the women left her to pee on the stick. When two pink lines appeared, Kassie's hand flew to her mouth. What was she going to do now? Chase had been cordial and professional to her at best. She didn't think he was going to be as pleased as Catherine thought.

She was a nurse practitioner; how could she have missed the obvious signs? Her hand traveled down to her stomach as if she could feel the tiny life inside. Butterflies hit her at the thought.

Not having time to dwell on it before leaving for court, she brushed her teeth again. The three women were standing right outside the door waiting for the results. She shyly held up the stick and they converged on her with hugs and reassurances.

"What am I going to do? Chase and I don't necessarily agree on things these days. He lives in Seattle. I'm here. I doubt he'd want to be a long-distance father."

"Listen, you don't have to figure out everything at this exact moment. Let it sink in and then sit down with Chase. You're not in this alone. He'll make sure you and that baby will want for nothing." Samantha guided her to a chair when she saw Kassie pale. "I'm sure you two will figure it all out. Just get through this trial first, so you can put it behind you. It'll be okay."

A few crackers and small sips of ginger ale and she started feeling like herself. "Now, in the morning, chew on a couple of crackers before you get out of bed." Catherine placed more crackers in her purse.

Maddie ushered Kassie into the shower, after which she sat at the vanity as Samantha took charge of her makeup and hair.

"The guys are downstairs waiting for you." Samantha handed her a ginger ale. "Small sips." Samantha fixed her lipstick and put a few small touches on her hair.

Maddie hugged her. "Don't worry, baby, it's all going to work out. Now go get this out of the way so we can celebrate."

Kassie felt Chase watching her as he sat in the seat beside her while Leo drove. Matthew sat up front and would occasionally glance back to give her a reassuring smile. Fiddling with her purse to occupy her hands, she leaned back and focused on the scenery outside. They entered through the back and waited in a small room until she was called. Chase escorted her into the courtroom.

Walking next to Chase, Kassie glanced to the defendant's side. Her ex-fiancé, Roger, sat with James. He smiled widely and watched as Kassie took her seat. Her supposed father-in-law wasn't looking as confident as he had in the past. His team of attorneys took up an entire table and the one behind him. All of them dressed in black, making it look like a funeral gathering.

Chase escorted her to the witness stand. Giving her hand a little squeeze, he smiled down at her. "You've got this," he said quietly and sat in a chair next to the stand. She held her head high and began answering questions from both sides. All the while feeling the heat of James's stare.

Breaking at lunch, she was immediately led to a secure room. Shadow brought her a sandwich from the local deli and unsweetened tea. She took one whiff of the tuna sandwich in front of her, and her body rebelled. Her hand shot to her mouth as she looked desperately about the room. Chase, seeing this so many times in his career, quickly grabbed the trash can. She emptied her stomach as he held back her hair.

"It's okay; you got through the worst part. You did good." Chase's voice was low and calming. She wanted to lean over and wrap her arms around him and let him take her back to the mountain. Where she felt safe and loved. Gripping the edge of her chair, she could only nod.

Shadow cleared the bathroom, and they escorted her across the hall. Chase took off his jacket so her knees wouldn't touch the floor as her stomach rebelled again. He handed her a wet paper towel and Saint brought in bottled water.

Concerned, Saint asked, "Do you want me to tell the judge she needs a longer break?"

Kassie shook her head. "No, I'm fine. It's just nerves, it'll pass. Let's just get this over with."

Saint waited until Chase silently communicated that it was fine before he moved.

Shadow returned to the secured room while Chase waited until Kassie adjusted her makeup and combed through her hair. She put her lipstick on and noticed Chase studying her.

"You're doing great. Don't let Stanton rattle you now." His voice was cool yet reassuring.

Placing everything back in her bag, she faced him. "When this is done, do you think we could talk?" There was a hint of a tremble in her voice, but she thought she had disguised it well.

His professional voice was in place and his face remained passive. "Let's just get through this trial. You made your decision and I wish you and Em the very best."

Shadow poked his head through the door. "They're convening."

Chase moved to the side to let her pass. She wanted to stay in the bathroom and tell him everything. But Chase's cool and distant stance prompted her to move along to the courtroom.

Questions were fired nonstop, leaving her tired and drained. Her fingers were sore from gripping the designer handbag so hard while she was on the stand. Finally, at five, the judge called an end to the first day. James Stanton's side had been aggressive, but most motions were denied. The evidence was stacked against him. It was the first day and her testimony had already buried him.

Kassie didn't acknowledge anyone as she was escorted to the car. She just wanted the day to be over with. Struggling to figure out how she was going to confront Chase concerning her pregnancy, she pushed the thought away and took a ragged breath as Leo started the SUV.

On the ride home, Kassie placed her head back against the headrest and was asleep before they made it down the block. Chase pulled a blanket from behind the seat and covered her. When they arrived at the mansion, she didn't even fight Chase when he unbuckled her and scooped her up into his arms. He felt her breath on his neck as she rested her head on his shoulder. God, he missed her. He reluctantly laid her on the bed and slipped off her shoes before laying a throw over her.

All three women converged as soon as he placed her on the bed. Maddie took her shoes from him, and Catherine volunteered to stay with her.

Samantha looked worried when he met her eyes. "She threw up at lunch. She hasn't eaten anything, so make sure she gets plenty of fluids and eats something for dinner."

Holding out his hand and motioning for Chase to gather the team, Leo talked into the phone in hushed tones. The team waited until Leo finished the call.

"There's been a development. Stanton was just rushed to the hospital with a heart attack. Shadow, I want you to get there and be our eyes and ears. Looks like our girl did good up there today. He's running scared. My contact says he's reaching out to dirty judges but right now, no one wants to be associated with him. His friend list just got shorter." Leo grabbed a bottle of water as he informed the team.

Shadow immediately left.

"Chatter indicates the bounty increased on Kassie. The funny thing is, there was a sniper dot on Emma at the courthouse the day Joe was shot. Now Emma's no longer a target. Something is brewing, so let's keep our ears to the ground and eyes open. Julio is doubling up on the security around the house."

Watching Chase, Leo continued. "Kassie requested that we move to Joe and Maddie's house. Now that Joe's doing better, there isn't any need to stay this close to the hospital. It's smaller, we can patrol it easier, there's a cottage to staff extra security and enough rooms we can reduce the number of people going in and out. I just don't have a good feeling about this. Everyone can be moved while we're with Kassie at the courthouse and no one will be the wiser." Leo waited for any objections.

Everyone agreed.

As the team filed out with their orders, Leo held Chase back.

"How's she doing? Shadow said she got sick earlier." Leo walked to the table that Kassie had requested the staff keep filled with drinks, snacks, and sandwiches for the teams. Maddie's cookies also filled a tray. He grabbed a couple of snacks.

"Kassie's rattled, but she did well on the stand. She asked to talk after this was over with. I don't think we have anything left to discuss. She's made her choices and I'm not even sure why she asked me to escort her to the courthouse when she prefers Cartwright."

"Did she say that?" Leo paused as he placed his water on a coaster and began opening a bag of chips.

"She didn't have to. I don't understand it, Leo. It's like the Kass I knew at the cabin is gone." He sighed as he sat in a chair across from Leo.

"How do you feel she's changed?" Unscrewing the cap off the water bottle, he took a long draw from the bottle and returned it.

"Look at this house. Leo, she says it's not about the money. Do you see the outfits she's been wearing? A few of those suits could build an entire wing of my hospital. Hell, the makeup alone could probably pay for all the linens. I can't give her this life, Leo. Not to mention this isn't hers, but her twin's. I don't think Kassie understands that even if James goes to jail, he has enemies. She'll always be looking over her shoulder. She didn't trust me enough to even hear me out."

Placing a couple of chips in his mouth, Leo thoughtfully chewed. "Brother, I want you to look around. Be honest with yourself. Is that what you see? Cause I'm gonna tell ya, man, I think you're way off base."

Rubbing his hand across his forehead, he closed his eyes. "I don't know anymore. Damn it. Maybe it was because it was just the two of us and we didn't have all this outside shit between us, I thought it was different. When I met her, she was a single mom just making ends meet with a sick kid. Now she's an heiress. I've spent weeks watching Cartwright hugging her, touching her, and spending time with her and she requests that I be assigned elsewhere. She doesn't want me here, Leo. Every time we talk, it ends up in an argument. She says it's not about the money, but that's all I see. This is the life she's going to be living. It's not even close to being on the mountain. I can't compete with this." Chase gestured around him. His voice lowered, "I caught Cartwright coming out of her room."

Leo's eyebrows went up at Chase's admission and quickly dismissed it. "Brother, let me give you some advice before you lose the most precious thing you have next to that mountain of yours. Have you ever asked Kassie how she feels? You want to know why she did this? My guess is that she spent three years questioning herself and she got way too comfortable with you. Things got messy with Hernandez and Matthew taking Em, she overheard part of our conversation, and your girl ran. She doesn't trust her instincts anymore."

Leo leaned in toward Chase. "You think she's changed? Go into the kitchen. She asked the staff to make sandwiches for the team when she's not here. As soon as she woke up from her nap, she found Emma, played with her and Melody, gave her a bath, and read her a story. She ate dinner in the kitchen with the staff as she made grocery lists. One of the staff members has a sick kid, she sent her home with pay and told her not to return until her child was feeling better. Right now, she's in there with Catherine and Samantha baking and making trays up for the men tomorrow. In the midst of everything falling apart around her, she knows them all by name. Kassie hasn't given any indication she has feelings for Cartwright. There could be a million reasons why he was there."

"I'm surprised Cartwright isn't in the kitchen with her. And I can think of only *one* reason why he would be in her room with the door closed in the middle of the night." Chase half rose from his chair, determined to make sure she got some rest. The grueling questions and attorneys trying to trip her up had taken a toll on her.

Leo indicated he wasn't done and gestured for Chase to sit down.

"He is. So is Saint. I'm trying to give you a different perspective. Kassie didn't ask for this. It was thrust upon her. You're probably the only person she's trusted for a long time. I should've never suggested you sleep with her. I regret that. When you made it clear she was yours that day everything went down, she became all of ours. Look around you. Does she look like she's happy? She's not the same woman I saw on Christmas day or the woman in those pictures holding Emma as a baby. She looks like a woman playing a part. If you don't get your head out of your ass and stop worrying about what you can't give her and focus on the one thing in the world that really matters....well then, brother, you never deserved her. And that's when Cartwright's gonna make his move."

Leo grabbed the empty bags and bottle and threw them in their respective recycling bins and exited the room.

Chase slumped back in the chair. Resting his elbow on the arm, he pinched the bridge of his nose. Everything that Leo said was true. Now he needed to figure out how to show his girl that he wasn't going to let her chase him off.

Chapter Ten

The next morning, the trial was postponed after Stanton's lawyers argued they couldn't proceed without the client present. The judge agreed. Leo directed Saint to check the judge's accounts as soon as the official handed down his decision.

Kassie had been quiet all morning, even when Chase informed her of the impromptu move. Gripping the bottle of ginger ale in her hand and peeling the label off, she seemed oblivious to everything going on around her.

Kassie's phone rang from an unknown number, startling her. She looked askance at Chase and Leo before they nodded for her to answer and placed the call on the speaker.

"Hello?"

"Hello Kassie."

Nausea threatened as she realized it was Roger. "Roger? How did you get this number?"

He laughed as if she had said something funny. "Have you forgotten how things work? Have you been gone that long?"

"What do you want?" Meeting Chase's eyes, he saw the panic in her face to hear from this man.

"Stanton wants to see you. Alone. He wants a private meeting in his room at the hospital in an hour."

Chase and Leo were shaking their heads.

"No." Her voice came out strong and confident, her chin lifted slightly with the encouragement of the two men. "Tell him that I don't plan on seeing him again until he rots in a jail cell."

"He wants to discuss Emma. He's aware of the hit. And Kassie? You know… he only asks once."

Her face went even paler than it already was. Her hands shook so hard that she nearly dropped the phone as Chase reached out to steady her. Taking the phone, he placed it up to his ear while holding her shaking body.

"Kassie will meet Stanton, but she won't be coming alone. I come with or the deal's off." He hung up the phone and placed it back in her bag.

The rest of the ride, the men were on high alert. Tension radiated throughout the car. It seemed to Kassie that Saint drove even faster getting to the house. Arriving at Joe and Maddie's, they exited the car when her phone rang again.

Leo and Chase flanked her as Kassie shakily pulled out the phone. Looking for permission from the two men, she placed it on speakerphone.

"Hello?"

"Kassie, it's James Stanton. If you want your daughter to live, you need to come to me immediately."

Running toward the house and speaking into his coms to Taco, Shadow indicated to the men that Taco had Emma and she was safe and sound.

Chase lowered the phone in her hand. "Emma's in the house. She's fine. Agree to meet but not until later this evening. We need time to secure the area."

At eight that evening, Kassie walked into the employee entrance of the hospital flanked by Chase, Leo, Saint, and Taco. They were headed to the hospital's administration executive offices. Julio's team was assigned the stairwell, ambulance entrance, exits, and rooftop, while Leo's team handled the elevators and the meeting.

Leo ordered Saint and Taco to sweep the floor minutes before their arrival. They worked out an escape route just in case Stanton tried anything. Chase pressed his hand to her back and steered her along the corridors.

Her alarmed eyes met his as she whispered, "Chase, I need to find a restroom." Panicking that she would lose the remains of her dinner in front of him, her pace picked up. Directing her to the closest one, the team fanned out, checking each stall. Shadow brought her a bottle of ginger ale as Chase held her hair back while she dry heaved. Feeling better, she rinsed her mouth at the sink while Chase dabbed her neck and chest with cool towels.

Looking into the mirror, she dug into her purse to fix her lipstick. Her hands trembled as she applied the color and placed it back in her bag. Chase gently grabbed her wrist and turned her toward him.

She avoided looking directly into his eyes, but he fixed her hair and tucked a piece behind her ear. Softly, he reminded her, "Take deep breaths. I'm going to be right beside you. Nothing's going to happen. The team has you surrounded and you're going to get through this, Princess."

Slowly meeting his concerned gaze, she found comfort in his familiar nickname for her and whispered, "Thank you."

He leaned in and placed a soft kiss on her forehead. Her hand gently rested on his chest as she inhaled the smell of oak and him. His hand drifted to the back of her head, kneading the tense muscles. Her eyes closed. She swallowed nervously.

"Let's get this over with, Princess. I miss you. I miss the us that we were at the cabin. I think we've gotten sidetracked with misunderstandings and assumptions. So why don't we go tell Stanton to kiss your ass and go home. Cause Kass, I'm not going anywhere."

Her startled eyes met his. She needed to make sure she wasn't dreaming. It had felt like they had been a world apart. Chase's thumb gently caressed her jaw while she unconsciously leaned into his hand. "I'd like that."

Taking her hand, he led her from the bathroom to the elevator, and up to the remaining floors, flanked by the team. She saw Leo lift his chin to Chase as he looked at their clasped hands and Chase placed his arm around her and pulled her close.

The team picked a room close to the fire exit. They sat facing the hallway. The rest of the team had fanned out and was stationed at each door. When the elevator dinged, one of James's lawyers pushed him out in a wheelchair with an oxygen tank attached. They were thoroughly searched before being allowed to enter.

Wheeling him up to the table, the attorney took the seat beside his client. James's dark black robe covered the hospital gown underneath. Sweat covered his brow and his coloring was a dusky pale, yet his cheeks were red as he fought for shallow breaths. It didn't stop him from still looking formidable to Kassie.

"As you can see, this isn't a setup. Mr. Stanton would like to speak to Mrs. Stanton alone," The attorney argued.

"No. That's not going to happen." Chase wasn't budging.

"You wanted to meet because of Emma. I'm here. What do you want?" Appearing calm, inwardly Kassie's stomach rolled as she met James's gaze.

"I'm going to jail." James's eyes bore into hers. "My lawyers informed me that your testimony will put me there at least for a little while but I've no intention of dying there. All I want to know before I die, is why you killed my son."

"What?" Looking in disbelief at his accusation, she gritted out, "I didn't kill your son! Do you think I'd kill my own sister?"

"You were the only one in the house! The staff was dismissed for the evening. You knew I was coming to visit you. I wanted a son!" His hand pounded on the table. "My son *needed* a son! You shot him!" His breathing increased as his face mottled in rage. Spittle flew from his mouth.

Chase pulled her further back and made it clear that James would have to go through him before he ever touched Kassie. Her chin went up and she gritted out her response to his accusations. "Don't you mean you were coming to rape me again? I didn't kill your son even though if anyone had reason to, I did! My sister was completely innocent of all this! She didn't deserve to die! Is this what I've been running from? You thought I killed Phillip?"

Stanton straightened in his chair while the attorney whispered something in his ear. He waved him away with annoyance. "I put the hit on you. But not my daughter. I didn't order that." There was no hint of regret or remorse in his statement.

Reaching for Kassie's hand under the table, Chase lent her support at James's confession. The attorney was trying desperately to stop Stanton from speaking.

"Leave me."

The attorney stood and left the room. After all, James only asked once.

James turned his attention back to Kassie. "You look a bit pale, Kassie." He smirked. Straightening in his chair, he slowly took her in. "You're still as beautiful as you were when you were carrying Emma. I see the morning sickness is not sticking to just the morning again?"

Kassie felt Chase's gaze land on her as James continued.

Stanton chuckled, "Ahh, I see you haven't told anyone yet. I'm sure Matthew Cartwright will be pleased. After being separated all this time, to finally be together and immediately start a family. It's almost like the past repeating itself. You were pregnant with my daughter when you married Phillip. Do you plan to marry Cartwright?" Watching her eyes widen, he continued. "Tsk, tsk, Kassie, I thought you would've learned by now. I know everything that goes on in my house and in my son's."

Refusing to look at Chase, Kassie addressed James. "We aren't here to discuss me. I want to know who wants Emma dead. You said you wanted to talk to me about her. Let's get this done." She felt Chase's hand slip from hers. Kassie didn't break eye contact with James even though her heart crumbled into pieces. This wasn't how she'd wanted to tell him. Finding out who wanted to harm Emma was the priority.

"Nothing will happen to my daughter. The hit will be called off on you." He sounded unapologetic that he was the one that had ordered it. "But I don't believe my order was the only one." His head drooped a little to the side before he straightened, determined not to show any weakness.

"In exchange for calling off the hit on you, I want to meet my daughter since I haven't seen her since she was a baby. I want updates on her on a monthly basis. It isn't up for discussion and I'm not asking."

"Emma's *never* going to know who you are. You're the man that raped her mother. I won't let you destroy her innocence or taint her in any way. You aren't calling the shots anymore. I am. You don't get to hurt my family anymore. Once you're gone, then there will be no one to carry on your sick legacy of destroying lives."

Tilting his head back and releasing a dark laugh, he looked at her. "My legacy is gone. My dead wife made sure of that when she sterilized my son. But I plan to get to know my daughter while I'm still alive. One way or another. And, Kassie, I have nothing to lose. Can you say that?" The glint in his eyes showed the threat he wanted to convey. She was tired of living in fear.

"She's *mine*." Kassie shot from her seat and leaned over the table. Chase rose as one with her as if James would have the strength to hurt her. He had already harmed her and her family enough for a lifetime. "*She's. My. Daughter.* You may have fathered her, but you've done nothing but bring misery to her and my life. Because of you, Emma was unable to get the medical care she deserved and suffered. I don't want you anywhere near her!"

"Motherhood suits you, Kassie. Matthew Cartwright doesn't know what type of woman he's getting." Chuckling, he leaned forward and stared up at the fiery redhead whose eyes flashed with rage. "I used to know a woman just like you, once. She had the same tenacity when it came to her son. But in the end, I won."

His attorney reappeared and Leo signaled that they would wait until Stanton was in his room before they exited. Taco and Saint escorted him down. Tension filled the air as she moved to look out of the office window. Chase hadn't said a word throughout the entire exchange. As soon as Matthew's name was mentioned, his hand had slipped from hers, leaving her all alone.

Pulling back the blinds slightly, Kassie stared into the parking lot. "I was planning to tell you, I found out recently. It was a shock, I needed time to get my head around it."

When he sat unmoving in the chair, the only way she knew he had heard anything she said was seeing his jaw clenched and his nostrils flare.

Flexing his hands, he stood and walked toward her.

She stammered. "I'm sorry you found out that way."

His face was taut with tension as he stared out the window. "Is it Cartwright's?"

"What?" The words barely came out. She stepped back as if he had slapped her. Nausea rose as her stomach fell, and she gripped the windowsill to keep from falling. Pain gripped her heart as she stared at the rigid man in front of her.

Leo opened the door. "We can head down now."

Glancing between Chase and Kassie staring each other down, Leo waited for one of them to respond. Kassie moved to the chair she had exited and gripped the back as she slid back down to keep her legs from quaking.

"Give us a minute." Chase's voice was clipped with anger. The temperature in the room seemed to have dropped.

Leo stepped outside the room. "I'm going to head down. The elevator will be waiting for you. It's locked. Come down when you're ready."

Moving forward and invading her space, his jaw pulsed in anger as he stared down at her. "Do you know how far along you are?"

Looking down in her lap, she slowly shook her head. When she raised her pain-filled eyes to meet his, she quickly blinked back the tears before she shakily whispered, "I think I'm around eight weeks."

She turned her head so he couldn't see the tears that welled, refusing to let him see how much he hurt her. This wasn't how she envisioned the conversation going. Surprise? Shock? Yes. Asking if the child was his… no.

Doing the math out loud, he said, "Eight weeks. That would put you at leaving the mountain after making love to me and leaving with Cartwright." He didn't say it, but the implication was there.

Bile rose in her throat, as he plunged an invisible knife deeper into her chest.

"I'm going to the restroom."

He started to follow when her hand shot out.

"No." She choked out. "The team swept the floor. No one's here, there's no need for your concern."

"Kass…I'm sorry. This is coming out wrong. Stanton seems to know a hell of a lot of things going on in the house. It doesn't matter, I still want us to work this out. I don't care if it's his, we'll work it out."

She inhaled sharply at his implication. "There's nothing to work out. I've *never* been with Matthew," she gritted out. "I'm not asking you for anything. You're not under any obligations to us." With her head down, she left the room and headed down the hall.

Kassie washed her hands and rinsed her mouth. Tears threatened but she refused to cry. She was already a single mom. Maddie and Joe would support her. She didn't need Chase Winters! Her hands shook as she fixed her hair and made sure her face masked all the hurt and confusion she was feeling.

Exiting the bathroom, she turned toward the office, intending to tell Chase she was ready to leave when a hand covered her mouth and nose with a rag. The last thing she saw was Chase looking out of the window before darkness consumed her.

Chapter Eleven

Running his hand through his hair and pacing the office, he checked his watch. The hurt on Kassie's face as she quickly exited the room made him feel like a complete ass. The impulse to run after her and soothe the hurt was strong. It was as if life had sucker punched him with a replay of his past with Rachel when she tried to trap him into marriage with a pregnancy and a child that wasn't his. Then aborted the baby when he insisted on knowing the due date. But Kassie wasn't like her. She wasn't trying to trap him. In fact, she tried everything to keep space between them.

Hanging his head, his mind raced through their argument. Eight weeks ago, she had fled the mountain the morning they made love in the barn. Mistaking her frenzied lovemaking as nerves, he realized she knew that she was leaving. She had been saying goodbye. He had been so caught up in making love to her, that nothing around them had mattered. Including the condom.

Frowning, he impatiently waited for her to return. Chase needed to make this right and apologize. He would reassure her that he believed her, that they would sort out this whole mess. It hadn't helped that his mind had replayed Cartwright coming out of her room that night with the smug look on his face on a daily basis.

The more he thought about it, the excitement at being a dad to Emma and this baby felt right. They'd have to figure out a few things, but he knew he wanted this baby. Most of all he needed Kassie and Em to complete him.

First, he needed her to know how much he loved her, and he was wrong. It was said in anger after weeks of watching Cartwright hugging her, holding her hand, and coming out of her room. He had fallen into

Stanton's trap. He let his own doubts and insecurities almost destroy the most precious thing he ever had.

Originally, he was waiting until this was over, Kassie wasn't going to change her mind about slipping into her sister's life. Not that he agreed with her decision, but he had no intention of letting her go. They would figure it out together. He had held off as Leo suggested. Now that circumstances had changed, he wasn't going to waste another minute. Checking his watch again, he knocked on the door of the bathroom.

"Kass, are you okay?" When there was no response, he assumed she was upset with him. "I'm coming in." He opened the door and found the room empty. Cold dread hit him. The hairs on the back of his neck went up and his adrenaline spiked as he tapped his mic while he rushed to the elevator. It was still locked. That meant she took the stairs.

"Leo, we've got a situation. Get to the secondary exit. Kassie took off. I'm headed down, start coming up. Have the team watch the exits."

"Copy," Leo replied.

He took off down the stairs, jumping over the rails. At the third level, he found Kassie's shoe lying on the floor beside a wet cloth. His heart pounded in his ears and his hand shook as he touched the mic.

"Leo, they got her!"

Taco gathered the cloth to see what Kassie had been drugged with. A thorough search had been done with no evidence of where she was taken or who had her. Julio was busy investigating the agents assigned to the stairwell. Chase's gut churned as the teams fanned out looking for any indication of where she was taken.

Hours later, the team regrouped at Maddie and Joe's. Matthew hacked into the hospital's security system. They watched the tapes over and over, looking for clues as to who could have taken her.

Saint leaned into the monitor and rewatched the tapes of each entrance and exit. "She was unconscious. How would you get an unconscious person out without being noticed when all the exits are covered?"

Chase jumped up. "The morgue!"

They crowded around the tape and sure enough, a man was rolling a hospital stretcher from the morgue to the parking lot. He grabbed Kassie and tossed her in the back of a hearse. Chase winced as he watched her get dumped like a sack of potatoes.

"Michael, make sure the go bags are stocked with extra medical supplies." He paced the floor, feeling at a loss that hours had gone by and he had no idea where she was. The look on her face before she left the office now devastated him. She wouldn't trust him to come for her, but he damn well wasn't going to let her down again.

"They're packed and ready." Michael replied.

"Damn it, check them!" Impatience and stress were taking their toll. He needed to find her.

Watching his friend fall apart, Michael glanced at the other team members before quietly asking, "What do you need me to add to the bag?"

All eyes turned toward him, and the room grew quiet. He gripped the back of his chair as he softly confided to his brothers. "Kassie's eight weeks pregnant. I don't know what we need to be prepared for, but we need to make sure whatever we have won't harm the baby."

Leo was the first one to place his hand on Chase's shoulder. "Congratulations, brother. Don't worry, we're going to find her. Saint will trace the plates and we'll find out where the asshole took her. You have my word."

As the night turned into the following day, there were no leads. The plates were stolen. All of Stanton's men were accounted for. Nothing came up on the dark web. It was like she disappeared without a trace. Chase paced the floors.

A week dragged by with absolutely no leads. Tension and worry could be felt throughout the entire house. Emma and Melody even felt the stress and played quietly with their dolls under guard. Joe and Maddie let the men work but were barely holding up under the stress. Catherine and Samantha took turns keeping the girls occupied and caring for the older couple. Both women were beside themselves but trusted the team would bring their friend back to them.

Chase barely slept since Kassie was taken. His mind kept playing the reel in his head when he had said the hateful words and the hurt look on her face. He knew without a doubt that she was carrying his child. He went outside to get some air while the men continued to scour through every lead. He looked up at the sky.

Come on, please give me some sign. Just one, Princess. I promise I won't ever doubt or leave you again. We'll figure this out.

Joe came out to the porch and watched the tortured man in front of him.

"Son, you need this more than me."

Chase took the shot of whiskey from Joe and downed it in one gulp. The burn hit his empty gut. He rubbed his hand through his unshaved beard.

"I'm sorry, Joe. I hurt her. She didn't deserve it." Chase's eyes burned from the lack of sleep. His skin crawled and he knew he was in desperate need of a shower, but he was worried about sleeping or not being available the moment they learned anything. He needed to get to his girl. Running his hand through his hair and pacing, Chase stopped to stand in front of Joe.

"Then I suggest you bring her back and do what every man on this planet does when they love a woman. You grovel." Joe patted the tired man on the shoulder.

"Nathan and I failed Kassie. But Little Bit, she's a lot stronger than Kassie ever was, she's a survivor. It took three years before she made it back home to us. From what I understand it was less than ideal, especially with Emma sick. That girl is fierce and determined. If you think she's this protective of her niece whom she loves as her own, just imagine how strongly she'll protect that child inside of her. She's just waiting on you to find her, son."

Joe left Chase standing on the porch.

There was a rush inside the house when Leo opened the door with the team in tow. Michael carried medical bags and the others were geared up. Leo threw his Kevlar vest at him.

"Suit up, we just got a lead."

Chapter Twelve

The day Kassie was kidnapped she woke up to find herself chained to a wall, lying on a mattress on the floor. Looking around to see if she recognized where she was, she watched her breath hanging in the air in the large, damp room. It was void of all furniture except for what she lay on and a small table with two chairs. A lamp connected to wires that ran across the ceiling gave off a dim light and a slight buzzing sound, making the room even more dismal. The dirt floor was the only indication that she was underground. She started yelling for help, hoping someone could hear her.

An hour later, her throat was dry and hoarse from screaming. No one was coming. She sat up against the wall and wished she had water to soothe her throat. She consoled herself knowing that the team would be looking for her. Even if Chase was upset with her, he'd never leave her. No. She trusted him to know he wouldn't leave her defenseless with a child. She needed to stay calm until he came for her.

Her thoughts were interrupted when she heard a key slide into the lock. She braced herself against the wall, looking for anything she could use as a weapon. There was nothing.

"Hello, Kassie. It's so nice to see you again."

Kassie's eyes widened in shock. "Roger! Let me go right now!"

"I don't think so. You've got a lot to answer for." He walked to the table, set a paper bag down, and threw a five-gallon bucket in the corner nearest to her. "You went to the FBI. All the while you were collecting evidence behind our backs. How did you get into the files?" He paused as he walked closer to her. "More importantly, what did you do with the ten million dollars?"

When Kassie didn't answer he invaded her space as she molded herself into the cold wall behind her.

"You cheated me out of your sister. It took me months to convince Phillip to give her to me. She would've been perfect. But you had to get involved and convinced Phillip to break the contract! I deserved that bitch!"

Seeing the crazy look in his eyes, Kassie remained silent. Something told her that nothing she would say would appease the angry man in front of her.

"Answer me, bitch!' His fist slammed into her face and her head hit the wall. Blood dripped from her lip and her cheekbone throbbed. The metallic taste filled her mouth as her ear rang.

"I didn't take any money, Roger, you're mistaken," she said, keeping her voice calm as she reasoned with him. "Maybe Phillip took it."

"I know it was you! You were in the office the day I gave the bank information to Phillip. Then two weeks later, it was all gone. Phillip and I had an agreement. He was planning to kill his dad and we were slowly moving the assets over. The only time money went missing was when you happened to be there. The day I confronted him about it, Phillip accused me of stealing from him and threatened to tell James it was me! Do you know what James would've done if he had found out what Phillip and I were planning? Where did you put the money?" Roger shouted.

Shrinking further into the wall, Kassie yelled, "I didn't take the money! If I had, don't you think I would've disappeared with Emma for good? Why would I have lived in the slums if I had ten million dollars?"

She tried using plain logic, but Roger picked up a metal rod and slapped it against his hand.

"I'm not going to ask you again. Stanton's legal team discovered the money missing because of this trial. I can only fudge the numbers for so long. Stanton will kill me. I need that money! Now where is it?" Roger loomed over her, his face distorted in rage and his eyes narrowed as he threatened her.

She knew there was nothing she could say that he was going to believe. She curled up in a ball and covered her head as he started striking her legs. She cried out in pain as she felt and heard the crunch of her bones as the metal rod hit her arm. she stayed curled up, making herself smaller to protect her child. The chain held her in place as he unleashed his anger.

Grabbing her hair, he then unlocked the cuff on the chain and dragged her to the chair. Pain from her arm spread through her body. She screamed. He slapped her across the face and leaned into her ear.

"I was planning on carving up that pretty face of yours so that nobody would want you again. Now, I think you'll help me work off that money." He laughed as he watched her tremble in fear.

"If you tell me now, I'll just sell you to the highest bidder." He took out a knife. "In fact, let's just see what you got hiding under there."

Panicked that he was going to cut her, she started to bolt from the chair. His foot struck out, causing her to faceplant on the ground, sending pain shooting through her arm. He stomped on her leg, causing her to cry out.

Dragging her back to a sitting position, she held her breath as he cut her silk top with the tip of the blade. Sitting perfectly still, she breathed through the excruciating pain, terrified he would cut her. Snapping the straps off her bra, he began to cut off her linen pants. They fell off like the wings of a butterfly and fell around the seat. A whimper escaped when the blade sliced into her injured leg. Smiling, he watched her face as he took the tip of the blade and dragged it up the limb until he got to her panties. He sliced into her skin slowly, causing a red river of blood all the way up her leg. She held the scream in. Stopping, his mouth twisted in an evil grin as he jerked the knife, startling her. As the panties' seam tore, Roger laughed as he started on the opposite side.

Her screams failed to get him to stop. She took a deep breath, trying to regulate her body's response. Knowing she was going into shock and thinking of the baby, she tried to bargain.

"If you let me go, I can write a check. I have access to Phillip's money. I can double it!"

He stood and walked around her chair as if contemplating her offer.

Out of nowhere, his fist connected with the other side of her face.

"Do I look stupid to you? Do you honestly think I'd let you do that and say we're even? You *owe me!*"

She felt like he had broken her eye socket. Feeling the blood running down her face, her eye throbbed, and she choked on the coppery taste of the blood in her mouth. Her body hurt everywhere.

"Please, Roger."

He grabbed her by the hair and kicked the chair out from under her. She fell on her leg. Yelling out as he kicked her in the back of the ribs.

"I'm a patient man. No one knows where we're at. I could keep you for months and nobody would ever know. But it'll be the longest time of your life and you'll be begging me to let you die. I'm going to give you some time to think about it."

The sound of the lock engaging echoed through the room. She gathered the clothing scraps he had thrown at her after he'd dragged her to the mattress and chained her to the wall. She dabbed at the cut on her legs and applied pressure in places where he had gone deeper. She made a makeshift sling for her arm out of her pant legs. Crying out in pain, she tried to align her arm the best she could and wrapped the remains of her shirt around what she could reach. Throwing the sling over neck, she braced it to her chest. Her arm throbbed with a pulse of its own. Taking deep breaths, she spit out the blood from her mouth and leaned against the cold wall.

Reminding herself that Chase wouldn't give up looking for her, she slid down to the mattress as her body wracked in shivers. Her hand moved to her belly.

"Don't you worry, your daddy's coming with a big bad team, and they're going to kick his ass. You stay with me, okay? Stay in your cocoon. I'm going to protect you, but I need you to stay strong baby."

With nothing left to do, she began counting down the minutes until Chase and the team came to get her.

The days seemed to be endless and she wasn't sure if she would make it until Chase and the guys found her. The stench from the bucket she used for her bathroom reeked throughout the room. There was only a small amount of water given to her to keep her from shutting down. Trying to hold on, she drank every ounce.

A new game of torture began daily as he questioned her. Bringing down two trays, he'd let her choose what she would be eating that day. Some days the plates were all empty, other days one held a slice of bread, or a bowl of rice. Reminding herself that the child she carried was counting on her, she would choke down as much as she could, without water, before he removed the tray.

His mental games were worse. Roger would drag her to the table and lay out cards, each with a different punishment, and make her choose what was going to happen when she refused to give up the location of the missing funds. He'd slam his fist on the table, making her jump when she took too long. She'd hesitantly pointed with her broken finger at a card. If she wavered, the punishment was twice as long. She didn't know if there was anything ever written on it, but he would slide the paper toward him and laugh as he read it and shake his head. Dread would fill her. She never made the right choices. If she had, she wouldn't have been there…

Entering the room, Roger dragged an empty bucket and placed it near her. Pulling Kassie up by her hair, he dragged her to the table and made her sit. Her chest was congested, and her breathing was raspy. Coughing hurt, yet she couldn't stop. Again, he made her choose a plate. She sat for a minute, trying to concentrate, when his hand slapped down on the table, making her jump. She raised her hand and pointed to the tray on the left. He grinned as he lifted the lid. The biggest juiciest steak she could've imagined sat in front of her. He grabbed the other tray and left the room.

The aroma of the steak filled the room, and all she could do was whimper as she was too dehydrated to cry. Finally winning the prize of real food, she couldn't eat it. Her face was swollen, and she could barely move her jaw.

With no windows to indicate night or day, she lost track of how many days had passed. For all she knew it could have been mere hours between his visits. Each time he became more desperate. Kassie's denial of the location of the money held the consequences of knife cuts, broken bones, and beatings. So far, she had three broken toes, two broken fingers, a broken arm, and a broken leg. She guessed her ribs were either cracked or broken because it had begun to hurt to breathe. But what scared her the most—Roger had strapped a gun to his belt.

When he tired of tormenting his prey, he left her lying on the cold dirt floor, not even bothering to tie her up. Where would she go? Her body was slowly shutting down. Kassie stared at the dim ceiling out of her one good eye.

"Sissy, are you there? Is Mama and Daddy with you? I need someone to talk to. Maddie and Joe will watch over Emma. I loved her as if she were my own. She's such a good girl." She whimpered and choked on her own sob. Her hand felt something on the floor, and she realized it was a clump of hair he had torn viciously from her scalp. She hugged it to her chest.

The ceiling light got a bit brighter. Kassie blinked. She was giving up. She let the weightlessness of her body take over.

A woman who looked similar to her bent over her.

"Hang on, Kassie, help is coming. I'm sorry, Lass. I know you're hurting, and I've sent Ivan to get something to help with the pain. I've dispatched my man to fetch the team of men looking for you and they're on their way. Don't give up. I've been where you are, I know the pain. The next time I see you, we'll both be free."

Kassie laughed, not knowing who this woman was. She had been around enough dying people to know that when a patient was in the dying process they would talk and see their loved ones or hallucinate.

"Help isn't coming. Look at me, I'm going to die. No one's going to find me. I won't get to see Emma grow up. I won't get to be with Joe and Maddie. My friends… Chase..."

The shadow of a man leaned over her and darkness descended. She felt the woman squeeze her hand and urge her to hold on…

Roger returned, dragging the five-gallon bucket that grated on her ears. He held the black metal pipe and struck his thigh lightly as he stared down at her as if deciding on what to do.

"I've waited long enough. If you won't tell me, I'll go get that brat of yours and you can watch me do everything I'm doing to you to her little body. It's your last chance, bitch, where's the cash?"

Swinging the pipe, he hit her on the stomach and arm. The sound of her bone crunching as her weak whimper filled the air didn't deter him as he continued to swing the rod. When she lay there motionless and no sound emanated from her, he stopped to catch his breath.

"Looks like I need to make a little trip. I thought knowing I was going after her, you'd break. You'd rather watch your kid get beaten to death before telling me where you stashed the money. The kid will be lucky that I beat her to death. You're a fuckin' lousy mom."

Kicking the bucket and making it fly across the room, he exited, leaving her limp and broken body lying on the floor.

Chapter Thirteen

"Milaya, why don't we save the girl if she means so much to you? We don't need some retired military team to come in, we have the men."

Flipping her braid over her shoulder, Victoria Stanton watched her men empty the rest of the warehouse of guns and drugs.

"No, Ivan. It needs to be them. I can't jeopardize my opportunity to bring James down. Kassie understood that when I gave her the information to bury him. We're too close to ruining the last of his contacts. I've got him grasping at straws financially to stay afloat. I've left him just enough so that he can keep his façade up a little longer."

Frowning, she put her arm around her husband. "I pray she makes it. I wish we had discovered her earlier. But I've had eyes on those men for a while now and they'll get to her quickly. We need to keep our attention focused on raiding his warehouses. He has innocent human beings being sold like cattle. I refuse to let them live that kind of life. Kassie wanted her revenge as much as I do. Those men can help her. I dispatched Ethan with a USB drive and coordinates; they won't waste time getting to her. We need to stay focused on our goals. He's a fool if he thinks I'll let him cheat me out of his death by having a heart attack."

Leo watched as Catherine and Samantha comforted Maddie as she broke into tears from worrying. The girls had gone to bed, and he watched as his brother went out of his mind with worry. They had exhausted all the leads and still combed every square inch of Stanton's home. James Stanton had been under the watch of Julio's team. Julio had so far uncovered two of his best agents being blackmailed. One of them had been assigned to the stairwell Kassie had been taken from.

The unspoken fear that he had Kassie ran through all their minds and time was of the essence. He ran his hand through his hair and took a sip of the now-cold coffee.

Saint opened the door and leaned over Leo, quietly speaking to keep from being overheard.

"A young man just appeared at the gate, insists he can only speak to our leader, and showed your picture."

Leo immediately went into action and ran to the gate. Shadow appeared relaxed while he lit a cigarette. If the young man thought for one minute that his life wasn't in danger, he was quite mistaken. Saint and Taco were already in position.

Ethan handed Leo the envelope.

"I was instructed to bring this to you immediately. It's concerning the woman you're looking for and I was to press upon you that time is of the essence. Don't waste time interrogating me or you might be too late." Then Ethan sped down the drive.

Wasting no time, Leo ran back to the house. He ripped the envelope open and grabbed the USB that fell out and handed it to Saint. The team gathered around. It was a video of the day the real Kassie and Phillip had died.

In the video, the real Kassie jumped up, desperately talking to whoever was in the room. The gun pointed to the floor, and she slowly went to her knees, begging for her life. Two shots were fired, Phillip's head fell onto the desk and Kassie fell to the floor. A few minutes later, they watched Kaitlyn—the woman they all knew as Kassie—enter the room and try to save her twin. They watched the anguish on her face as her sister whispered to her, and the pain at watching her sister die.

A somber mood fell over the team as they watched a younger version of the woman they knew transform before their eyes, instantly carry the world on her shoulders.

Even though they knew what her sister had whispered to her, watching Kassie realize that her life was going to be forever changed, was an eye-opener. Especially to Chase. He saw the devastation and the lost look in her eyes as she listened to her sister. Realizing that she never had a choice, she needed to remain Kassie. He finally understood what she had been trying to tell him all along.

They watched it over and over. Shadow spotted the first clue.

"Look! They're the same shoes that Roger guy was wearing. He killed them!"

Saint grabbed his computer and began delving into Roger, hoping to find where he might have taken Kassie.

Chase leaned in. "Why would Roger want Kassie dead? Or Emma? It doesn't make any sense."

Saint pulled out a stack of documents from the envelope "Because he wanted her sister. He wanted to groom her as Phillip had done to Kassie. There's even a contract between Roger and Phillip. It wasn't just about Kaitlyn, it looks like Phillip was getting ready to push his father aside and make his own alliances. Roger was going to be a part of it and Kaitlyn was part of the deal. Kassie convinced Phillip not to go through with the agreement. Roger must not have been happy that the contract was broken. Without Phillip and no male to continue the family, Roger would be next in line to take over. He couldn't have predicted that Kaitlyn would take Kassie's place."

"That doesn't explain why he would want Emma gone," Leo stated.

"I think Roger was tying up loose ends, getting rid of anyone that could claim the family name. I don't think he knew everything in this will. He'd already aligned himself with James until he realized Phillip was getting ready to seize control. When Phillip died, his father wasn't any wiser to his plan and he's now James's number one man. He stood to take over when James died. Having Kassie and Emma suddenly show up alive would've ruined his plans."

"Where would he take her?" Watching Saint work his magic on the keyboard, Chase was getting antsy. He couldn't stand still; he was ready to go get his girl.

"I think we need to get Cartwright involved. He's a better hacker than I am. The dude has skills. The coordinates on the USB show a plot of land. There's nothing on it. I can figure it out, but Cartwright would be faster." Saint directed his comment to Chase, knowing time was a factor.

"We do whatever it takes to get her back." Swallowing his pride was easy if it meant that he could get Kassie back.

Leo made the call and the men looked over all the documents left in the folder while they waited for Cartwright to give them any information he could find.

Fifteen minutes later, Matthew Cartwright called back with the information they needed. He came across some documents concerning property an uncle willed to Roger. It appeared to be an old farmhouse thirty miles away, with a river that was easily accessible. As soon as the team saw the outline of the property, they knew there was more going on there than it seemed.

"We just need to figure out where he's got her. If the paperwork here is even close to the truth, we'll only have a very limited time to find her before he knows we're on site. We can breach security, but I'm concerned about the time." Rubbing his hand through his scruff, Leo pondered the situation.

Chase sat straight up. "No. We've got something to help with that. We have Rollo."

Feeling like they were on the right track, Leo patted his friend on the back.

"Let's roll out. We gotta get our girl."

Rollo came running out with a vest already attached to his chest. Chase opened his side of the truck and the dog jumped in. It was time to bring Kassie home.

Chapter Fourteen

Kassie's life flashed before her eyes. Laughing in the kitchen with her mom, Maddie, and her sister as they made cookies. Watching movies with Joe and her dad. Nights with Emma playing Candyland and Go Fish. Chase…

Just when she thought she couldn't feel anything, her heart hurt.

She waited for death to come. Feeling the wetness between her legs, she guessed that the baby was gone. Deep in the pit of her stomach, rage built. She lost her child and now he was going after her sweet Em. She screamed as loud as she could, knowing that she wouldn't be heard.

"Can you hear me, Sissy? Answer me! Do you see what's happening to me right now? What did you do with that money? I'll tell you what you did, you got me killed. He's going after Emma and I can't protect her. Help me save her!"

Silence answered her. Broken and unable to shed any tears because of the lack of fluids, she mourned the loss of her family and everything she had been denied experiencing. She yelled into the empty room again.

"I'm dying, Sissy, and you don't even care…"

A voice from far away reached her ears. The voice sounded like her own, but it wasn't. A warm glow seemed to surround her and for the first time in a long time, she wasn't cold.

Listen to me! You need to hold on. You have to fight. Get the gun. Do you hear me, Sissy? You fight!

The glow started to disappear.

"Don't leave me, Sissy, come back!" She heard the click of the door and this time she didn't even care. "I'm so sorry, baby."

"Are you talking to yourself again? I told you, *nobody's* going to come." Dragging her by the hair to the bucket on the side of the room, she didn't even feel it. She didn't scream or fight. She was waiting for him to pull the gun and shoot her as he had done her sister. He bent down to prop her up. She was a complete rag doll as he tried to get her to stay upright.

The word *fight* rushed through her head. She had to be hallucinating at this point.

Fight!

There it was again.

Grabbing her arm, Roger jerked her upright. All the training that Chase had taught her kicked in and she envisioned him talking in her ear, instructing her on how to disarm someone with a gun. Her body remained limp until she snatched the gun quickly from the holster. Surprised, Roger reeled back as a shot fired through the room.

Wheezing from the broken ribs and holding up the gun that seemed to weigh a ton, she aimed it at him.

"You killed my sister. You helped kill my parents." He began to back up.

"You aren't getting out of here alive." He backed into the chair and stumbled. "Nobody's here to help you and if you kill me, you'll lie here for days and die an even slower death than what I've planned for you."

"Maybe so, but I'm sending you to hell first." She aimed the gun, and another shot rang out. He laughed.

"Looks like you are having problems seeing me." He chuckled cockily. "You're going to run out of bullets and then I'm going to make you suffer more."

He started to advance, and she thrust the gun forward. There was a noise behind the door. Roger looked behind him and started toward her quickly. She closed her eyes and let out a breath, relaxing her stance as much as she could, just as Chase had taught her.

With what little energy she had left, she screamed, "My name is Kaitlyn Abigail Reynolds. You killed my sister, and this is for her."

Pulling the trigger twice, she heard his body hit the ground. Sliding against the wall, she fell to the floor as she waited for death to come. It was close, she could hear the voices coming for her…

Chapter Fifteen

"Go find her, boy," Chase desperately pleaded to the canine. Sniffing the shirt, Rollo took off at full speed through the tunnel. Ten minutes later, he alerted to a find. Guns drawn, they raced ahead. When they got to the door, they heard Roger talking. Rushing the door, Leo entered first, followed by Chase, Shadow, Saint, and Michael. Guarding the tunnel entrance, Taco and Matthew called for an emergency evac, not sure what they would find.

Leo burst through the door with his gun drawn and nothing could have shocked them more.

"I'm Kaitlyn Abigail Reynolds! You killed my sister, and this is for her!"

The second shot rang out and Leo dived to the floor. The team followed suit as the third shot hit its target and Roger dropped to the ground, shot through the chest. Rollo made a beeline to Kassie, then licked her face and whined as the team crowded around her. Chase took off his shirt and covered her.

"Kassie! Oh God, baby, I'm right here!" Reaching for Michael's bag, he began pulling out supplies, trying to find a place to insert an IV. His hands faltered. Michael grabbed the bag and began to search for a vein, instructing Saint and Leo to do the same. Kassie was severely dehydrated.

"Chase, I got this." Michael reassured him, "Just talk to her."

"Hold on baby." He brushed her hair off of her face and noticed big chunks missing. "We're going to get you out of here. Emma, Maddie, and Joe are waiting for you to come home. Stay with me, Princess."

Kassie's eyes fluttered open in surprise. She weakly whispered, "Thank you for coming for me. Tell them I love them."

"No. Keep your eyes on me, Princess." He took in her battered body and the blood smeared all over the floor. His voice broke as he braced her head while they placed a collar around her neck. "Please don't leave me, Kass," Chase pleaded.

Leo took her blood pressure and showed it to Michael.

Shaking his head, Michael dug into his bag and threw a blood bag to Leo and another IV kit. "She's lost a lot of blood, her BP is low, Chase." Taking a blanket from the bag, the team spread it over her as her body shuddered.

"Keep talking to her." Michael pulled more things from his bag and threw stuff toward her feet to Saint. They started working their way around. Saint was efficiently bandaging her hands and legs while Leo got the portable cot ready to transfer. Michael silently conveyed to everyone there except Chase that she was not looking good, not that they needed confirmation.

Michael started taking inventory of her most immediate needs. "Her ankle, arm, and fingers on her left side are broken. Breath sounds indicate she's most likely got broken ribs and possible pneumonia. Lacerations on her back and legs. There's a couple of deep ones, but most are thin. Her stomach is distended, possible internal injuries, so we need to be cautious in picking her up. We can't risk puncturing the lung. I'm worried about that leg and her toes. Chase?"

Chase nodded, while his eyes pinned on Kassie. His voice was thick with emotion. "How far out is the helo?"

Kassie weakly held up her hand. Chase took it gently in his. "I lost the baby, I'm sorry." Her eyes conveyed her sorrow.

Leo clapped him on the back "It'll be here in ten. Just enough time to get her out of the tunnel."

"Let's not waste time." Michael barked out orders as time was of the essence. "Saint, hold the IV and blood bags. Leo, let's do a two-man lift until we get to the entrance. Taco can pull her through as we lift." He touched his mic. "Be as gentle as you can, Taco."

"You got it, brother. I'll treat her like the most precious thing on earth." Taco replied.

Leo grabbed the morphine stick from the bag and injected Kassie.

Chase whispered encouraging endearments in Kassie's ear as tears fell. Waiting for Michael to complete his ministrations, he looked about the room. Blood was smeared everywhere, and chunks of hair lay around the room. A bloody pipe lay on the floor next to an empty bucket. The room smelled heavily of ammonia. If Roger hadn't been dead, Chase would have killed him without a second thought. He didn't deserve to live.

Saint finished getting Kassie secured to the cot.

"Let's get her out of here. Saint's going to have to help carry her. I'll carry the supplies," Leo ordered as the team scrambled to action.

The fifteen-minute flight was silent as the team watched her chest rise slowly with each breath. Leo called Catherine to have her break the news to Joe and Maddie. She would bring them to the hospital while Samantha stayed with the girls.

Upon landing, the team jumped out and began to assist in transferring Kassie. Chase refused to let go of her hand as they wheeled her to the trauma unit. Michael and Taco followed directly behind.

Saint was the first one to notice that Leo hadn't moved. He stood by the helo and waited.

Leo lay on his side and watched as Kassie disappeared through the glass entrance. "Saint."

"Yeah, boss?"

"When Kass gets out of this damn place, you're in charge of teaching her how to shoot." Agitated, he scooted closer to the door.

"Chase worked with her on the mountain." Peering into the cockpit, he watched as his brother slowly moved.

"Well, apparently the bastard forgot to explain to her that she should keep her eyes open when she's shooting a target."

"Well, she hit the bastard." Noticing that Leo was hurt, Saint leaned in and grabbed his arm to help him.

"Yeah. She did. But she also shot me in the ass." Annoyed at being struck in the butt out of all places, he gritted his teeth from whining about the pain.

Saint raised his head and barked out a laugh. Shadow joined him as they assisted him out and into the hospital.

Chapter Sixteen

Chase put his face directly into hers. "Princess, I know it hurts. I need you to fight with everything you've got. I'm going to be right here beside you."

A flurry of activity began all at once as they wheeled her down the hall. Another doctor was talking to Chase. Squinting to avoid the light, she noticed that Michael and Taco were at her feet getting people out of the way.

Chase disappeared! Where was he? *He said he wouldn't leave!*

Panic assailed her as the room full of strangers moved her lifeless body like a ragdoll and began poking and prodding. *Don't touch me! Don't touch me!*

The heart monitor sped up.

Chase reappeared dressed in scrubs. "It's okay, Princess. I just needed to get washed up and into scrubs. I'm never leaving you, again."

They placed the mask over her face as she fought to stay awake and to see Chase until the last possible moment. His forest-green eyes never left hers as if he were transferring some of his strength into her beaten body. As the drugs pulled her under, she started to lose the battle with consciousness. Kassie's eyes fluttered, and she thought she heard Chase whisper, "I love you."

A week went by as the team took turns watching over Kassie. Unrecognizable, she was covered in bruises, cuts, and her spleen was removed. Three fingers were splinted. Casts covered her arm, wrist, and leg. Multiple concussions were discovered after a CT scan. Because of the pneumonia, she was placed on a respirator to let her body rest and heal.

Sedating her to give her body time to recover. Everyone set about making sure she woke up comfortable and safe. Catherine bathed her battered body. Samantha washed the blood from her hair with the help of a bedside wash tub and cut it in a style that would cover the gaping bald spots until her hair grew back in.

Refusing to leave her side, Chase took in every nick, slice, bruise, and chunk of missing hair. Reminding himself of how he let her down and made him even more determined to heal her broken heart.

The days seemed to drag by, and the nights were even longer. Nine days. He hadn't seen even a sliver of her beautiful blue eyes. Watching the heart monitor and checking her vitals were the only things he could do, and it was taking its toll. His brothers were always close. They shoved tasteless sandwiches at him and forced him to leave long enough to shower. Chase knew they spoke to him, but he couldn't comprehend what they had said as he focused on Kassie.

On the tenth night in the wee hours of the morning, he thought he felt her hand graze the side of his. He waited. Nothing. He leaned over and brushed the side of her cheek, careful of causing her any additional pain.

"Hey, Princess, I need you to open those baby blues. Emma misses her mama. Joe and Maddie are getting worried. Don't let that bastard win after all this. You told me a while ago that your mama said that love was the only thing worth fighting for. I need you to come back to us, Princess." Chase pleaded. "Fight for me even if you want to give up."

"Thank you."

Chase looked up to see Maddie standing there watching him. Her long gray hair was braided to one side. She wore a pair of black sweatpants and a long grey sweater. The light from the hallway lit her body from behind and she looked like a beautiful angel.

"I can't stand this damn waiting." An exasperated Chase ran his hand through his overgrown beard. "I'm sorry, I know this must be hell for you and Joe."

She walked into the room and scooted the chair closer to the hospital bed. She brushed her hand lightly on top of Kassie's head.

"I couldn't sleep. I felt like she needed me, so I came over. It's nice to know she made such devoted friends while she was in Seattle."

"I saw the pictures in Joe's office. I couldn't tell her twin and her apart, but it sounds like they were night and day." Chase quietly conversed with her.

Maddie smiled. Reaching for Kassie's hand, she began to lovingly stroke it as she dabbed a bit of lotion from a jar. She passed it to Chase for him to use it where he could on the other hand. "I love both my girls. Kassie was so full of life and energy and never had the patience to work for anything. I swear she gave us all gray hairs from an early age." Maddie chuckled. "Then we got Little Bit here. She'd take her time and do whatever she wanted to learn over and over until she got it down pat. There's no such thing as a perfect child, but she was full of goodness and light."

Chase huffed. "I hate to break it to you, Miss Maddie, but I think she's been making up for it since you last saw her. She's been a royal…I'm sorry I don't know why I'm telling you this now."

"Oh, I imagine she was a handful." Maddie giggled. "She gets that from her mama. She's loyal to a fault. If you threaten her family, she comes out like an old mama bear."

Grabbing more lotion, she moved toward Kassie's feet. "I think toward the end, her sister realized what her mistakes had cost the people she loved the most. There's no doubt in my mind that Little Bit loves Emma as her own in every single way that counts, but it was unfair of her sister to put that duty on her. She never got to live her own life. She never got to be like youngins her age."

"She's a very good mama. Emma has truly been blessed. Kassie's one of the strongest women I've ever met. She's also one of the best nurses I've ever worked with. I've never met anyone like her." Chase squeezed Kassie's hand.

Maddie hand soothed Kassie's forehead as she spoke. "Sugar, I know you're in there. You can't hide, baby. I know you're scared but it's time to wake up. Ole Joe is pacing a hole in the hotel carpet. Now you tell your sister and your parents, you gotta come back home. You have a baby to tend to. They'll watch over yours, while you take care of Em. Now say goodbye and come back to us, Sugar. We need you." Maddie's stern voice held a firm motherly tone with a hint of a scold.

"You think she's given up?" Chase's expression was that of someone that lost all hope.

"No baby. She's still with us. She just likes where she's at right now. We need to remind her of what she has at home. And no, I haven't lost my mind. We just think of the dead and the living a bit differently where Joe and I come from. When you first brought her in, she was talking to her sister. She kept saying things… I just think maybe they've been catching up a bit. But now it's time to come back." Her face was full of worry, but her voice was strong.

"Maddie, I can see why Kassie thinks you and Joe are the most amazing people." They shared a grin across the bed at each other. "I thought I felt her move her hand earlier, but I waited, and she didn't do it again."

"Don't give up yet. Just keep talking to her. Tell her what she's got to live for."

Maddie quietly left the room. Chase bent over and applied lip balm to Kassie's dried lips. "Princess, I need you to wake up so we can figure out this whole mess. I want you and Emma to come back to Serenity with me. I want you to help me with the hospital if you want. We could raise our family there. I never asked you how many kids you wanted. I don't care how many we have as long as Em isn't an only child. I have always wanted a brother or a sister. Of course, Maddie and Joe are welcome, too. I'm sure you'll have a lot of catching up to do. If you don't want to move, we'll build a hospital here. Whatever you want. Open your eyes, Kassie. Just open your eyes, please."

He sat down and grabbed the jar of cream he saw Samantha put on Kassie's face and started to gently apply it. It was then that he saw her hand move. For the first time, he allowed himself to hope.

Chapter Seventeen

Kassie heard everything Chase said. It took her some time to find her way through the fog as she moved toward his voice. She struggled to get closer to him, the closer she got, the more people she heard. Her head throbbed and her eye felt like she had a big cake of mud attached to it. *Where am I?*

She managed to get the other eye to open but the light hurt, and she immediately closed it again. Someone shut the blinds.

Kassie slowly opened her eye and heard Joe and Maddie's immediate response as they thanked the Lord and cried. Chase kissed her forehead gently.

She raised her hand to touch her face, but Chase caught it in his.

"Easy, Princess. Your face is swollen, and I don't want you hitting your eye."

Kassie's hand roamed down to her stomach, immediately feeling the loss of her child. Looking at Chase for confirmation of what she already knew, he shook his head. As if unable to say the words, he raised her hand and kissed the inside of her palm. A tear slid down the side of her face as she watched emotions play across his. He softly swiped away her tear with his thumb.

Maddie leaned over her, smothering her with kisses as she spoke gentle, consoling words. Joe waited his turn and placed a kiss on her forehead. Choked-up and full of emotion, he whispered brokenly, "Welcome back, Little Bit."

Kassie took a moment to look around the room. She saw Catherine staring sadly at her while Samantha wiped her eyes. Leo's face held a look of pity. Saint stood at the edge of the doorway with a toothpick in his mouth, his gaze went to the floor when her eyes landed on him.

While Maddie and Joe held her hands, the people in the room conversed around her. Something was wrong. Listening to them talk, everything was painfully cheerful. The room became stifling as she watched their faces and glances of concern toward her, yet no one addressed the elephant in the room.

Could they just leave her alone for a while? *Go away! Leave me alone,* she screamed in her head. No one listened. She closed her eyes and willed them all away.

Three days later, Kassie took in the meal tray the aide set in front of her. She hadn't spoken since she had woken up, much to the concern of her family and friends.

Catherine had found a designer hospital gown in dark blue with pink and white flowers embroidered on it. The matching stretchy headband hid the missing patches of hair in the front, making her appear normal regardless of the multicolored bruises on her face and body.

Chase leaned against the door and watched as Kassie stared at the food. Wincing, she hesitantly picked up a spoon. Chase mentally made a note to have the others watch for signs of pain as Kassie refused to indicate when she was having headaches. He walked further into the room.

"Nurses make the worst patients."

She was startled and dropped the spoon.

Smiling to put her at ease, he placed a heavenly smelling bag on the table.

"Maddie went home today with Joe. They'll come later this afternoon. She made this for lunch."

He pulled out a bowl of butternut squash soup with homemade rolls and fresh butter. He slathered butter on the roll and tore off pieces to feed her. When she made no move to eat and stared longingly at the food, Chase picked up a soft piece of bread and brought it to her lips. She swallowed hard before she slowly took his offering as if he would snatch it away.

"We need to discuss a few things, Princess." He gave her a bite of soup and she closed her eyes. "Open your eyes, sweetheart. I need to see them while I talk to you."

Her eyes opened immediately, and she stared at him. He didn't miss the terror in her eyes at his command. He softened his voice and tentatively sat on the bed. Continuing to feed her as she made no move to help herself, he watched her reactions closely as he broke the news.

"Stanton was sentenced three days ago. He's been sentenced to twenty-five years in prison. No possibility of parole." He frowned. "The hits have been called off but we're still looking into that, so security is staying in place."

She finished half a bowl of soup before her eyes began to close on their own. Chase had all kinds of bells going off in his head. She hadn't spoken. Her face held no expressions. She was just… there. He needed to talk Maddie and Joe into getting her assessed for depression and PTSD. He covered her and kissed her head.

She had fallen back to sleep. Or at least given the impression she had. Noticing that every time she wanted out of a conversation, or the room got crowded, she seemed to fall asleep to escape anyone asking questions. Not finding any reasons for her inability to speak, the doctors surmised Kassie was using it as a coping mechanism.

They discussed briefly bringing Emma in to see her, but Kassie adamantly shook her head and refused to let the little girl see her in this state. She would be spending months in rehab for her physical needs, but Chase felt that she needed help to process everything that happened.

He watched as she finally opened her eyes.

"Maddie is coming to visit with you while I run some errands today. Would you like me to pick anything up for you, while I'm out? Would you like a good mystery or a classic to read or something special to eat?"

Kassie's face turned panicky. The heart monitor sped up and Chase watched as she gripped the sheets. He removed the remaining food and wondered what the bastard had done to her to cause such a reaction over such a simple question. He kissed her forehead and left the room to find Joe.

Maddie walked in and was changing the flowers in the vase when she noticed Kassie was watching her.

"Well, there you are, Sugar. Did you have a nice visit with Chase? I brought you some apple pie."

"Maddie."

"You spoke! Let me call the doctor!" Maddie rushed to hit the call button.

Kassie shook her head and grabbed Maddie's hand.

"What is it, *Cher*?"

"Chase."

"I'll call him. He's gonna be so happy to hear you!"

"No."

Maddie looked startled. "What's the matter?" She placed both of her hands over the trembling young woman's hand. "Talk to me."

"Don't. Want. To see. Him." Kassie shook her head and stared at the floor.

"Why? He's been so worried," Maddie lightly admonished. She was surprised by Kassie's request when Chase had been nothing but devoted to her.

"I. Can't. See. Him. Just can't." Kassie faltered.

Tears fell down her face and Maddie wiped them away. "I'll call Joe and have him handle it. You just need to concentrate on healing. We'll figure it all out, Sugar."

Chapter Eighteen

Chase had taken Emma and Melody out to lunch and to a nearby park to give Catherine a break and settled the girls down for a nap. Glancing at his phone, he noticed the text from Leo asking him to stop at the hotel suite before visiting Kassie.

Opening the door to the suite, Chase's brows went up in surprise to find Leo and Joe waiting for him. Immediately, his concern was that something was wrong.

"Is everything all right with Kassie?"

"Son, she's doing fine. I just need to chat with you for a spell." Joe handed him a drink. "Down it, 'cause you're gonna need it."

Confused, Chase tipped the drink back and set the glass on the table. "What's going on?"

"Chase, my Little Bit is going through a heap of troubles right now and she's asked that you not come in to see her anymore."

"She's talking!" Genuine delight lit up his face before Joe's announcement hit him.

Joe passed him another drink. "Now, hear me out."

"Yes, sir." Chase mechanically downed the drink, his body going numb with Joe's announcement. "Sir, I'm a little confused. Kassie asked not to see me?"

Joe nodded his head. "Yes. That psychiatrist you sent over says she is suffering from PTSD and depression, just as you thought. Now she's asked not to see you. I imagine this is most likely to do with whatever was going on before her kidnapping."

Chase hung his head. "Yes, sir." He took a moment to gather his thoughts. His chest straightened and his shoulders went back as he bore all the responsibility for his actions. "I fucked up. We had words…the day she was taken." He looked Joe square in the eye. "I hurt her. I was planning on talking to her about it and then Roger kidnapped her, she's been recovering and there hasn't been a good time to talk about it at the hospital."

"You got the women folk up in that hospital room buzzing around Little Bit and circling their wagons. I'd not be doing my duty if I failed Nathan and Abigail Reynolds right now. It seems the two of you are constantly at odds. I know you've been here for her, but if you're causing her stress, I'll have to honor her request."

Kneading his forehead, Chase sighed as he faced the older man. Looking at Leo, and getting a head nod from his brother, Chase reluctantly spoke.

"I'm not going to lie to you, sir. I disagreed with her decision of staying Kassie. James is always going to have enemies. I didn't want Kassie looking over her shoulder all her life. I know it's not about the money, but I can't give her this type of lifestyle." He paused before he admitted his biggest transgression. "I asked her if Matthew Cartwright was the baby's father."

Leo slapped the back of Chase's head and Joe's mouth hung open. "Well, take comfort in the fact that God made dumber men than you! What in the hell made you do something so stupid?" Joe slammed his glass down on the table.

Chase felt like he was back in his father's study getting a lecture after he had been caught doing something he shouldn't have at school.

"Sir, I honored her request to stay away. Kind of. I walked the perimeter outside. I watched Matthew with her for days and caught him coming out of her room when I fetched Rollo. When Stanton let the cat out of the bag about her being pregnant, he assumed it was Cartwright's too. I offered to raise the child as my own. Kassie denied sleeping with him. I let something from my past cloud my judgment. Wanting to give her time to heal from this ordeal, I haven't tried to speak with her. I don't know how I'm going to fix things if she's refusing to see me." Chase waited for the condemnation from Joe, already feeling at a loss on what to do about Kassie.

Joe was quiet as he studied the man before him. "Little Bit's hurtin' son. Her sister and she were as thick as thieves. Her twin took advantage of her, and this is why Little Bit is lying up in that hospital bed right now." Joe walked to the hotel room window and looked out at the storm gathering in the distance.

"I know Little Bit like the back of my hand. She did all this for her sister and her family. She'd do anything for little Emma. But now, for the first time, she has choices. She's scared. It's up to you to convince her otherwise. You and I are of the same mind concerning Stanton and I worry about what this will mean for Little Bit down the line. What's done is done and we'll be there to support her no matter what."

He turned and filled his glass with another draw of whiskey and refilled Chase's. "I don't think Matthew means anything more to Kassie other than a connection to her sister. That's not to say I haven't had worries myself about the friendship."

"Now we got all this *gris-gris* going on." He shook his head. "We all make mistakes son, and I'm sure Kassie has regrets too. I've seen how much you care for her, and I know what hell a man goes through when the woman he loves is hurt and he couldn't save her. But she deserves to be happy and if you can't fix this, I expect that you'll allow her to find the happiness she deserves."

Chase held out his hand. "I promise you, sir, I'll do everything in my power to make this right. If I can't make her happy, I'll let her go. I'd like to talk to her one more time before she makes any decisions."

Joe swallowed down his drink and took Chase's hand and shook it.

"I'll talk to Little Bit. I can't promise more than that. I'm not gonna lie, son. You're going to have an uphill battle. I've seen that haunted look in her eyes. I know you didn't put it there, but I think you're going to have to fight those demons to get to Kassie."

Chase looked Joe in the eye. "I don't care if I have to go to hell and back, I'll chase Kassie's demons away and make sure she has her life back. Even if that doesn't include me." He swallowed hard at the thought of losing her.

Nodding, Joe gripped his hand. Then Chase exited the room, already making plans. His girl had taken flight physically in the past. But now, she was fleeing from the monsters in her head. He would ensure she'd never have to run again…

Chapter Nineteen

Kassie lay in the hospital, a shell of her former self. Earlier that day, the doctor had come in to speak to her alone.

"As you are aware, Mrs. Stanton, your body has been through a lot of trauma. It may take a while, but there's no indication that you won't be able to walk normally again with physical therapy. What I want to discuss with you is your health moving forward. There was a lot of internal damage. As you know, we removed your spleen, and performed a D&C. Your kidneys are functioning on their own, and you're healing nicely. Unfortunately, there's a lot of scar tissue and the chances of having any more children are very slim. There are advancements and ways to conceive, but the reality of the situation…"

Kassie hadn't heard anything past that. Another blow to her already fragile mind. She lost her child and wouldn't have another. Chase talked about having a family. Now, that was something else between them.

She refused to talk to him about everything that occurred. If she opened her mouth to speak, all she would do was scream. The terror, the days of fear and loneliness, the stress of wondering if Chase was there now out of guilt, overwhelmed her. Remembering their conversation before she was taken, she was sure he had no intention of continuing their relationship. Especially when he had asked if the child she carried was Matthew's.

A movement in the doorway caught her attention. Joe stood with his hands in his pockets as he watched her with pity in his eyes. She looked away, tired of everyone looking at her as if she were fragile. When they thought she was asleep, they discussed her and made decisions about her future without asking what she wanted or needed.

"There's my Little Bit." Joe smiled as he walked further into the room.

"I thought you were lost in your thoughts and I didn't want to disturb you." He came closer to the hospital chair that they had propped her up in and pulled a chair next to her.

"Maddie tells me that you don't want to see Chase. I gotta say, *Cher*, I'm a bit surprised. He's been here throughout this whole mess." Kassie began shaking her head and he put his hand up in the air to stop her. "Let me have my say, and I'll let you have yours."

Scowling, she looked away from him, but he waited until she begrudgingly gave her attention back to him before he began. "I know some personal things have transpired between you and that young man. My understanding is that some mighty hurtful things have been said and I get that you'd be upset. I'm not taking his side either. But I'd hate to see you miss out on something special. He's asked to see you and talk to you one more time and has agreed to leave you alone if that's your wish. Will you see him?"

Knowing that she couldn't have kids was even more reason to push Chase away. She wasn't going to deprive him of his dream of raising a family on his mountain.

The last few weeks he hadn't left her side. Even when she pretended to be asleep to keep from interacting with him. But now, more than ever, she couldn't allow him to see the cracks. She needed him to go before she completely fell apart and he blamed himself. Seeing the guilt in his eyes that he hadn't kept her safe from Roger was more than she could handle. It wasn't his fault. James Stanton and his colleagues were evil.

Knowing she needed Chase to leave before the cracks began to show, Kassie agreed to meet him.

Chase knocked lightly on the door. "Good evening, Princess."

He waited until she bade him to enter. He closed the door and locked it so they wouldn't be disturbed. Sitting on the edge of the bed facing her, Chase quietly spoke.

"I was trying to hold off this discussion until you were feeling better. Princess, we need to discuss what happened. I don't want to lose you or Emma."

Biting her lip, she looked down toward the foot of the bed. "I appreciate all you've done. Chase, it's time for you and the team to return home. It's time for all of us to move on. Joe can handle our security."

"Kass. I'm not talking about your protection. We'll table that discussion for now. I want to talk about the day I found out you were pregnant." Lifting her chin with two of his fingers, he waited until she met his gaze. "I have a confession to make. I didn't leave when you were at the Stanton estate. I stayed on the grounds and worked security outside." Her eyes widened at his admission.

"Day after day, I saw you with Cartwright. The way he looks at you, touches you, and always seems to be in the same room when you're around. That, coupled with the fact you didn't seem to mind his presence and never asked to see me, led me to some very wrong conclusions. I saw him come out of your room one night when I fetched Rollo. When Stanton assumed the baby was also Cartwright's, it sent me over the edge. I know the child was mine. I should've never doubted you."

No wonder he thought she had slept with Matthew! If only they had talked earlier! No, she couldn't veer off course now. She avoided eye contact.

"I'm sure the announcement came as a shock. I didn't have any intention of hiding it from you. I'd just found out myself, the trial was going on and I thought it best to hold off the discussion until after."

Sighing with relief, he watched as she gripped the blanket and twisted it in her hand.

"I just lost my head. I know it's not the best excuse, but it's an honest one. I admit I was wrong." He cupped her chin. "I'm sorry I hurt you."

Swallowing hard, she tried to break the news to him as gently as she could. "We were brought together under extreme circumstances. My life is here and yours is on Serenity Mountain. The baby is gone and it's time we all got on with our lives. It's time for you to start your dream. I know you'll be very successful, and I wish you the very best."

Straightening, he asked, "So did you agree to meet with me with your mind already made up?" His jaw ticked and he gripped the edge of the bed.

She closed her eyes and scrunched her nose to keep the tears from falling. There was no easy way to say what she needed to. She needed to make sure he knew there was no chance of them ever being together.

"We don't know each other. I admit, I should've trusted you and insisted that you listen to me that day at the barn. I was scared for Emma and worried they would send a team up the mountain. I didn't want you hurt. Both of us know this relationship was based on deceit. I pretended to be my sister and you pretended to care about the single mom and her kid to gain information. I don't think that's solid ground to build anything on. We were cut off from reality and our feelings got away from us. I have no intention of allowing myself to mistake those feelings for anything else."

"Princess. I disagree. I know you. You know me. You can't deny what we had at the cabin. There was no pretending." Chase struggled to remain calm.

"No. I don't." She shook her head, "I was playing a part. My name is Kaitlyn and you got to know Kassie. You made judgments based on my sister life, while not knowing a single thing about me." Keeping her voice firm, she continued. "We were stuck together on a mountain for months, and things happened. But we're back in reality now, and we both need to accept it and move on."

"Don't do this, Princess. You don't believe that any more than I do. You weren't playing a part when we made love. You told me everything on that mountain. That was you."

"Me?" She laughed out loud. "How would you know? If it was me, then why didn't you trust me? You talk so much about me trusting you, Chase. If you knew the *real* me, then you wouldn't have doubted whose child I carried, not for one second. I'm not even sure if *I* know the real me. I've been Kassie for so long I don't know where I end and she begins. But I *do* know that I'm not Rachel and I wouldn't have tried to pass a child off on you that wasn't yours."

"I know that," he whispered, sounding ashamed of himself for uttering those words that day.

"I asked not to see you anymore because I'm no longer your responsibility. I was a job. A few months from now, you'll be helping someone just like me. You'll be building your dream." Her voice cracked but she kept firm. "I need to make a life with Emma. One that doesn't include Seattle or Serenity."

"I disagree. Don't I get a say? We made mistakes. We can start slow and—"

She shook her head. "No. No, Chase. You don't know me. You asked me if this was about the money. Then you don't understand why I need to stay Kassie. You didn't trust me enough to know I would've remained faithful to you. Our entire relationship was based on a lie."

"Kass—"

"I think it's time you go." It took everything she had to make her voice sound strong.

"Don't do this. You're running. Love doesn't run. You taught me that. I'm not going anywhere. You're scared and I understand that. A lot's happened in a short amount of time. Fight with me, yell at me, but don't give up on us."

"There is *no* us. Right now, I need to focus on me and Emma."

"I don't believe you, Princess. Why now? I've been by your side day and night. What changed? Talk to me," Chase pressed.

"I don't have anything to say," she whispered and looked down in her lap.

"This is for you. Because I *do* know you." Pulling a silver bracelet from his pocket, he held each charm on his thumb as he went through them one by one. "The night we fled to my mountain, you were terrified, and I never left your side. Every morning you'd wake up and watch the sun come over the mountain and lift your face." The charm held a mountain with a sun rising.

A German Shepherd was next. "You were terrified of Rollo, and we overcame that fear together. Now, he's your best friend."

Pointing to a bee with rhinestones, he said, "You tried the best honey in the world and enjoyed every cup of tea with it."

Smirking, he pulled out the coyote. "You fought off coyotes until Rollo and I could get to you. Kassie didn't do that. *You* did."

He pulled out an angel holding a golden heart. "I know you're upset with your sister. But if it hadn't been for her, I would've never met you. She brought us together and I'll always be grateful to her for that. Now she's watching over our child," he pointed to the heart, "as you watch over hers."

Finally, a silver Christmas tree with tiny colored stones appeared. "I made love to you, not your sister. I love you, Princess. No matter what name you call yourself."

Gently clasping the jewelry around her wrist, he set her hand down. "I'm not giving up. Whatever has scared you, know I'm here. I hope this reminds you of our mountain, of all we went through, and we're still here together. I'll give you the time you need. When you're ready, I'll be here."

With that, he leaned over and pressed a kiss to her cheek and exited the room. She fingered each one of the symbols of their experiences, faintly smiling at each memory. Clutching it close to her chest, she cried.

Chapter Twenty

A day later, Kassie flew to the best rehab facility in the country. Suspecting that Chase had something to do with it, she agreed to go if her friends returned to their lives. They couldn't stay and watch her day after day. Frankly, she was sick of the looks and silent communication between them when they didn't think she was paying attention.

Maddie, Joe, and Em were staying close by. She allowed Emma to visit and explained that she was in an accident and it was going to take a long time before she felt better. Leo and the team refused to leave, and it took all her willpower to keep from asking about the only missing man from their group.

Luckily, she was able to hide the panic attacks. When she felt one coming on, she would make her way to the bathroom and turn the shower on. Working in the healthcare field, she knew this wasn't smart, but she wasn't willing or ready to speak to a therapist.

Leo was a pain in her ass. He had no problem harassing her when she wanted to give up. He pushed, prodded, and aggravated her to no end.

Saint and Taco's rotation was always fun. Every Tuesday night, Taco would show up to relieve Saint and announce, "Taco Tuesday!" as he carried in a paper bag filled with the best tacos she had ever eaten. Saint would come in with her favorite candy bar or ice cream.

Shadow was the quiet one of the bunch. As much as she enjoyed Saint and Taco, she enjoyed the downtime with Shadow more. She didn't feel the need to talk or make conversation. Michael would tell stories of the kids he treated and always checked on Emma. Julio's team alternated between her and Emma.

The nights were long as she tried to stay awake to keep the nightmares from coming. Dark circles appeared under her eyes. She was losing weight and knew she looked unhealthy, but food held no appeal. At the same time, she started to hide food in her closet. An apple here, or crackers there. Just enough in case they didn't bring any. She didn't know why she had the compulsion, but it made her feel better.

At the beginning of the third week, the cracks in Kassie's armor were starting to show. Between the anxiety and the lack of sleep, she was losing her grip on her tightly controlled demeanor in front of the team. When Emma, Maddie, and Joe would come to visit, she plastered a smile on her face and pretended that everything was peachy. Joe would cast a worried glances at Maddie but neither said a word, much to her relief.

Starting her exercises early, she stretched her leg with the rubber bands. The task was more difficult, with her broken arm still aching, but she was determined. Her leg throbbed as she bent it, and her fingers could barely grasp the stretchy rubber band. She smiled across the room as an older gentleman rose from his wheelchair. He grabbed a black metal cane.

The next thing she knew, it slipped out of his grasp, hitting the concrete floor. The sound echoed and clanged off the hard cement floor. Kassie's mind immediately flashed back…

Roger walked toward her with the black metal rod. "Where's the money?" Whack! Whack! The crushing sound of her bones breaking pounded in her ears. The sound of the pipe hitting the chain that held her… Whack!

Her arm shot out as she fell to the floor and curled into a ball. Someone was screaming. She covered her ears. Hands grabbed at her. *Don't touch me, don't touch me!* She couldn't breathe. Black dots appeared around the edges of her vision as she felt the blood racing through her veins and her heartbeat pounded in her ears. Blackness consumed her as someone picked her up.

Thirty minutes later she opened her eyes to find a concerned Leo staring at her. Her body felt sluggish and tired.

"Do you want to tell me what happened in the therapy room?" He quietly asked.

"I don't remember." She lied. "I need to get back to the room and finish my exercises." She started to rise when he gently pushed her back down.

"I was a SEAL for a long time. I know when I see PTSD and I think you do too. It's okay to admit that you might need to talk to someone. Even the strongest soldier sometimes needs a helping hand."

Pulling herself up to a sitting position, she scowled. "It was a one-time thing. I must've been overdoing it." Grasping at straws, she prayed he'd believe her.

"PITA, I think you're fooling yourself. When you're ready to talk, let us know." Leo squeezed her hand.

"PITA?" Kassie eyed him in confusion at what he called her. "Chase calls me Princess."

"Chase calls you Princess because that's what you are to him. To me, you are literally a pain in my ass, therefore PITA." Leo walked out of the room as she giggled at her new nickname. At least he wasn't treating her like a piece of glass.

That evening, Kassie pretended to be absorbed in some television sitcom she'd turned on to keep the men from talking to her about the incident. Shadow cast her weary glances from the doorway but remained quiet. By one in the morning, she couldn't keep her eyes open. Leaving the show on so she wouldn't have to face the dark, she laid her head on the pillow.

Drifting off and thinking of Chase and the mountain, Kassie wondered how far he was in building the hospital. She even missed Rollo. She wished he was on the side of her bed so she could sleep knowing he would stand guard. She turned and adjusted the pillow underneath her head and readjusted her arm. Peeking through the slits of her eyes, she saw Shadow exchange shifts with Julio's agent. With one last glance in her direction, he took off down the hall.

A hand flew over her mouth and nose, cutting off her air. Kassie struggled, trying to get her arm from under the pillow. She felt his hot breath and a deep voice whispered in her ear. "This is a message from James. He wants to see his daughter and he only asks once." He roughly shoved her head into the bed and was gone in a flash. Kassie gasped for air, then she screamed. Shadow came running, looking for the threat in her room.

Kassie pointed toward the door. Unable to speak, feeling the terror that she had held at bay, she grasped her throat as if she couldn't breathe. Shadow rushed to her side. She could hear him talking but he seemed so far away…

When she came to, Leo, Shadow, and Taco stood over her. Their set jaws, firm mouths, and set stances told her she wasn't going to be able to easily dismiss them. But she had her own agenda.

"Leo, I want your team or Matthew on Emma's security. Not Julio's." She pushed the call button and waited until a nurse appeared. "Please call Dr. Fields. I'm leaving AMA. I want the forms as soon as possible. Leo, please arrange for us to leave immediately." She swung her legs out of the bed with some difficulty.

Saint stopped her when he placed his hands on her shoulders.

"Whoa, Missy, ain't you rushing it just a tad bit? We got Miss Emma and your family covered. All you need to do is focus on healing."

"If you don't let me go right now, I'll leave on my own free will. Leo has talked Joe into keeping you here with me but if we don't leave in the next hour, I'm leaving without you and hiring my own private security!"

Saint stepped back, stunned at Kassie's outburst. Leo said something low to Shadow and he exited the room.

"Clear the room." Leo's words were immediately obeyed. Coming to the edge of the bed, he pulled a chair up next to Kassie.

"Wanna tell me what's going on? You know the care plan said you would be here a while. Now all of the sudden the day after having a panic attack—" Kassie started to interrupt but he held his hand up. "No. I've seen enough men to know exactly what this is. I'm not going to listen to that bull you're going to tell me about not remembering."

Kassie's entire body was humming. Her hands were visibly shaking so she placed them under her thighs so Leo wouldn't notice. The narrowing of his eyes let her know she hadn't fooled him one bit.

Joe rushed into the room. His usual pressed shirt had been hastily buttoned and his white hair was messed up as if he had just rolled out of bed.

"Little Bit, what in the tarnation's going on? Why's Shadow coming to get me and telling me we're leaving?" Confusion was written all over his face as he saw Leo sitting next to the bed.

Kassie could barely maintain her control. "Joe. I want to leave now. I want to go home. We can continue therapy from the house. Leo doesn't want to go, be ready to leave as soon as Dr. Fields releases me." Her voice wavered.

Joe exchanged looks from Leo's angry face to Kassie's stressed and gaunt one, the two were in a battle of wills.

Finally breaking eye contact, Leo spoke. "We'll be ready to roll but if you think this is over, PITA, you've got another thing coming."

She concentrated on the wall behind him. "Please make sure Emma is always with one of you. I'm going to get dressed. Joe, make the flight arrangements?"

Scratching his head, Joe nodded and exited the room.

"If you'll excuse me, I need to get my bags packed and dressed." She slid from the bed, hanging onto the wall as she made her way to the bathroom. Her legs shook and it took every ounce of energy to close the door. She slid down the wall and sat on the cold floor and took deep breaths before the anxiety attack took over.

Dr. Fields wasn't happy that his patient was leaving. He tried everything he could to no avail to convince her to stay. Finally having had enough, she used the card she had seen her sister use when she wanted something done without any question. Making her voice firm, she set her steely gaze upon him.

"Dr. Fields, I'm Mrs. Kassie Stanton. I assure you that I can employ whatever you feel my medical needs are from my home. You, however, will no longer be employed if you don't have those forms in here within the next thirty minutes so I may leave. This is not up for discussion."

Leo eyed her speculatively as she played with her already packed bags.

She had slipped into a long dress that covered her scarred legs and continued to ignore him as she kept her icy demeanor. When the nurse came with her paperwork, she scribbled her name and handed the forms back to the nurse.

Saint rounded the corner with a wheelchair.

"It's a long walk, and the way you're determined to hightail it outta here, I got you a faster ride." Grinning widely, he winked at her. She smiled right back at him and then threw a smirk over her shoulder at Leo as she sat down and allowed Saint to push her.

They loaded onto the private jet that Joe arranged. With Emma buckled next to her, Kassie leaned against the cold glass of the airplane window. The anxiety hadn't decreased by leaving. Determined to hide it from Leo and the team, she waited until Emma fell asleep before covering her and heading to the bathroom.

By the time they landed and loaded the cars, Kassie was on edge. Leo loaded Maddie, Joe, and Emma in one car with Taco and Saint while Shadow loaded her in the second. Sliding into the driver's seat, Leo started the car. The night surrounded them as they made their way to the house, making her anxious. Clutching the door, she tried to control her breathing, so it didn't sound as loud in the silence of the car.

"Okay, PITA, what the hell is going on? You look like you're ready to fall over any minute. I think you're whiter than a ghost. I'm beyond serious when I say, I think you should've stayed at rehab."

"You know what Leo? I'm tired. It's been a long day and I seriously have a problem that you continue to boss me around like I'm five years old. I'm a grown-ass woman. I can get the same therapy here. You need to go home. You can't babysit me forever, you know!" Kassie's outburst startled even her.

Leo pulled the car to the side of the road. Then, he jumped out and stalked to her side. Yanking the door open, he leaned into her side of the car.

Shadow slid to the passenger side behind Kassie and quietly said, "Boss."

Kassie couldn't control the panic that struck her, even knowing that Leo would never hurt her. She saw how effective he could be in an interrogation by the way she felt intimidated at that moment. She shrank back into the seat. His nostrils flared and his jaw ticked, yet when he touched her hand, it was as if she was made of fragile glass.

"This isn't you, PITA. In the last twenty-four hours, you've become an ice princess. I just watched you order an AMA by threatening a doctor's job. You were absolutely rude. Ordering Joe about like he's an employee instead of a second father to you. Every week, Chase sends you flowers, and you don't even acknowledge or respond. If you think I missed the panic attack on the plane, you're sadly mistaken. You're gripping the door as if you are going to jump out at any second after ordering this ridiculous move. We're staying right here until you talk."

Looking into the night, the cool air, and Leo looming over her, panic was starting to set in at his threat of staying there. Water pooled in her eyes, her lips began to quiver, and she fell apart right in front of him.

Stunned, Leo looked sheepishly at Shadow in the back of the vehicle. Unbuckling her and pulling her to his chest, his eyebrows went up when she wrapped her arms around his neck and big heaping sobs wracked her tiny frame. Running his hand across his face, Shadow looked at his boss, pulled out his phone, and started texting.

"I'm sorry. Every time I close my eyes, he's there. I killed someone. I'm supposed to save lives. When will this ever end?" Sobbing, she clung tighter. "I was so rude. But I just wanted to get out of there. That man scared me, and I didn't want anyone else hurt."

"Whoa." Pulling away from her, Leo grabbed a wad of tissues and wiped her nose. "What man are you talking about?"

Hiccupping, she turned her watery eyes toward Leo. "Last night, Shadow left. Someone put his hand over my mouth and told me James only asks once. He wants Emma." She blew her nose and talked into the tissue. "I don't think I can run away again."

Shadow leaned forward. "The male nurse that came in last night? He's been there since we arrived and was background checked. Or Julio's agent? Why didn't you tell me, sweetheart?" His voice was soft and comforting, different from his normal gruff and to-the-point answers. "Shit."

Kassie hiccupped, "I didn't want you hurt. I didn't know if anyone else was there."

Leo sighed and ran his hand through his hair and pinched the bridge of his nose. "You know we're highly trained, right?" He nodded to Shadow. "Get Saint and Taco back on the next flight. Call Chase and Michael, get them here, pronto."

"No. I can't see Chase. Please, Leo. I don't want him to see me like this." Narrowing his eyes, he looked at her questioningly.

"Darling, you lost me. That man was by your side when you looked like you went ten rounds in a boxing match, and you've healed since then. You look a helluva lot better than before." He pushed the hair away from her face so he could see her expression.

"I'm begging you. I can't let him see me. I'm…broken. He deserves someone that can give him everything. That isn't me, Leo."

Glancing back at Shadow, he watched Shadow shake his head back and forth. Frowning, he helped her get buckled in.

"I'll assign him elsewhere for the moment. But Kass, sometimes what we think someone needs, is the complete opposite. Don't wait too long to find out that you were what he needs the most." Her head went up to look into Leo's eyes.

"I'm sure that Chase is busy with the hospital and it's important to him. That needs to be his priority." She tried to convince herself. She couldn't see Chase. She could hide some of her anxiety from the team, but he'd see right through her.

Settling Emma in Kassie and her twin's old room, in her sister's bed, the little girl was excited that she was having a sleepover with her mama. Not wanting to place fear in Em's head about sleeping in the dark, she had laid in bed covered in sweat and shaking until she heard the even breathing of her daughter, indicating that she had finally drifted off. Letting go of the edge of the blanket, she quietly rose out of bed. She made her way across the room to the bathroom and flicked on the light. Splashing cold water on her face, she closed her eyes and counted to fifty. Her daughter was safely ensconced in bed, blissfully unaware of how bad things can happen in the dark. Unfortunately, Kassie was well aware of the monsters that lurked there.

Chapter Twenty-one

The third night after arriving home, Kassie experienced her first night of terror.

A hand clamped over her mouth and nose, and she was unable to move. Unable to breathe. She could see Shadow, yet she couldn't call out or grab his attention…

She sprang from the bed screaming bloody murder. Leo was the first one to arrive to see a hysterical Kassie hiding in the corner of her closet and a crying Emma. Maddie quickly removed the frightened little girl, wrapping her up in a blanket and murmuring soothing words as Joe and Leo attempted to calm Kassie. She was trapped in her own little world and couldn't fight her way out. An hour later, the sedative she was given had finally taken effect, and Leo watched over her.

The next morning, Kassie woke and made her way slowly down the stairs to an astonished Joe and Maddie. Little Emma started crying and ran to hug her mother's legs. She wrapped her arms around her daughter, completely confused as to why Emma was upset and reassured her.

Two nights later, Shadow rushed through the door again as Kassie began babbling nonsense and begging someone not to touch her. Emma was removed. Again, the next morning, Kassie came down the stairs with no knowledge of what happened.

Dark circles appeared under her eyes. She didn't remember the dreams, but she knew something was happening that she couldn't explain. Joe and Maddie explained what happened. Anxiety ate at her as she realized she was the monster in the dark for her daughter. Calling a sleep specialist in Corpus Christi, Kassie packed a bag to prepare to spend the night at the hospital. Her hands shook as she folded her clothes and grabbed all her essentials for the overnight session.

Leo sat on the opposite bed watching Kassie. "PITA, we're going to be in the room with you the whole time. You've got this."

Nodding to acknowledge his reassurance, she continued to stuff things in a bag. She didn't want to go to another hospital. The staff at the last one had been thoroughly vetted. Yet James had found a way in. What if he tried again? Swallowing down nausea that threatened to come up, she shot Leo a small smile at his worried frown.

When she arrived at the hospital, Kassie was given a gown and asked to change. Her eyes widened when the nurse asked Leo to leave, and he steadfastly refused.

"I'll turn around after you step away and are within my eyesight, ma'am, but I'm not leaving her." His brown eyes met Kassie's as she smiled in relief.

Hooked up to the electrodes, she lay on the bed watching the machines. Fighting sleep in fear of what was to come, she gripped the sheets by her scar-covered thighs and began to grip and dig into her legs.

Leaning over the bed, Leo gently took both her hands in his. "PITA, I'm not moving. If I'm not here, one of the team will be. Let go. Breathe with me."

She hadn't realized that she had been holding her breath. Blood was rushing through her veins, and she felt numb. She gave him a tiny nod as her vision clouded over with black dots. A few minutes later she was out. Leo nodded as Chase walked in the door and brushed the bangs from her eyes. Giving the man a chin lift, Leo guarded the door.

Roger was screaming. She was chained to the wall. "Where's the money? Dragging the bucket over, he placed her leg on top of it to cut a thin line with the razor-sharp knife. Slowly dragging it down her thigh. Her broken leg screamed in pain as she fought to keep the bone straight as she screamed for someone, anyone to help her. Roger stood and laughed as he began to carve into her leg again while he stepped on her broken one. She begged and pleaded for the pain to stop.

A voice broke through. "Princess, you're here with me. We're sitting in the window seat overlooking Serenity Mountain. The flowers are blooming. The sun is shining on your face. Come back to me, Kass. Fight it, sweetie."

Her cries quieted as she reached for the voice. Shaking her head, she called out, "You can't love me, I'm broken. I ruined everything."

The voice hushed her. "No. You fought for your daughter. You did everything, right. I'm right here, Princess." The scent of oak surrounded her. With those comforting words, she drifted back off. Every time the monster threatened, the voice kept it at bay…

Dr. Levy sat at his desk and explained to Kassie she was suffering from PTSD and night terrors. He prescribed sedatives for bedtime and antidepressants for the daytime. Embarrassed, Kassie put the prescriptions in her purse and left the office.

"What did the doc say?" Leo fell into step next to her as she made her way to the awaiting car.

"It's nightmares. They'll pass."

Refusing to look into his eyes, she slid into the backseat and buckled up. Saint passed him a silent communication from the front as his eyes narrowed at the whopper of a lie she'd told. The entire team had been present when the machines registered the nightmare coming on. The needles spiked and went crazy as she struggled between the veil of the nightmare and reality.

When they returned home, she cheerfully greeted a concerned Maddie and Joe, telling them the same fabrication. Taking Em by the hand, she went into the living room and played a game with her and avoided the adults lurking outside the room.

"Emma. I need to talk to you. Mama's been having some yucky dreams lately and I know I've scared you. I didn't mean to, but sometimes I don't know when it's going to happen. I was wondering if maybe you'd like to have sleepovers at the cottage until I feel a bit better? Uncle Saint, Uncle Shadow, and Uncle Taco would be there with you. Emma, you know how you say Uncle Taco, but his name isn't really Taco? Uncle Derrick's name is Uncle Leo, he was named because he's like a lion! So, you need to call him Uncle Leo from now on."

Emma continued to play with her gingerbread man. "That's so cool! Does that mean Uncle Taco is named after a Taco? What about Dr. Chase? Will he be able to watch me?"

"You'll have to ask Uncle Taco. Dr. Chase is working on the hospital right now to help our military, and it's important." Kassie's heart lodged in her throat at the thought of Chase being there. She closed her eyes thinking about how safe she'd felt when he'd wrapped his arms around her. But she'd screwed everything up. She should've talked to him. No. It was better, he could find someone who could give him a family.

Attempting to maintain a routine, Kassie would bathe Emma and read her a story before one of the men would retrieve Emma for her sleepover. The team set up their sleeping arrangements and were surprisingly good with Emma. Saint played Go Fish with her daily and Shadow taught her how to play hide and seek which strangely imitated his way of blending into the background and moving about the room without being noticed. She understood how he earned his nickname. So far, the living situation worked, but it wasn't a long-term solution.

Kassie smiled and laughed on cue. She even agreed to a shopping trip with Maddie so she could reassure the older couple she was getting a grip. As soon as they arrived at the stores, the team spread out, covering the women but allowing them to enjoy themselves. Picking up items and walking around the store, she was aware of everyone who came near her. Frequently glancing around as if she were looking for something, her eyes would search out the members of the team.

Two hours later, Maddie suggested they stop in for tea at the local tea shop. Kassie quietly excused herself as one of the men checked the bathroom. She smiled at Taco as he held the door open for her. As soon as she entered, she turned the lock and vomited all over the toilet. Sweat ran down her neck, dots appeared at the edge of her vision as she fought for control and slid down the wall. Shaking, she dragged herself up and placed a wet towel on the back of her neck and rinsed her mouth. A firm knock on the door made her jump.

"Everything okay in there, PITA?"

Readjusting her lipstick and making sure her hair was in place, she unlocked the door and shot a fake smile at Leo as he scanned hers.

"Of course, I just needed a minute. Do you think we could stop at the bookstore? I want to pick up some books for Em." Pretending to place her lipstick back in her bag, she waited for his response.

"Sure." Leo sighed. His concerned eyes scanned her for any indication that she wasn't okay.

Sitting back at the table, she chatted with Maddie as if she hadn't a care in the world. They visited the bookstore, and she made a couple of purchases. Once they were headed back to the house, she could finally breathe.

Feeling like a complete failure as a mother and a burden to the older couple, she was starting to sink further into depression. She knew the signs but had ignored them, hoping they'd go away. Refusing to see the therapists that Chase was sending wasn't helping. She just wasn't ready. Now, rarely speaking, she walked around the grounds until she tired herself out and would sleep in the old treehouse that her daddy and Joe had built for her and her sister. Something needed to change. She was restless, bored, and could tell this was affecting Emma too. The normally cheerful child was becoming more and more disruptive.

Once a week without fail, a flower arrangement appeared with a letter from Chase. Her heart dropped into her stomach at the mere thought of him. She missed him. Had his life returned to normal? How was the hospital going? Had he seen her friend Samantha? How was the town doing?

Sitting down in the living room, she looked at the table that held a new flowerpot with little yellow flowers and green leaves. It was cheerful and bright. Everything she wasn't. The night before, she'd woken up drenched in her sweat, her heart pounding in her chest, and ringing in her ears. She fought sleep by digging her nails into her thighs to keep herself awake. She kept the charm bracelet Chase had given her in her pocket. When she felt an attack coming on, she would caress each charm as if it would magically make the anxiety disappear.

"Mama! Gran Maddie asked me to give you this." She placed a letter in her lap. "Can we play Candy Land?" Looking hopefully at her mama, Emma waited for her reply.

"I'm sorry sweetie, Mama isn't up to playing a game right now." A monotone voice had replaced her previously cheerful tone that had been reserved for her daughter.

"You never play with me anymore!" Emma stomped off and Kassie sighed. Emma's tantrums were getting worse, but she honestly didn't have the energy to deal with them. Maddie and Joe would handle it.

It gave her plenty of time to sink into her own little world and be invisible. She didn't have to worry about anything. She could stay numb. It was better than feeling anything. She stared at the letter on her lap, knowing who it was from and that opening it would make her feel something that she didn't want to feel.

Kassie,

These are called Marsh Marigolds. They grow along the lake. I know how you loved fall with the changing of the leaves, but springtime is a time for new beginnings. New flowers of all different colors pop up all over, providing an amazing view of color and hope. It's also referred to as cowslip. What I like most about this flower is that it reminds me of you. It's strong and resilient and can take care of itself around the lake. But even in a drought, this little guy can still flourish. It might lose its leaves, but the bloom is just as beautiful.

I wish you would answer me. Princess, there's so much to talk about. I'm here whenever you're ready…

Chase

Sighing and squeezing her eyes shut to push away the emotions each letter brought her, she fingered the delicate flowers and tried to imagine them around the lake.

Sounds emulated from the kitchen. Getting up to investigate, she opened the door and found Joe at the stove teaching Emma how to make Mickey Mouse pancakes. There was more batter on the two of them than in the bowl.

Maddie held a plate of bacon and patiently waited while Kassie got it situated in her hands before letting them go. "Just in time to help set the table. Chef Emma and Joe made us a wonderful breakfast. Would you mind getting out the syrup and butter?"

She set the bacon down and noticed an extra plate had been added. She picked it up to return it to the cabinet.

"Leo's coming over to join us for breakfast," Maddie announced as she noticed Kassie's confusion over the extra dinnerware.

Kassie inwardly groaned. He pushed her to no end. He barked orders at her as if she was part of his military team. He pissed her off daily and refused to leave. Now that he had moved temporarily into Maddie and Joe's old house next door, they welcomed him like family.

"Good morning, PITA. Good morning, Ladybug!"

"Good morning, Uncle Leo! When is Dr. Chase coming home?'

Leo watched Kassie's face carefully. "I'm not sure, Ladybug, but hopefully soon. He misses you and your mama something fierce."

Kassie's nose scrunched up as she pretended to concentrate on spreading butter on her pancake.

"Did he get my last drawing?" Emma asked hopefully.

"Yes, he did. He said he's going to hang it up as soon as he gets home, or maybe your mama will take you to go see Dr. Chase."

"Yay! I wanna ride the horses! I'm glad he asked me to take care of Rollo. He plays ball with me because Mama's too lazy."

"Emma!" Admonishing the little girl, Maddie gave her the mama stare.

Emma slammed her fork down on the table. "It's true! All she does is sit. She never plays with me anymore! I hate you!" she yelled at Kassie before jumping up from the table and running from the kitchen.

The adults were silent. Kassie closed her eyes and took a breath. Her body started to hum. She didn't want to have another attack in front of Leo. He'd seen too many of them to count. She placed her napkin on the table to go after her daughter.

Maddie placed a hand on top of hers. "Let me handle Emma. Why don't you play the piano for a bit? Or go for a walk?" She smiled as if everything was fine. Nothing was ever going to feel normal again.

Chapter Twenty-two

A month passed.

Kassie made her way slowly down the stairs of her childhood home. She was walking without too much pain. She could move her fingers and hand. The cuts and bruises had slowly disappeared, and her hair was starting to grow back. Her body was slowly healing even if her heart and soul felt empty.

Tonight, she was going to break the news to Maddie and Joe. She woke up and grabbed her phone to scroll through the daily news. The headline read: *James Stanton Escapes Prison.* Dropping the phone, she immediately headed to the bathroom to vomit.

How could he possibly have escaped? She needed to leave. Her sister had put her family in danger, but she refused to put Maddie and Joe on Stanton's radar again. James only asked once. She was damn sure she wasn't going to give him a chance to get Em.

Dinner had been a quiet affair up until Kassie mentioned that she and Em were leaving.

"What? Why would you even consider that right now? You're still healing!" Maddie protested. Joe sat silently in the chair staring at her as if she had lost her mind. Shadow shoveled food into his mouth while he watched the show.

Leo placed his fork on the table rather loudly. His mouth was set in a firm line as if he was biting his tongue to keep from telling her his feelings on the topic. Glancing at Emma, he made sure her attention was on the mashed potatoes she was playing with, completely unaware of the tension at the table.

"Did you have a place in mind? Were you planning to let us help you plan a move or were you going to pack a bag tonight? Or are you planning to repeat your move on Serenity Mountain?" His eyes narrowed and he crossed his arms as he waited for her response.

Flinching at the barb she replied, "I contacted a few places. But I haven't figured everything out. I believe I'm capable of making my own decisions."

"Just barely," Leo gritted out, unable to contain his anger. Emma looked up at the change of tone in his voice.

Sliding away from the table, Joe kept a firm head. "I think it's best if we table this discussion once Ladybug gets her bath and story." He gestured toward the little girl who was watching them.

Panic was hitting her as she weighed her options. Should she take Emma and disappear? Em's medical condition was controlled now. What if something happened while she was on the run? Julio had offered to help her. If she ran, she could never return. Thinking of the older couple and the friends she'd made, her stress level compounded. Excusing herself to get her daughter ready for bed, she knew as soon as Leo escorted Emma over to the cottage, the trio would appear at her bedroom door.

Frustration grew as she let Emma play in the tub while she picked out their pajamas. The home that was once full of love and laughter no longer brought her joy. All she felt was impending doom and the walls closing in. Even the bedroom was a constant reminder of the sister that had put her in this predicament.

She got Emma dressed for bed and read her two books. Then she sent her along with Joe to the team's cottage. Then she quickly threw on a blue silk robe trimmed in white lace with flowing sleeves and a pair of slip-on sneakers. Taking the steps quietly, she snuck into the kitchen, grabbed a flashlight, and slipped out the back door. Sweat began to form and her hands began to shake as soon as she stepped outside into the darkness. Determined to make it to the one place she had avoided since her return to Texas, she carefully walked the winding path. When she was out of sight of the house, she turned on the flashlight. Further down the path, she finally arrived at the large dome-like structure. Roses twined around the huge columns. Jasmine covered the wall at the back of the structure. The honeysuckle was placed in a semicircle around the front, only leaving an opening wide enough for the brick path.

Three graves lay underneath, side by side. From left to right were Nathan and Abigail Reynolds and the last grave read Kaitlyn Abigail Reynolds. She dropped to her knees in front of her sister's grave, the one person she blamed for everything.

"Sissy, how could you do this to me? Did you realize what you would put me and your daughter through? Did you even think about it? I'm so... so...*pissed!* You *left* me! I told you, I didn't want to switch that day! If you hadn't insisted, I'd be the one lying in that grave and you could've been free to live your life with Emma! *Why Kassie?* Do you know what I've been through? Do you even care that I've lost everything? I *despise* being you!"

It felt good to finally vent to the one person that had caused her all this misery. She continued to rail at her sister. "I'm *lost!* I can't find my way back. Are you happy?" Sobbing, she hit the concrete in front of her. "I can't sleep because of the monsters lurking in the dark. I can't eat. All I think about is those days of eating nothing or choking rice down to nourish my child only to *lose* it because of your greed! *Money*, Kassie! Was my child's life worth it?"

Sobs wracked her body, "I don't know who I am anymore! But I know I don't want to be you! I've already lost Chase, but I'm not giving you any more of my life. My dreams can't come true but something good will come out of this!"

The eerily quiet of the night was all she heard.

Crawling to where her parents were, she tearfully touched their headstone. "Mama and Daddy, I don't know what to do. I'm surrounded by people, but I'm alone. I can't tell them! I tried being good, so you didn't worry about me, but I hate being her! I don't want fancy clothes and cars. I just want to be me! What should I do? Where should I go? Why can't I be me?

Curling up into a ball she lay at the foot, praying by some miracle that they would answer her pleas. Her heart pounded and she felt dizzy and fatigued at the same time. She clutched the flashlight as it began to flicker indicating the batteries were low.

Kassie let out a cry. She couldn't be stuck in the dark. Dragging herself up from the cold stone, she frenziedly shook the light. Panic welled up inside of her.

"Princess."

The sound of Chase's voice sent a wave of warmth through her body. Turning around, Kassie gasped at seeing Chase standing there. Kassie's legs took flight as she sobbed and threw her arms around him.

"I sent you away. I don't believe you're here." She squeezed her eyes shut and opened them again.

Chase pulled her back as his hand cupped her cheek and he swiped a tear away with his thumb. "Wherever you go, I go."

Closing her eyes, she felt him pick her up and start down the path toward the house. Breathing in the smell of oak and mint, she closed her eyes and prayed he wasn't a dream.

Chapter Twenty-three

Chase swiped his hand through his hair and paced the living room of the cottage that was just a short walk away from where Kassie was sleeping. "Jesus, I don't know how much more I can stand! She isn't getting any better mentally or emotionally and Emma's even affected. Not that I blame her, she's trying to get Kassie's attention."

"Joe and Maddie are taking Em to the beach in the morning. Kass is going to be out for a while, why don't you go sit with her?"

Chase let himself in through the kitchen and upstairs to Kassie's bedroom. Leo followed him. He went to the bathroom and got a washcloth and wiped down her tear-streaked face. She had dug her nails into the sides of her thighs. He gently dabbed them clean and washed off her nails.

"We need to figure out a new plan," Leo said. "She refuses to talk to the therapists that you have visit. Hell, she barely talks at all. Maddie and Joe are concerned. It's been all over the headlines that Stanton escaped. They're worried that if given the opportunity she'll take Em and run again. I increased security, as soon as Saint was alerted." Leo watched his friend lovingly take care of his woman.

"I know. This isn't working, Leo, she's barely taking the medications unless Maddie hands it to her."

"I'll have Taco watch Em while we meet Joe and Maddie tomorrow when they return. Come down once you get her cleaned up, we'll figure out our next steps." Leo exited the room to give his brother time alone with his thoughts.

Chase went back to smooth Kassie's hair out of her face.

She was back in that room again. Her body shivered even though she was coated in sweat. He got closer to her with the metal pipe, and she couldn't move away, her hand was chained to the wall. She had to protect her baby! Whack! Whack! The metal rod hit her arm and side. She cried out. Terrified that he would kill her this time.

Something cold was placed on her head. The voice that always seemed to drive Roger away, was calling to her.

"You're safe. It's a nightmare, Princess. You're home in your bedroom. Come back to me."

"You're trying to trick me. I pushed you away and told you to leave."

"No, baby. I'm right here with you. Do you want to talk about it?" Caressing her cheek, Chase waited for her to respond.

A single tear fell down her cheek. "I couldn't get away. He chained me to a wall. I lost our baby."

"That wasn't your fault. Once you recover, we'll go to the mountain and have a memorial. We'll place a plaque on the family tree so everyone will know how much our baby was loved."

Kassie was quiet for a moment.

"I should've trusted you and none of this would have happened." She whispered regretfully.

"We don't know that. I made mistakes too. Please come back to me. I need you." He pleaded with her every single time. She shook her head.

"I can't come back. It hurts too much. Emma hates me. You're not here. You're just a dream…"

He would be there to chase away her demons even if she didn't realize it.

On a nightly basis, Chase would sneak upstairs and sleep in the bed across from Kassie's.

When her nightmares came, it was the only time she talked. Whispering encouraging endearments, he would hold her and keep the monsters at bay. In her self-induced world, Kassie believed Chase was a figment of her imagination.

Sometimes she would sob and confess tidbits of what had occurred during her captivity, other days, she cried that she missed him. He detested the deception, but it was the only way he could be near her. It was the only way he knew that she was still there somewhere. Trapped in her own mind and struggling. He wasn't giving up. Somehow, he'd break through to her.

Maddie and Joe returned home the next day after going to the beach. Emma was a bear and the couple looked exhausted. Dinner was quiet. Maddie took a tray to Kassie's room and Emma fell asleep as soon as she finished her meal. Leo scooped the little girl up and dressed the little sleepyhead in a nightgown and tucked her into her bed. Taco stayed to watch over her so Leo could meet Chase, Maddie, and Joe.

Making his way into the kitchen, Leo grabbed a towel to help Joe with the dishes. The man had aged while watching Kassie fall deeper into her world. Chase came in through the back door. Joe pulled a plate from the oven and placed a meal in front of him.

"Eat son, while we talk."

Chase thanked him and dug into the homemade food. Maddie arrived a short time later.

"It's been two months. How long are we going to let this continue? Kassie was more engaged with Emma while recovering from the scalpel wound in Seattle when I first met her. No wonder Em's having meltdowns. I'm sorry Joe, this isn't working." Chase couldn't hide his frustration and worry.

Joe sighed. "I know, son. Maddie and I've worried ourselves sick. It was bad enough losing her sister, but I feel like we're losing Little Bit too." Comforting her husband, Maddie put her arm around him as he took her other hand.

"I've stayed away because she requested it and I hurt her. I fully acknowledge that. But you can't deny that she's calmer when I'm here. I don't think I can stay on the sidelines anymore. I love her. I don't want to keep deceiving her and I want her to know I've been here." Determined, Chase made his intentions known. He didn't want to add to their stress, but the current situation wasn't working.

The couple exchanged a look. Maddie stood and placed her hands on each side of Chase's worried face. "You've proven to us how much you care for her. We know if anyone can pull her out of this, it'll be you, we've no doubts. Now go to bed Sugar, because tomorrow will be another day and I think it's time you let Kassie know you've been here."

The next morning had started eerily quiet. Agreeing that it would be ideal to wait until Emma went down for a nap before Chase made an appearance, Leo brought Em over for breakfast. Kassie hadn't come down for the meal and even Em could feel the tension in the air.

"Uncle Leo?"

"Yes, Ladybug?" He took a bite of his eggs and waited for the little girl to voice the question she had been chewing on since she sat down at the table.

"What's wrong with my mommy? Why is she so sad? She doesn't want to play with me anymore." Emma's head hung down and Leo placed his fingers underneath her chin. When she raised her watery eyes to meet his, his heart nearly broke.

"Baby, your mama loves you more than anything on this earth. I know it doesn't feel like it right now, but she does. Do you remember how much you missed her when I took you and Melody on a vacation with Auntie Cat?"

Emma nodded her head up and down.

"Do you remember how bad your tummy felt before Uncle Michael put your pacemaker inside it?"

Again, the little girl nodded.

"Well, your mama had a bit of an accident and now all the outside has healed but her inside is still sore like your tummy was."

"Can Uncle Michael put a pacemaker in her tummy to make her feel better too?"

"No, sweetheart. It's not her tummy that hurts. It's her…heart. And that part of the body takes a long time to heal, so we have to be patient and love her and remind her we know she's going to feel better."

"So, we need to love her, and she'll feel better like when Uncle Michael fixed me?" Emma's hopefully questioned.

"That's right, sweetie, so we just have to be patient until she feels better. Can you do that?" He ruffled her hair to get a giggle out of her.

"Yes. I know! Mama loves flowers. I'm gonna go pick her some in the garden!" She hopped down and started to run out the back door, calling for Maddie.

Chapter Twenty-four

Emma knocked on the door and walked slowly inside, proudly holding the bouquet that Maddie had helped her pick. Kassie was in the bathroom with the water running. Impatiently waiting to surprise her, Emma surveyed the room looking for the perfect place to set down her flowers that were tied with a pink ribbon and placed in a pretty jar. Her eyes fell on the tall dresser across from the bed. Searching for something to help her reach the top, she set her present down and went into the hallway in search of something that she could climb on.

Walking into the room across the hall, she found a five-gallon bucket Joe had been using to store the painting supplies he was using to paint Emma's room across from Kassie's. Quickly removing the items, she dragged the bucket across the hall.

Opening the bathroom door, Kassie heard the scraping of the bucket. *A flash of a memory of the five-gallon bucket grating across the floor as Roger sat on top of it and pressed his foot on her broken leg went through her mind. Then he took a knife and thinly sliced her skin. The river of blood made a pattern in the jagged dirt floor.*

Oh God! He's in the house! Hide, Hide!

She ran back into the bathroom and slammed the door as the sound of the bucket grew closer and closer. She turned the lock and scrambled into the tub. Her hands went over her ears. *Make it stop! Please make it stop!!* The bucket dropped, startling Kassie more. *Please don't let Roger find me!*

Her body shook in desperation. He was going to get her! She wasn't going back, she'd rather die! Her eyes latched on to the razor sitting in the tray. She desperately grabbed it, clutching it like a weapon. She screamed her terror as she heard him banging at the door and yelling. *Somebody help! Help!*

Leo called Chase to let him know that Maddie was making lunch for Em and that she should take a long nap after being outside most of the morning picking flowers. Hearing the commotion upstairs, he ran through the kitchen, into the entryway and practically ran over a visibly shaken Emma. That's when he heard Kassie screaming.

"Chase, something's going on with Kassie!" He grabbed Emma by the shoulders. "Ladybug, stay here! I'll be right back, it's ok!" He handed her his phone and took off in a dead run. Maddie and Joe followed quickly behind.

"Leo, what is it, what's going on? Damn it, I'm coming over!" Chase demanded.

He heard the sniffles. "Dr. Chase. Can you come and fix my mommy's heart? Uncle Leo says it's broken and she's sick on the inside. You made her feel better before. Please, Dr. Chase! I just took her flowers, and she started screaming." Emma was crying now. "I want my mama."

A hand caressed her head, and she looked up to find Chase standing there holding his phone. Getting on his haunches, he was at eye level when he calmly hugged the little girl.

"Ladybug, I'm here. Go into the kitchen with Saint. I'm going to help your mama now."

"Yes, sir." Chase handed her off to Saint who promptly headed toward the kitchen so Emma couldn't hear or see anything else going on. Chase headed in the direction of the hysterical screams. He could hear Joe and Leo trying to talk to Kassie, but the hysteria grew louder.

"Fuck this. Stand back, Joe." Leo kicked the door in as Chase rounded the corner of the room.

Maddie exhaled deeply. "Oh Jesus, Mary, and Joseph! Please help my baby!"

Chase was already in the room. Kassie fought Leo tooth and nail.

"I'm not going back! I'd rather die! I'm not going to let you hurt me anymore!" She brandished a razor in front of her like a weapon. Leo positioned himself in front of the older couple so they wouldn't get hurt. He grabbed a towel and started toward her.

"Princess. It's me. Chase." Chase came forward and pushed Leo back slightly. "You're safe, baby. You're here with me, Maddie, Joe, and Leo. Listen to my voice. Roger can't come near you. Remember, you shot him,

Kass. He's not going to hurt you or your family ever again." He took a small step forward and her arm jerked the razor toward him in a defensive move.

Kassie was huddled in the tub. Tears streaming down her face. Even though she was looking directly at them, she was trapped in her nightmare. Shaking her head, she replied, "You can't be here. I don't want you to see me like this…" She sobbed. "I can't let James have Emma! I can't do this anymore!"

"No, Kass. I'm right here. Do you remember telling me what your mama said? Love was the only thing worth fighting for. I'm not going anywhere, baby. I'm fighting for you."

She shook her head in denial as the tears continued, "You can't love me now. I lost the baby. He hurt me…" She gasped as another memory flashed before her.

Roger stood on her broken leg and laughed as she screamed in pain. The metal rod struck her stomach, and she felt the blood seep between her legs. Her chance of having children died with every strike. He struck again, damaging her ribs. He broke her. She was broken…

She waved the razor in front of her, shaking her head. "No, don't love me. I can't give you what you want."

Chase rushed her. He grabbed the razor from her hand. Hysteria overwhelmed Kassie as she struggled for survival.

"Grab the sedative!"

Leo took off. Chase climbed into the tub with Kassie and crossed her arms over her chest. He began to whisper close to her ear and Maddie and Joe took in the scene and held on to each other in complete loss over what to do.

"Princess, take this for me." He held the pill close to her mouth, he wasn't sure if she would accept it. Thankfully, Kassie opened her mouth on command and Leo pressed a glass of water against her lips. Chase continued to croon to Kassie and stroked her hair. Leo wiped her face as her eyes closed.

"Oh Lord, what are we gonna do?" Maddie cried. She wiped her nose with a tissue Joe handed her. His face was distraught with worry. Maddie crossed the bathroom floor to hold the precious face of her goddaughter. "Lord, please tell us what we need to do to help our baby girl." She wiped Kassie's unconscious face and caressed her cheek. "Don't nobody deserve this, especially my sweet girl, she didn't do anything but good."

Joe leaned over his wife and helped her to stand. "We ain't gonna fail her, Maddie. We just gotta figure out a way to reach her. Don't you lose hope. Our girl's in there and she's a fighter. We gotta stay strong for her until she can stand on her own. We'll figure it out, my love."

"Joe, do you still have that power of attorney?" Chase asked.

"Yes, it's still in place while she's incapacitated. What are ya thinking, son?" Chase looked at Leo, then back to Maddie and Joe.

"I need your permission to place her under my care. I'm taking her home. I'm taking her back to Serenity Mountain."

Chapter Twenty-five

Joe handed Saint the last suitcase to load onto the company jet as he spoke with Leo and Chase. "We'll give you a few weeks to get settled and we'll follow with Ladybug."

Chase carried an unconscious Kassie onto the plane with Leo at his heels. He laid her gently on the soft leather sofa and strapped her in. "Can you stay with her? I need to do something before we leave."

Leo nodded as Chase exited the plane and headed to the car. Emma sat in the back with Maddie next to her. She stared dejectedly at the plane and watched as Chase came to her side of the car. She hadn't spoken since the incident. He opened the door and gently unbuckled her and pulled her from the car seat.

"Ladybug."

Emma's sad blue eyes, a replica of Kassie's, looked up at him. "This isn't your fault, baby. Your mama's insides hurt really bad. That's why she was screaming. I'm going to take her up to the mountain and make her feel better. But this isn't like the last time. You're going to come in two weeks. She might not feel good for a long time, honey. But you'll be there to help me make her feel better. She told me that love is the only thing worth fighting for and do you know what?"

"What?" Sniffing and wiping her nose on her sleeve, Emma looked up at Chase.

"She loves you so much that you're going to be the best medicine for her. I need to take her to some doctors, and you can't stay with her right away. But you'll be close, and we can go for horseback rides, play with Rollo, and you can meet Bear and watch how he sweet talks the bees into giving him all that delicious honey."

She looked up hopefully. "Mama isn't mad at me?"

"No, Ladybug, she loves you more than Maddie's cookies! Do I have your permission to take care of her and love her until you get there?"

She threw her little arms around his neck. "Yes, Dr. Chase, you can make her feel better and love her. Then when I get there, we can love her together and she'll feel better faster!"

Chase hugged the little girl and returned her to the car seat. He squeezed Maddie's hand in reassurance. Joe waited by the plane stairs. Chase shook his hand, and the older man pulled him in for a hug.

"Take care of my Little Bit, son." His voice broke and he quickly straightened up. "You best be going."

Chase nodded at the distraught man. "I promise you, I'll do everything in my power to love her, care for her, and protect her. I have no intentions of letting you or her down, sir."

Joe nodded and stepped back to allow Chase to ascend the steps.

Chase sat across from Kassie on the flight home. After sending emails and texts to have everything ready for their arrival, he finally shut the computer down. Leo was giving orders to the team.

Chase vaguely wondered if Kassie found out about Stanton's disappearance and if it was the catalyst to the breakdown. He may not have been directly involved in what happened to Kassie, but he had done enough damage to cause her to worry about Em for a lifetime. Matthew and Taco were staying in Texas and would follow with Emma and the Richardsons in a couple of weeks. Julio and two of his trusted agents would alternate as needed.

Shadow and Saint would meet him at the cabin. He hadn't known what he would have done without the team over the last couple of months. They had alternated guard duty and entertained Em to give Maddie and Joe a break. Chase offered to pay the team.

Leo had shaken his head. "We've done enough government jobs we can afford a break and I've got some ideas to run by you once we get back. I know you've got your hands full. The team has been following the leads from Mayor Thorton in Seattle and they've made some breakthroughs. The feds have made sure that as long as we are supplying them with the information, they'll supply us with funds."

Jake had been there to meet them when the plane landed. Kassie was still out and the sad look in Jake's eyes conveyed how sorry he felt for her.

"Don't do that." The sharpness of Chase's voice caught Jake by surprise.

"Don't do what, son?"

"Don't feel pity for her. If you bring that shit up the mountain, she'll feel it. We need to be strong for her and we've spent the couple of months letting her stay comfortable in her cocoon. Now we're going to shake things up. It's my only chance to get her back, Jake."

"If anyone can help her, it's going to be you and that mountain. Now let me tell you what I have, and you tell me what you need."

On the way up the mountain, Jake gave him a SITREP of everything on his email list.

"Dr. Meyers will be up at the mountain as you requested tomorrow. I gave her the payment information you told me to go over with her. As soon as she heard it was Kassie, she refused the amount. She said she'll discuss the arrangement with you later. I made a reservation at the inn for her to stay at. Widow Anderson's home is up for rent, and I got the keys. It needs cleaning. Catherine and Samantha said they will tackle that this week before the arrival of Kassie's family. I don't understand why you don't want them to stay at your parent's cabin."

"Because I'd like Leo to stay there." He hadn't bothered to say the words just in case he needed help with Kassie.

"Bear brought over honey, fresh bread, and some fresh fish from the lake. He put it in the freezer. We've already stocked you with beef and pork to last you six months. Samantha cleaned your cabin and got everything that you requested. The books you wanted from the library are in the living room."

"Thanks, Jake. I think we're going to get settled tonight. Starting tomorrow morning, no communication unless it's by text. I don't want any noise."

"We got the memo. I sure hope this works." Jake glanced in the rearview mirror to see Chase's tired green eyes staring back at him.

"So do I, Jake. So do I."

Chapter Twenty-six

Kassie burrowed farther into the blankets. Even as the numbing feeling of the medication left her body, she knew something felt different. She didn't hear Maddie in the kitchen getting breakfast ready or Emma's little giggles as Joe told her the joke of the day. She didn't even hear Leo's insufferable voice yelling at the bottom of the stairs to get her lazy bones down for breakfast.

The scent of bacon tickled her nose. She pulled the covers off the top of her head. Her eyes widened as she shook her head trying to clear it. *I must be dreaming…*

"Good morning, Princess. I hope you slept well. Would you like to come sit in the window seat and watch the sunrise while I finish making breakfast?"

Still surprised and confused, Kassie didn't respond. Placing two trays by the window seat, Chase set a mug full of steaming hot mint tea on one. Not bothering to wait for her reply, he exited the room.

Noticing the robe at the foot of the bed, Kassie slowly removed the covers from her legs. She put the warm dressing gown on, grabbed the blanket from the chair, and padded to the window.

She eyed the tea with a frown. She couldn't control her hand's shaking sometimes and would spill it. Maddie had started pouring her tea only three-quarters full and it was always just warm enough to drink. This mug was hot. She leaned in to feel the steam tickling her nose and the smell of mint awakening her senses.

Climbing into the window seat and propping herself up with pillows, she burrowed herself behind the curtain. She wrapped the blanket around her and carefully steadied the teacup with two hands on her knees as she anticipated the sunrise coming over the mountain. *I'm dreaming. This isn't real. But I'm going to enjoy this moment.*

A movement next to her caught her attention. Chase sat opposite her in the window seat waiting for the sun to rise. His eyes stayed focused out the window and he hadn't acknowledged her existence. *See, it must be a dream. He doesn't even know you're here.*

The sun rose and Kassie held her face up to the warm rays filtering through the window, taking in the beautiful colors around and below her. It had started as a dark orange and splashes of dark red, pink, and yellow created a work of art.

Closing her eyes, she soaked up the sun. Her lips formed a tentative smile as she reveled in the warmth and security of the mountain. Expecting for it to be snatched away in her dream, she was going to enjoy it while it lasted.

Once the sun rose and she finished her cup of tea, Chase stood. "Breakfast is in the kitchen whenever you're ready."

She watched him walk out and heard the clanking of dishes. Slowly disentangling herself from the covers, she made her way to the bathroom. Performing her morning routine, she washed her hands and pulled her hair back into a ponytail. Her gaze fell on the shower, the memory pulled her in…

Chase lathered conditioner into her hair and massaged her scalp. Leaning in and enclosing her in the safety of his arms, he murmured, "God, I love your hair, princess." He gently tugged it, making her lean farther back. Beginning with a soft kiss on her lips, he left a searing trail down her jawline. Tenderly nipping her neck as the water surrounded them, a low growl came from him as he watched the shiver go down her body.

Kassie bit her lip as she moaned. Oak body wash filled the air as she lathered his shoulders and slowly drew patterns on his chest as he held her in his arms. "I never thought it could be like this," She admitted in wonder at all the things he made her body feel.

"It's not always like this. This is special, Princess." Nuzzling her ear he whispered, "It's us."

Her hands worked their way down until they reached his stiff cock. Now it was Chase's turn to groan, eliciting a giggle from Kassie as she took her time washing him thoroughly. He stepped directly into the spray and rinsed off. Picking her up just under her butt, Chase placed her against the heated shower wall and grinned evilly as he adjusted the multiple shower jets where he wanted them and held her body as the water hit her clit as he fingered her pussy slowly.

"Chase." She moaned his name as her breathy sighs became full-on pants as Kassie got closer to exploding. Suddenly, he removed the streaming water, causing her to whimper in need. "Don't make me wait. Please. I need you."

Chase slid the condom over his swollen cock and entered her slick sheath, slowly rocking back and forth, bringing her close to the edge and then backing off. Her nails dug into his back, pulling him closer to her. Pulling him further into her. "Ahh." Kassie moaned as he went deeper.

He attacked her mouth in an onslaught of kisses and she half screamed, half moaned her orgasm into his mouth. He took his time and continued to explore her body and shifted her to bring her into a deeper position on his cock.

"I can't get enough of you, Princess."

She tilted her head back as the fresh sensation brought on a whole new experience of pleasure. "Good." She smiled seductively at him.

Always controlled and in control of her, his hand gently went around her neck, making her feel helpless but he never once added pressure. He stepped back and then tilted her body slightly so only her shoulders and head were touching the wall. With his hand still on her neck and the other holding her up under her butt, he adjusted his controlled rhythm to a series of longer, slower strokes. Her eyes went wide as she screamed, and he emptied himself inside her.

"You're mine Kassie. Don't ever forget that," Chase demanded.

She rubbed her arms and squeezed her eyes tightly. Wiping away the memory of something so sweet and loving. Knowing she couldn't have that again. Chase had made her feel so beautiful. There was nothing beautiful about her now. She was ugly on the outside with all her scars on her legs. Inside, there was nothing but black and darkness. She hid in the shadows. Nobody would find her. Nobody would hurt her, ever again.

Opening the closet door, she found her clothes placed neatly next to Chase's on the dressing vanity. Searching through the pile, she found her favorite leggings that Samantha had given her. Next to her pile lay her favorite Navy sweatshirt of Chase's. Picking it up, she inhaled the scent of him. Slipping it over her head, she sat in the closet afraid to open the door, to find it was all just a dream. Her breathing increased, and she squeezed her eyes shut as the blood started to pound in her head, making her dizzy. The corner of her vision started to fade to black. The closet door opened slightly. She whimpered.

Trying to give her some space, Chase waited in the kitchen. When she failed to come out, he went in search of her.

Nothing had prepared him to find her in the corner of the closet cowering like a small child and trying to make herself even smaller. He crouched down on his haunches and calmly spoke.

"Hey, Princess. You're having a panic attack. We're on the mountain. You're safe." Keeping his voice low and comforting, he continued. "Take a deep breath, baby. Now let it out." He repeated it three more times until he could see she was gaining some focus.

"Good girl. You did a great job, that one didn't last as long. You took control. I'm going to give you a few minutes to gather yourself and I'll be waiting in the kitchen. Breakfast is ready."

It took all of his strength to walk away from her. But he'd stood by and watched Maddie and Joe cater to her every need. It was with the best intentions. But his girl was hiding in there and was getting too comfortable to come out. They took care of all her worries and responsibilities, leaving her no reason to fight.

He took a sip of his coffee and ran his hand through his hair after fifteen minutes, wondering what the hell he should do next when she hadn't come out of the closet.

A noise behind him caught his attention. She stood at the bar holding onto the back of a chair. She was still pale, but she was back in control. He turned and placed a plate in front of her and smiled.

"Hi, beautiful. There you are. I wasn't sure what you wanted and I'm starving. There're pancakes in the oven with the bacon and scrambled eggs with biscuits on the stove."

He turned around and began to place food on his plate. Her grimace when he had called her beautiful hadn't gone unnoticed. He added that to the checklist of things to talk about with Claire, the therapist from Seattle.

Gripping the plate with two hands, she made her way over to the stove. Chase saw the plate shake but made no move to take it from her. She scooped out a small helping of eggs. Glancing back at Chase, she pulled apart a biscuit. Looking wearily at the oven and back at her plate, she cautiously opened the oven and removed a piece of bacon. Making her way back to the kitchen table, she sat across from him.

Looking at her plate, she picked up her biscuit and realized the butter was next to him. Chase pretended to concentrate on his cell phone as he shoveled the eggs into his mouth, waiting for her to ask him to pass the butter. He gripped the fork tighter when she looked away and ate the biscuit dry. Disappointment filled him.

When they finished eating, he grabbed her plate and took it to the sink. He didn't turn around but began to give her the options of the day.

"I thought you might like to take a shower, so I'll take care of the dishes. When you're ready, I thought you might like to walk the lake. The Marsh Marigolds are in bloom, and I thought you'd like to see them. I'm going to grab a shower in the guest room while you decide."

She turned back to her room, closed the door, and locked it.

Frowning, he took another sip of coffee. Knowing he had a key if he needed to enter the room, he left her alone. If it made her feel safer, he wasn't going to let it deter his plans.

Chapter Twenty-seven

Chase came out of the guest room to see Kassie sit on the sofa to go over all the books from the library. Knowing she liked the classics, he had gotten her six. Kassie ran her hands along the spines of the books as she read the titles. Placing them neatly on the table, she stood when she realized he was there.

"You'll need a jacket, it's still a bit chilly on the mountain. I think Samantha left you one in the coat closet. I need a few things from the barn. Why don't you come out when you're ready?" Putting his boots on, he went about his business and walked out the door.

Kassie stood in indecision. Walking over to the window she looked over the mountain and the lake, pressing her face against the glass and allowing the coolness to seep into her skin. The curiosity about the Marsh Marigolds finally won out and she went to grab her shoes.

Finding the jacket and a pair of light gloves in the pockets, Kassie hastily put them on. In the back of the shelf in the closet, she found a white hat with a fluffy ball on top. She pulled it over her head and made her way to the barn.

Chase watched Kassie wrestle with herself at the table in her indecision to ask him for the butter. Watching her choose her food had been excruciating. He wondered why he hadn't noticed this when they were at Joe and Maddie's. Then he realized it was because Maddie either fixed Kassie's plate or took a tray to her on days she didn't come down. His girl was afraid to make choices. He knew partially what that bastard had done to his woman, and watching her deal with the aftermath made him want to kill Roger all over again.

Leaving her in the house was difficult when he was fighting the urge to see what she was doing. He impatiently waited to see if she would come. Busying himself with pitching fresh hay, he fought the urge to go back inside. Somewhere deep inside, he knew the Kassie he loved was there, just afraid to come back to the light.

The barn door opened. She cautiously stuck her head in.

"Hey, Princess, perfect timing. I just got Scarlett and Rhett all setup." She glanced at the horses and back at him. He casually closed the gate. "There're some carrots in that bucket over there. Rhett is black and Scarlett is red. Watch Rhett, he likes to nip."

She stood at the edge and watched him. He walked to the bucket and grabbed a carrot and handed it to each horse. "Just let me wash up and we can be on our way."

Walking slowly toward the horses, she was startled when Scarlett pushed her head through the stall door and made her presence known. Jealous that Scarlett was hogging all the attention, Rhett craned his neck around the corner to make sure he got an equal opportunity for adoration. Kassie giggled at their antics.

Chase returned from the basin and Kassie froze when she saw him holding a five-gallon bucket. Stark terror filled her eyes, and she started backing toward the entrance, never taking her eyes off the bucket.

"Easy, Kass. Remember where you are." He followed her gaze to the bucket and placed it behind the tool bench out of her sight.

Taking a step toward her, he stopped as she edged closer to the door, ready to bolt. "Princess. Let's go for that walk. I promised to show you the marsh marigolds." She practically ran out of the barn. Chase closed the barn door and watched her from the corner of his eye. He sighed in relief. *Remember, Winters, slow and easy.*

Walking toward the trail, he slowed to give her time to catch up. When they made it halfway around, he took the path to the gazebo his dad and Jake had built for their wives. Opening the door, he removed two water bottles and a couple of soft protein bars from his pack. She followed him slowly inside then she sat in the chair closest to the door.

Scooting the food and drink in front of her, he reminded her, "Eat sweetheart, we need to keep your strength up."

Walking halfway around the lake was the most physical exertion she had done in months. Occasionally stopping to give her a rest, Chase told her the names of a flower or spoke conversationally, saying Bear could probably tell her what medicinal property each one held.

Watching her pick at the food and grip the water bottle, he noticed when her eyes started to droop. Wanting her fresh for her visitor that afternoon, he got up and opened the door.

"Princess. Let's head back to the cabin for a break, we don't have to do everything in one day." Not waiting to see if she followed, he started down the dock. She waited until he was a few paces ahead, then opened the door and followed.

Chapter Twenty-eight

When they entered the cabin, Kassie took off her boots and placed them by the door and hung up her jacket and hat. She stood in indecision on what to do next. Disgust filled Chase. Not at her. At the monster who had made her the shell of the person she once had been. Walking to the fridge, he pulled out the pasta and salad from Jake and the bread that Bear had dropped off.

Heating the meal, Chase handed her the bread, a cutting board, and a knife. Grasping the knife, she carefully cut the slices as if she were afraid of making a mistake. It looked as if it was taking all her brain power to concentrate on cutting even slices. Working on her confidence was going to be one of his priorities.

He placed the food on the table, and when she finished the bread, he took it, placing the butter next to his seat. Sliding into her chair, she took a small amount of pasta and a small slice of bread, then searched for the condiment. When she realized it was near him, she tore the piece into sections and chewed slowly. Disappointment surged through him. *Easy, Winters, baby steps.*

When half of her lunch was finished, she placed her bowl and silverware into the sink. Going back to the table to retrieve her plate, she then threw away her bread and stood by the sink in indecision.

"I'm not done eating. Why don't you grab a book and read a bit or take a nap?" Chase said.

Turning toward the living room, she gingerly sat on the couch and picked up each book again and read the titles, finally deciding on *Jane Eyre.*

After placing his dishes in the dishwasher, he ventured over to ask if she would like a blanket and found her asleep sitting straight up. Grabbing a pillow, he tenderly lowered her to the couch and covered her with a blanket.

For the first time in months, he was able to take stock of how she was doing physically. Most of the time he only got to see the bruises and cuts and how they were healing from the light of a nightlight or if Maddie took her for a walk, he could see the mottled bruises all over her face and arms. Leo updated him, but it wasn't the same as seeing her in person. How her cheeks were sunken in, her eyes were gaunt and had lost their sparkle. Her bouncy, fiery, red hair hung loose, thin, and dull around her shoulders. Placing it in a ponytail at the back of her head, she wouldn't allow anyone to touch it since Samantha cut it.

Going over his checklist of things he needed to discuss with Claire, Chase's mouth formed a thin line. Kassie had to hide her hair when she was running from the dirty agents. It was the one thing she'd asked Samantha to give back to her when Chase had taken her for a spa day. Imagining it gave her a closer connection to her sister, he wondered if that was why she refused to do anything with it now. Hearing her confession to her twin and parents that night at their graves had been heart-wrenching. Hopefully, Claire could help her navigate her feelings concerning her sister. He'd never forget the day she saw herself in the mirror for the first time in the hospital.

Kassie had been awake for three days and hadn't said a word. The nurse had left the hospital tray over her lap after removing the untouched food. Carefully sliding the tray open, Kassie flipped the mirror up. It hadn't been her face that she was concerned with, it was her hair. She touched the chin-length version and tears had run down her cheeks. Samantha took her hand.

"Hair grows back. It won't be like this forever. I cut it so it will grow back healthy and full again. It will be an easy style for you to handle during physical therapy and won't tire you out to wash. It's only temporary, sweetie."

Samantha had left the next day, and Kassie refused to see either of her friends again. He didn't think it had anything to do with her hair; she was trying to isolate herself. If she could've figured out a way for the team to leave, she would've dismissed them too. Fortunately, Joe had stepped in and left her with no choice. Hopefully, today would be a turning point. He grabbed his phone and updated Maddie and Joe. Just as he finished, his phone rang silently. Leo's name popped up on the screen.

Taking the call to his room, he picked it up so it wouldn't disturb Kassie.

"What's up?"

Leo's voice was full of tension. "We got some movement on our investigation in Afghanistan. Taco, Saint, and I are leaving at sixteen hundred tonight. I called Julio to get a team for Emma. He's coming personally with another agent." Chase knew that finding out what had happened to their brothers had been one of the priorities of the team.

"I wish you luck, Leo. I hope the lead pans out." He truly hoped that the team found some closure on what happened while they were on their mission.

"It's more than a lead. I can't get into it now, but I'm going to be gone for a month at the minimum. I hate doing this to you now. Michael will help out on the weekends and Cartwright's in town. He volunteered to be there when Michael can't."

"When and who invited that asshole?" Agitated, Chase paced the room. Although Matthew was instrumental in finding Kassie, Chase didn't trust him around her.

"I did. He's good at the cyber stuff and I need someone with his skills on the team. He's the one that found the lead on the Afghan information. I know your feelings toward the man, and I don't blame you, brother. But right now, we don't have much choice and I believe he has Kassie's best interest at heart. He's agreed to keep himself scarce unless you need him."

Chase just grunted a reply. He couldn't think of any situation in which he would be desperate enough to call Cartwright for help. "I'll see you when you get back. Be careful, brother."

"I'll try to check in on you and Kass. And Chase…" Leo's tone changed from all business and held a bit of emotion.

"Yeah?" He tiredly replied.

"Good luck, brother." Ending the call, Chase stuck his phone in his jeans and got to business.

Placing a pair of clean pajamas in the bathroom along with Kassie's toiletries, he thought about driving her down the mountain and stopping at Samantha's. Maybe a short spa day and being around her friend would help. Plus, Samantha could report back anything that she was concerned about since Kassie refused to say she was in pain. Her limbs would occasionally swell, and after several times of Leo finding her huddled over the toilet, Chase had deduced she was suffering migraines. It was as if she felt she deserved the pain.

A soft knock on the door let him know that his visitor had arrived.

He opened the door and let in the tall blonde. Professionally dressed in a black pantsuit and a pair of red-rimmed glasses, she smiled as Chase took her hand. Indicating the sleeping woman on the couch, he ushered her to the table and formulated a plan.

"I'm assuming you've had time to read the records and the recommendations from the psychiatrists and therapists?" Holding up the coffee pot and a bottle of water, he waited for her to choose.

Indicating the water, Claire replied, "Yes, I did. Thank you for sending everything over. I'm sorry for what's happened to her, but I won't be charging her for treatment with the amount on that check Joe sent me. It was way too much. I'll charge my standard rate, with a schedule of three mornings and three afternoons. One day off for right now. This way, I can handle my patient load in Seattle. The only other expense that I'd like to have covered is my stay at the inn. I want to be close just in case we have a breakthrough, or she's having a difficult time."

Chase nodded. "Consider it done. If you think she needs anything else, let me know. You also read that she's refused to talk to every therapist we've brought in?"

Nodding, Claire smiled at the anxious man in front of her. "She's lucky to have such a supportive family and group of friends. But ultimately, this is going to be on her, Chase. I can provide her with the tools and support, but she has to decide to fight."

Raising up from the couch, Kassie noticed the visitor sitting with Chase. Claire stood and confidently walked toward the couch. Kassie stood and shot Chase a menacing look.

Blocking her exit, Claire stood in front of her. "It's good to see you, Kassie. I've missed you at the hospital."

Chase stood and walked toward the couch. "Kass, I invited Claire to come and talk to you. I thought you'd be more comfortable talking to someone that you knew."

Claire cut him off. "Thank you so much for inviting me." She walked over to her briefcase and pulled out a list. "Here's the list of everything I'll be needing. You can go ahead and get those items now. Kassie and I'll be fine catching up without you."

Chase looked momentarily confused. "I think I'll just hang around the barn and I'll have Jake pick up the items on your list."

Claire shot him a bright smile. "No. No, I need you to go get them. I realize you're a doctor, but I think you forgot that there is this thing called patient confidentiality. Kassie and I need to feel safe here. I can't allow you to come in during our designated time. We won't expect you back for at least an hour."

Kassie's head shot up and she angrily shot both of them dirty looks before she walked into the master bedroom and shut the door. Then the lock clicked.

"I think I should stay. She's had some meltdowns and panic attacks. It's taken two of us to handle it. I don't want her to—"

"I assure you, Dr. Winters, I know what I'm doing. You need to stay away for the next *three* hours. I mean it."

Chase took a deep breath and looked at the woman in front of him. "That's a long time." His voice was barely above a whisper. He swallowed. "I won't lie, I'm worried."

"Kassie needs to feel safe to talk and trust me. As much as you don't want to hear it, you're also part of her issues. I read the notes you left me. You in your own way have enabled her. All of you have, with completely good intentions. I think you've realized this, or you wouldn't be doing this drastic of a change with her care. Please let me do my job."

"She doesn't talk, Claire. Not because she can't. She's said a few things, but there are days she doesn't speak at all."

Placing a comforting hand on his arm, she reassured him. "She's been through hell. It's not going to be easy. Go run some errands and get out of this cabin. I've got this. Trust me."

Nodding, he glanced at the bedroom door before he walked out the front door, closing it behind him. Turning his truck in the direction of Serenity, he headed to Jake's.

Jake took one look at his godson's face, opened the door wider and ushered him in. After he settled in a chair with a glass of whiskey in his hand, Jake sat down next to him.

"Okay, son. Tell me what's on your mind."

Chapter Twenty-nine

Looking at the clock, Kassie smiled smugly to herself. It had been over an hour and there had been no sound from the other parts of the cabin. The last thing she'd heard was Chase's truck going down the driveway. Staying hidden in the window seat, she had waited for the time to pass looking out at the mountain. When the second hour passed, and no noise came from the other room, she decided to get a glass of water.

Opening the door, she only took a few steps before she spied Claire in the chair by the fireplace with a book in her hand.

"I was wondering if you were ever going to come out. I've been dying to see what the view from the master bedroom looks like. The drive up the mountain was beautiful, you must really love this place."

Kassie's nose scrunched up in annoyance. Claire ignored her and walked into the bedroom. Irritated that Claire was invading her private space she followed her into the room.

Taking a seat in the window before Claire descended upon her territory, knowing it was childish, Kassie protected the spot she had dreamed about all those miserable days. Knowing how well Claire broke down walls because she'd referred her toughest patients to her, Kassie was determined Claire wasn't going to get through hers.

"This is a lovely space! It's peaceful and quiet and the view is gorgeous. Is this where you feel the safest?" Claire asked, sitting down across from her.

Kassie didn't respond, knowing what Claire was doing. She was *not* one of her patients and didn't want to talk to anyone. She feared that if she started talking, all the venom from everything that had happened would spew out and she couldn't stop it. This way she had control.

"Augh, I see you aren't going to talk. That's okay. I'll just sit here and enjoy your company." Sighing forlornly, Claire continued, "I saw José just last week and he was asking about you. Catherine and Melody were at the grocery store yesterday. Melody is such a cutie. How's Emma doing? Chase told me the pacemaker has done wonders for her. I'm so happy for you."

A million questions about José popped into her head. She missed her best friend and Melody. And Emma. Not once since she had woken up here had she given Emma a single thought. It was almost a relief. Seeing the hopeful look in Emma's eyes every morning wishing that her mama was somehow going to reappear that day was almost too much. Didn't they understand? She'd died. Twice. Once with her sister and once in that cold, damp room.

She closed her eyes and relived the moment she had talked to her sister while she lay on the cold, damp, floor, waiting to either die from her injuries or from Roger shooting her. She hadn't cared.

Fight! Sissy, you have to fight!

No. She wished that she hadn't fought. Roger was going to kill her, and she had been ready to accept her fate. The pain had been too great. She'd been hurt physically, mentally, and emotionally. When she lost the baby, there was nothing left but a dark black void. It was there that she hid in the shadows and could silently scream her terror.

When she was at the hospital she had tried to let go. But her sister's voice kept invading the dark. She dreamed of her twin talking to her.

No. You're not ready. I need you to take care of Emma. Chase needs you. Go have the life you want. I'll take care of your son, you take care of my daughter. We'll see each other someday.

She didn't know why she'd even thought of that. She hadn't been far enough along to know whether she had carried a girl or a little boy. But in her heart, she had felt she had lost a little boy with Chase's hair and green eyes.

"Do you want to share that thought with me?"

Slowly facing Claire, whom she had forgotten while she was lost in her memory, her eyes narrowed, and she knew she had to push her away. Claire could make her feel when all she wanted was to stay numb.

"Go away." She crouched farther into her seat so the curtain provided a small amount of protection, a wall between her and her new enemy.

A glint of determination shot through Claire's eyes as she smirked at her friend and coworker. "I'm not going to do that. You've managed to get all those doctors to give up on you. But I'm not just anyone, I'm your friend. I'm not giving up because you'd never give up on me, Emma, or José."

It was Kassie's turn to flash a look of stubbornness. Shaking her head, she firmed her mouth in a tight line, indicating to Claire she had no intention of cooperating. Instead, Claire laughed.

"I'm going to be back in the morning. Chase said you went for a walk today. I think we should walk so you can show me that lake. I'm almost jealous that you have such a wonderful view compared to my apartment where Mr. Jenkins sits on the patio and smokes his daily six packs of cigarettes." Claire shivered in disgust. "Be ready at nine, and if you aren't, I have no problem dragging you from your bed."

Kassie rolled her eyes. She had seen Claire do just that and she had no doubt Claire would have no problem doing that to her.

They sat quietly and looked out the window. Claire didn't intrude on the rest of her peace. She wondered about the people Claire mentioned. Were they alright? Her heart ached when she thought of Em. Maybe, just maybe, she could talk to Claire just once.

Chapter Thirty

Two weeks later, Kassie was meeting with Claire and progress was being made. Walking around the lake twice a day made her leg grow stronger. Her face had filled out, she had rosy cheeks and didn't look as haunted. Even her hair had grown. Rollo followed her everywhere and she preferred the dog's company to his. Chase reminded himself that it was still positive even if it was baby steps.

Maddie and Joe arrived in town with Emma and anxiously awaited news that there had been an improvement. Maddie secretly dropped off some gardening tools and flowers for the front of the cabin and some plants for a small garden bed.

That morning he nearly lost his patience when she refused to ask him for the butter and ate her toast dry. It was as if she wasn't sure she was making the right choice by asking. It had become a game. Every morning, his new mantra became "ask for it, Kass, just ask me to pass the butter." Disappointment filled him as he watched her deny herself the tiniest pleasures.

Spending her days curled up on the window seat in his room, she read the books he had gotten her. When she finished the last one, he'd told her he could drive them into town to the library so she could pick out her own books. She promptly set the books on the table and didn't touch them again.

Impatience was building and he didn't know how much more he could take. Three weeks wasn't a long time in the scheme of things but watching her lose herself and all her passions broke him.

Today she walked out of the bedroom wearing a T-shirt and jeans.

"Good morning, Princess. You got a special delivery last night. It's on the front porch." He turned around and poured himself some coffee figuring he had a fifty-fifty shot of her going to see what it was.

Sending the morning update text, his gaze followed her as she opened the door to find the small crates with colorful flowers and a box of cute little yard décor. She bent down and picked up each flower and looked at the name. She rummaged through the box. Her hands slid over the garden tools as if itching to use them and jerked her hand back.

Unable to handle watching her another day without finding a way to reach her, he jammed his phone in his back pocket.

"I need to take the horses out. I won't be long." Chase addressed her curtly.

Going out to the barn, he saddled Rhett. Urging him down the drive, he pulled out his phone. Pressing Matthew Cartwright's number, he waited for the man to answer.

"Kassie's at the cabin. I need to get some space. Can you keep an eye on things?"

"Sure, man. Take your time. I got eyes on her now," Matthew replied civilly.

"I'm sure you do" Chase muttered under his breath. Urging Rhett into a full run, he couldn't help but think of how much he wanted his team back.

Kassie watched Chase disappear from her sight. She knew he was frustrated, but healing from trauma wasn't going to happen overnight. Walking back into the cabin, she picked up a book to read. Ten minutes in, she was bored out of her mind. She headed to the bedroom and crawled up in her window seat and tried to lose herself as she had done for the last few weeks. Not even three minutes later, the cabin walls started closing in.

Looking outside at all those colorful flowers from the front window, she slid on a pair of rubber boots that she'd discovered in the closet. Telling herself that it was supposed to storm later and the rain would be good for the flower's roots, she cautiously made her way outside.

Bending down and reading the labels, she sorted out the plants according to sun or shade, then placed them in groups around the porch and sidewalk. Changing her mind, she replaced some plants with others trying to find the best places for them. When finally satisfied, she grabbed the tools and started digging. With each stab into the ground to dig the hole, she took out her frustrations and thought about Chase's hospital.

Claire had left a notebook for her to write her feelings in. It sat on the dresser. Instead of her feelings, she had sketched drawings while she sat in the window seat as she envisioned the hospital and support buildings. A dormitory cabin with a central kitchen and each room having a separate bath for staff that worked doubles or didn't want to make the drive home. Chase mentioned having a training facility to teach new skills or trades. Sketches of the backside of the mountain held her drawings of a service dog training area, a miniature subdivision of smaller cabins for military members who progressed in treatment but weren't ready for the real world. The more she thought about it, she added on to Chase's hospital. A unit for troubled teens was placed on the opposite end with notes in the margins about having the teens help the soldiers and vice versa.

Thunder rolled across the mountain and before she knew it, all the flowers were planted. A small fraction of satisfaction crossed her mind as she looked at the colorful entryway. Looking toward the raised garden bed, she noticed the small assortment of vegetables for the planter boxes. Pouring the soil into the empty beds, she began to place the tomato and pepper plants. Clashes of thunder and flashes of lightning lit up the sky and rain started coming down. Needing to finish what she started, she stabbed the dirt faster, adding the plants.

"Kassie!"

Hearing someone calling her name, she ignored them, there was no time to stop! The thunder clapped as lightning spread across the clouds as the rain began to come down in buckets. Her clothes clung to her, but she refused to let it deter her.

"Kassie, get inside!" The wind whistled through the trees, loosening her hair from the ponytail and hair flew into her face. Rollo began to bark and took off down the drive.

Grabbing another plant, she dug another hole in the dirt that had turned into mud and packed the roots in. Two hands touched her shoulders. Sheer panic hit her. She grabbed the small spade and brandished it in front of her.

"Don't touch me!" Screaming in fear at the unfamiliar hand on her.

"Kassie, get inside, darlin. The weather's getting bad! You gotta go inside!" Matthew insisted as he grabbed her arm and started to pull her toward the house.

"No, no, no!" Flinging her body sideways, she knocked them off balance in the front yard. Mud clung to them both.

"Kassie, darlin', I'm not trying to hurt you, you can't be outside!" Yelling against the wind, he tried to get a grip on her leg, causing her to panic.

Dragging herself out of the sludge and thrashing to get away as the sheets of rain pelted her, she screamed.

The sound of horse hooves caused her to turn and look down the driveway. Chase's hair was plastered to his head, his face red with rage. He jumped off the horse and headed straight at Cartwright. He picked him up by the collar with one hand and struck him hard in the jaw with another.

"You just couldn't stay away from her, could you!" He struck again.

Matthew struck back and both men fell into the mud. Kassie's beautiful flowers were crushed as they rolled over all her hard work, exchanging punches.

"Stop it! Stop it!" she screamed, as the two men continued to take turns beating each other to a pulp. Matthew defended himself and Chase let out all his rage.

Whacking a broom at the two men, she continued to beat them until they separated. Flushed from the exertion and out of breath, she yelled, "I said stop!"

Surprised by the force of her voice, the two men stopped hitting each other. Daggers shot from her clear blue eyes as she brandished the straw broom like a weapon. Breathing heavily, she dared either one of them to start up again. Her hair whipped around her and for the first time, Kassie felt something. Anger, frustration, fear, but more importantly, she felt powerful.

"Chase Winters, stop beating my friend up!"

A snicker escaped Matthew as he watched her warily as she stood over them ready to smack them again.

"And you!" She turned her attention to the mud-caked man.

"I'm not my sister! I love you as a friend, Matthew. If you can't reconcile that I am not who you wish me to be, then we can't be friends."

"Kass—"

"No! Don't Kass, me! I didn't pay attention to what the others were saying. You want me to be *her*! I want you to be part of my life and am grateful for your help in finding me, but I can't be what you need. You deliberately provoked Chase knowing he was watching me and led him to believe we slept together! I won't tolerate that anymore. Now, are you going to be my friend or not?" She stood with one hand on her hip and her legs apart, still holding the broom while she awaited his answer.

"Yes, Kassie. I apologize for creating any misunderstanding between the two of you." He stood and offered Chase a hand up as Kassie brandished her broom higher, ready to pelt him if they started again. Lightning hit the sky.

"I'll care for the horse. I'll leave you to Kassie." Matthew grabbed Rhett's reins and led him into the barn.

Now that she'd garnered their attention, she threw the broom on the ground and frantically began to repair the damage to her beautiful blossoms.

Stooping beside her, Chase calmly apologized.

"I'll replace the ones that we ruined, don't fret about it, Princess."

She shook her head wildly as water ran down her face, and he wasn't sure if it was rain or tears. Hair stuck to her face as she continued to work. His eyes followed her hands as she frantically shoved the roots back into the sludge.

"They'll live, Princess, because somebody cares about them and wants them to grow despite what they went through."

The roar of the wind increased, and lightning struck close by. He knew they were on a limited amount of time. He moved to her right side and began scooping divots in the dirt while she painstakingly cultivated the broken plants.

Holding out his hand to help her up, he expected her to refuse or avoid it. His eyebrows rose when she gingerly placed her hand in his. She stood and looked up at his face, using her other hand to shield the water from her eyes.

"Why? Why are you doing this?" she shouted.

Momentarily at a loss for words, Chase stood in the rain. His eyebrows furrowed in confusion.

"Because I want you to feel better, Kassie, to heal and be whole again." He pulled her hand to his chest. Just as her hand reached him, she jerked it back as if she had been burned.

"Then what, Chase?" Her chest heaved as all the torment over the last few months bubbled to the surface.

Stepping closer to her, and watching her take a step back, he tried to explain. "I don't know what you mean, Princess." Looking up at the sky and back at her, "Do you think we could go inside and have this discussion? In case you haven't noticed it's storming."

"No! I don't. You don't get to say what's best for me. I have a brain, you know!" Rain drenched them both and she shivered.

"Kass, you're cold, let's get out of the rain." Yelling over the wind, he tried to get her to move but she pulled back.

"I don't understand. Why are you doing this to me?" she cried.

Standing in front of her, he pulled his jacket off and tucked it around her. "What, Kass? What am I doing to you?"

"Acting like you care. *You hurt me!*" She threw his coat at him.

Guilt showed in his eyes and he picked up the coat, holding it loosely in his hand. "Yes, I did. I'm sorry, Kassie."

"I don't want you to be sorry! I don't want your guilt! Don't you understand?" Balling her fists, she continued to beat his chest until she tired herself out. Holding onto her wrists, he held her as she fought him.

"No! I don't understand, Princess. I'm damned if I do and damned if I don't! I know I hurt you, baby. If I could take that day back, I would. I stayed away as you asked. I watched you almost die. I don't know what you want me to do!" Pushing back the hair plastered to her face, he held her steady and tried to give her the warmth of his body as hers was wracked with shivers, but she refused to go inside.

"You accused me of not trusting you!" She sobbed. "But what about you, Chase? Why didn't you trust me? You didn't ask me what I wanted! At first you thought I wanted the money, then assumed I wanted to live like my sister. I hated every minute of it! And you accused me of sleeping with Mathew! Did it ever occur to you that he was the one person that I could talk to about my sister? No. You treated me like I was the same as Rachel!"

"I was wrong. I know you don't care about the money. I was worried that I couldn't give you that kind of life. I'm trying to fix it now, so you can have the life you want."

"You don't get to *fix* this, Chase! You told me how you felt obligated to marry Rachel because you were with her all that time. I don't want you trying to fix me because you feel obligated out of guilt!" The wind whipped around the two of them, but Chase held his ground.

Making sure she heard him over the storm, Chase yelled, "Is that what you think? You think I'm with you because I feel guilty?" Invading her space, he cupped her soaked face. "Yes, I feel guilt, remorse, and pain. Because I love you, damn it! I don't want to see you hurt."

"You can't love me, Chase!" Gripping his wrists, she held on tightly to him. "I *don't know* me. I carry my sister's name, but I'm Kaitlyn inside." Sadness filled her eyes. "You can't love me, I'm broken!"

"I don't give a damn about who you call yourself. You'll always be mine. That's all I care about. After watching the video of your sister telling you about Emma and seeing you in that hospital bed, I couldn't care less what you do with your name or the money as long as you're on this mountain sharing your life with me!"

Kassie started to say something and shut her mouth. Backing up, she headed toward the front door and left Chase outside, alone.

Chapter Thirty-one

Placing food and water in the buckets and some toys in the stalls to occupy the horses, he grabbed his jacket to exit the barn. Thunder shook the ground and the rain sounded like nails were hitting the building. Sliding open the door, he saw the trees whipping and bending in the wind, stirring up debris. He stepped outside and grabbed the handle to pull the door closed, completely engrossed in his thoughts of Kassie and how he was going to get through to her.

Out of nowhere a thick limb from the tree next to the barn cracked and whipped in his direction. He tried to shove the door back open to escape. The branch struck him, and it was too late. Blackness surrounded him.

Kassie shivered as she shoved the sodden clothes onto the floor and turned on the shower, letting the steam fill the room. Tipping her head back and letting the hot water run from her head down her body, she grabbed the bottle of lavender shampoo and washed her hair. She enjoyed the feel of scrubbing the top of her head. It was as if her body had come back fully alive. Glancing at the hand that Chase had held, she longed for his touch.

"They'll live, Princess, because somebody cares about them and wants them to grow despite what they went through." She pondered that thought as she cleaned the mud under her nails.

It was taking Chase a long time in the barn. Kassie dried her hair and as she started to place it in a bun, she let her hands drop. She looked closely in the mirror to see the same woman who stood there months ago.

That woman had been happy and glowing with love and possibilities, this one knew how ugly the world could be.

Thinking back, she thought about the day Chase had rescued her and how things had gone terribly wrong. When he found her, she was so relieved, thinking she wouldn't die alone next to Roger. God, she missed him. Waking up, she realized they'd deemed her a "failure to thrive". Maddie hovered and clucked over her and took over Em's care. Her friends and family shook their heads and whispered when they didn't think she was awake. When she woke, she could see the pity in their eyes. It was easy to slip away and let them. She didn't have to think about anything.

Chase had attempted to wake her.

"Hey, Princess, I need you to open those baby blues. Emma misses her mama. Joe and Maddie are getting worried. Don't let that bastard win after all this. You told me a while ago that your mama said that love was the only thing worth fighting for. I need you to come back to us, Princess." Chase had pleaded. "Fight for me even if you want to give up."

Chase had never said anything about loving her before the incident. He'd asked her to fight out of guilt. They never discussed the baby. When she found out she couldn't give him the family that he wanted, that had been the last straw.

Emma. How she missed her sweet, beautiful girl. She longed to stroke her hair and read her a story as she lay across her lap. A pang of guilt ran through her. Emma was the only one who hadn't looked at her with pity. Her innocence was still completely intact and if anything, she'd acted out because she didn't understand why her mama was gone.

Glancing out the window, Kassie saw the barn door was cracked open and Chase was nowhere in sight. He should have been in by now. Pacing the living room, she watched the clock and bit the skin around her thumb. Her gut kept nagging at her. Something was wrong.

She pulled her boots from the closet and grabbed her rain jacket. She opened the door and staggered as the wind caught it, threatening to slam it farther open. Pulling it shut, she made her way to the end of the porch. Something was by the barn. It was then she could hear Rollo barking furiously next to the object on the ground. Fear struck her.

She clung to the railing as the tempest around her increased. Her body weight was no match for the force behind the gale. Letting go of the railing, she ran toward the barn. The force of the wind knocked her to the ground, and she crawled closer.

It was Chase! She saw the tree limb stuck into the other side of the door and realized what happened. Immediately, she took inventory of his body. Rollo lay down next to his master and whined. Checking his pupils, she gently probed his head. Hysteria bubbled beneath the surface when she discovered the blood behind his scalp. A huge gash was on his hairline and that would require stitches. She ran her hands down his body to see where he had put his arm up to guard himself against nature's weapon. It held a jagged cut. Brushing the caked mud from his skin, she noticed his body was a block of ice.

Kassie knew there was no way she could get him up to the cabin. She ran against the wind back to the house and into the bedroom. She jerked the sheet off the bed and headed to the bathroom. She filled a bag full of towels, soap, and a spare change of clothes for Chase, then she bolted to the back of the closet and grabbed his medical bag. Kassie rushed back outside.

Rollo stood and barked as he saw her weaving her path back to them. He ran toward her, then waited until she had a firm grip on his collar and led her back to the unconscious Chase.

Bracing a towel to support his head and neck, she gently rolled and tucked half of the sheet under him. She rolled him the opposite way and retrieved it from underneath. Sitting in the mud, she took a few breaths as the adrenaline kicked in and she removed the heavy limb from the track. Tying the makeshift stretcher at the end as a handle, she tugged and pulled.

Repeating the process, she did it again and again. Rollo grabbed the other end and helped her tug. Breathing a sigh of relief when Chase's feet cleared the doorway of the barn, she slammed it shut.

Water droplets fell from her hair as she grabbed the scissors and started cutting his shirt and pants off. There was no way she was going to be able to move him to remove the sodden clothing. When she got to his shirt pocket, she felt the hardcover of his phone.

Desperate, when Jake's phone went to voicemail, she dialed the one person she knew would come.

Chapter Thirty-two

Leo and the team had returned the night before. After three days of no sleep, he crashed immediately. After planning for the team to bug out again the following week, Leo headed toward Serenity Mountain to check on Chase when the hellacious storm hit. He had just pulled into the town limits when his phone rang. Glancing at his dashboard, he noticed Chase's name pop up.

"Leo."

"Leo?" Kassie's voice cracked on the other end. "Help me."

"PITA? Where are you?" He demanded.

"In the barn. Chase is hurt. Hurry."

Leo pressed on the accelerator. "I'm on my way, Kassie. I'll be there in about fifteen minutes. Are you safe?"

"Yes. Chase is injured, I can't move him." Her voice conveyed her worry.

"I'm coming. You take care of my brother, Kassie. I know you can do it. Do you hear me?"

Leo couldn't see her nodding her head up and down. She hung up the phone and continued to get Chase out of his clothes. After drying him off, she pulled on his pants and cut his sweatshirt in half to cover him. His temperature was low. Gathering piles of hay, she hoped it would help to warm him up as she wrapped his injuries.

The door that had seemed to weigh a hundred pounds easily slid open as Leo's frame filled the doorway. He looked at his friend and nodded toward her.

"You did good, Princess. What's the SITREP?"

"Tree limb hit him in the back of the head. His pulse is steady, I think he has a concussion, and two cuts that need to be stitched."

"Let's brace his head and neck and I'll get him up to the house. Can you help me? I'll come back out and get the barn locked up. There's a tornado getting close, we gotta hurry," Leo urged.

Kassie nodded.

Leo easily lifted Chase like a sack of flour, as Kassie held on to Rollo and ran to open the door to the cabin. Rollo and Leo followed as she ran to the bedroom. She pulled down the blankets and placed old towels by his head and arm.

She got to work cleaning the cuts and just finished stitching his arm when Leo's voice startled her.

"Damn, PITA, I didn't know they taught nurses to stitch. I think you did a better job than Doc."

"I'm a nurse practitioner." Biting the tip of her tongue, she cleaned the gash on his forehead and adjusted the light. Her eyebrows furrowed in concentration as she sewed. Washing off the clumps of mud stuck to his head, she worried if Chase was warm enough.

She grabbed another blanket and laid it across him. "He needs a hospital. I don't know if he has a concussion or worse. I don't know how long he was laying out there."

"We can't leave until the tornado passes the area. The last thing we need is to be stuck outside. You did a great job. Go get out of your wet things and warm up."

Running into the kitchen, she poured two cups of coffee and placed them next to Leo and Chase. She gathered her clothes from the closet, then rushed to the shower and washed quickly. Throwing his Navy sweatshirt on, she smelled Chase's scent. He smelled like home.

Thunder rattled the house and lightning flashed through the room. Thankfully, she was back in the bedroom when the power went out. Kassie sent a worried look in Leo's direction.

"Don't worry, the generator should kick in shortly. Being up in the mountains, Chase is always prepared."

Just as predicted, the power kicked back on.

"I need you to hold him here so I can check the back of his head too," Kassie said as she rolled Chase to his side.

"Just tell me what you need. I'm taking orders from you." Leo winked at her trying to reassure her. "For once."

A groan came out of Chase as Leo returned him on his back. Kassie checked to see if his temp had risen and softly patted his head with a cool damp cloth. He probably had one heck of a headache, but she didn't want to give him anything until she knew what they were dealing with.

He slowly took her hand and kissed the inside of her palm. Longing washed over her. She could feel the scruff on his face as it scraped her hand and fingers. He turned his face toward her, grimacing in the process.

"Stay still. A tree limb hit you. We're waiting out the storm and then you'll have to go to the hospital. I'm pretty sure you have a concussion," Kassie cautioned.

His eyes widened and a lopsided half grin, half wince crossed his face. "Welcome back, Princess. I'm so proud of you."

She sat back a little bit. Leo moved on the opposite side of the bed. "You gave us quite a scare. The tornado has passed so we should be able to leave soon." He glanced at Kassie with a half question.

She wasn't ready.

Kassie focused on Chase. "I can't go. I'm not…" Waiting for his anger, she fully expected him to fight her.

He took her hand in his. "It's okay. I'll be right back."

"You didn't tell me your girl could sew. You better be happy it wasn't me. I can't stitch a straight line for shit. She has a steady hand."

"I might have to talk to her about going back to school and becoming a doctor. What do ya say, Princess? You're an amazing nurse. I watched you in Seattle and your attention to detail in your charting. You could even hold off discharging patients you get a soft spot for." He tried to grin, but a wince was all that appeared.

"I thought about it, but I had Em and it's a lot of work." She didn't bother to say she was also on the run.

"But you were alone then. You aren't alone anymore. You got me, Jake, Maddie, and Joe, the team, and this town loves you. Only if you want it; there's nothing wrong with you being a nurse practitioner. You're a damn good one."

Smiling, she wrangled all the wet and soiled towels to take to the laundry room. The weather had calmed, and the wind had all but stopped. It was time to let him go.

Leo slowly helped Chase into the cab of his truck while Kassie fussed, adjusting pillows and clean towels around him. She covered him with a blanket.

"I'm coming back. Will you be here when I return?" His worried gaze caught hers.

"Let's see how hard your head is." She added, "I need to see Em."

"Ladybug, Maddie and Joe are in town. I'll have Jake bring them up."

She shook her head. "No. I need time to think… I…don't know…"

"Would you like to talk to Claire? She's staying in town too. She could help you sort out some of your feelings. I'm not pushing, Princess. You weren't brought here to be a prisoner. We take this on your schedule. I just want to know that you'll be okay." Leo climbed into the driver's side of the truck and started it.

She took a step back and held the door. "Will you have someone call me to let me know how you're doing? What the doctor says?"

"Absolutely, then I'm coming home." She knew he was waiting for her to say she would be there.

Climbing the stairs to the porch she watched Leo back out of the drive. Rubbing her arms, she tried to shake the void left by Chase's absence. Kassie cleaned the muddy clothes and sheets and remade the bedding. She made a cup of tea with honey, then crawled into her window nook and placed her phone on her lap. Clearing her mind, body, and soul, she picked up the phone and dialed.

"Dr. Claire Myers speaking."

"Claire. It's Kassie." There was a slight pause on the line.

"Hello, Kassie. What can I do for you?" Claire's cheerful voice held a note of surprise.

"Chase got hurt. Leo is taking him to the hospital. Could you come to the cabin? I want…to talk."

"I'll be there in twenty minutes." The line disconnected.

She stared at the number pad and ran her hand over the top. She took a deep breath and dialed.

The phone rang half a ring when Maddie picked it up.

"Sugar, is everything all right?" Her worried tone came over the call.

"Hi, Maddie. I'm okay. I don't want you to worry about me. I need to talk to Em."

"Of course, Sugar. Joe is out on the porch swing, reading a book to her. She gets more like her mama every day." Kassie could tell that the older woman was crying and trying to hide it.

"I'm sorry, Maddie. Don't worry." Kassie reassured her.

"I'm not worried, my sweet girl. You're a Reynolds, a fighter. Everything's gonna be just fine. Let me get Em."

A few minutes later the sweetest voice she had ever heard came over the phone.

"Mama?" The voice was tentative and sounded a bit scared.

"Hey, baby girl. How's my Em?" Kassie mustered all her old self back into her voice.

Silence left a big gaping hole at the end of the line.

"I'm so sorry, Em, that I scared you. I wasn't feeling good that day. It wasn't your fault. I love you."

"You're not mad at me?" Her daughter's worried voice made her stomach drop. She would change that.

"Oh baby, I could never be mad at you. I love you more than Twix!"

The tinkling laugh that followed made her heart sing. "I love you more than Milk Duds!" Emma shouted into the phone.

"I was wondering if maybe I could see you tomorrow? I've missed you terribly." Kassie waited for her to respond.

Emma got quiet. "Did Dr. Chase fix your heart? He promised he would make you feel better."

"He did Em. I'll see you tomorrow and I can't wait for one more sleep to see you."

"Goodbye, Mama. I can't wait to see you tomorrow!"

"Me too, sweetheart. I love you."

She took a deep breath and looked at the serene landscape the rage of the storm had threatened to destroy. But when the furor left, the beauty and the peace of the mountain had persevered.

Chapter Thirty-three

Claire Meyers sat on the opposite end of the window seat. She now knew this was Kassie's favorite place in the whole world. "Where do you want to start, Kass?"

"I don't know what I'm supposed to do."

The therapist watched her patient as she took a sip of the delicious tea. Kassie squished her nose up in deep thought.

"What do you want to do?" Claire asked and set the tea on the tray to grab from the batch of cookies Maddie had sent over.

"I want to take back my life. I'm tired of everyone feeling bad about what happened. We need to move on. They hover. I can just *think* something and the next thing you know, it's done for me."

"That's a fair statement. They were really worried about you. You didn't speak. Do you think that they would have stopped if you would have asked?"

The thought had never occurred to her. "I allowed them to do it. I was numb."

"Do you think they carry some of the blame for what happened?" Cocking her head to the side, Claire waited for Kassie to process the question.

Kassie readjusted herself in the seat. "The team wasn't at fault. It wasn't their space to guard. Julio's man was being blackmailed and left the site. Nobody could have known Roger would've done that. Even I was shocked when he showed up in that room."

"You know those men, Kassie. At one time, they alternated who was watching over you. Do you think they cared whose responsibility it was? Or did they care more that you got hurt on their watch? Maddie and Joe look to you as the daughter they never had. Your friends were extremely worried about you. But you don't mention Chase."

"Leo takes everything so seriously. He would have found this to be a major "FUBAR" as he would say. I don't blame them. I love Maddie, Joe, and my friends. I know they were doing everything out of love. I didn't ask them to stop because it was easier not to deal with it all. Chase, I don't know…"

"But you blame yourself. What did you do wrong?" Claire persisted.

"Where do I start? I should've talked to Chase and waited for the team to come up with a plan. If I would have confronted him that day, I wouldn't have left the mountain."

"Do you think Roger would have stopped if he hadn't gotten to you that day? Would he have found a way to get to Emma?"

Kassie absorbed the question. "No, he would have found a way and I wouldn't have wanted him to get his hands on Emma. If he had to take one of us, I'm glad he got me."

"Of course, you wouldn't want Emma hurt. You're her mama and that's what parents do. They protect their children."

Kassie pressed her forehead against the cool window.

"Kassie, is that why you stopped talking? Because you felt this was your fault?"

Kassie closed her eyes. "All my life I've tried to be what everyone else needed. My sister was a handful, so I tried to be good so my parents wouldn't worry. She talked me into switching with her so I could pass her tests in school. Then it was so she could go out with different guys. After she married Phillip, she switched with me so she could leave the house to meet Matthew. I didn't know at the time that was what she was doing. When she was dying, I had to be what Emma needed. I didn't like it. I don't regret being there for Emma, but I should've stopped long before that." Kassie readjusted herself.

"I couldn't understand why she wouldn't leave. She adamantly refused and we fought. We had just made up that day. I hadn't been there for an hour when she convinced me to switch places to go see Matthew. Then she was killed. My sister pushed me into a relationship with Roger and encouraged me to marry him, knowing what he was like. If I hadn't found out he was cheating and broke off the engagement, I would've been imprisoned in the same life I tried to get her to leave."

"You know you can be mad at her, right? It's even healthy to be mad at her."

"I'm mad at myself. I feel like I've never had any control over my own life. I sacrificed myself to protect my sister, then I had no choice but to run with Emma. Then Leo and the team took over once I was found by James. Then Roger, he…"

"Say it, Kassie. Say it and get it out there. Don't let it have power over you any longer."

"He didn't rape me, Claire. Thinking I was Kassie, he was repulsed to have sex with me because he wanted a sweet, innocent, naïve girl named Kaitlyn. Roger was more interested in getting the money and exacting revenge on Kassie for changing Phillip's mind."

"What else did he do? I saw the medical reports. Purge it."

"Roger beat me, carved me with a knife, broke my bones, and starved me. The monster sat on my broken leg as he cut me. If I took too long choosing my torture for the day, the punishments lasted forever. He made me choose my meals. Most of the time it was nothing. Sometimes a slice of plain bread. But all I cared about was protecting my unborn child."

"Yes. You protected your child. And. You. Survived. I'm sorry about your baby. Now you don't have anything holding you from living your life. You have protection from the team, or you can hire someone else. Kassie, you're free to live your life. What do you want to do?"

"I would just like to lead a normal life. As Joe would say, I want to turn all this *gris-gris* into something good and get rid of all the bad."

"Does your life include Chase?" Claire inquired.

"I don't know. I don't want him to be with me because he feels bad. I know he feels guilty about what was said in the office before I was taken. We made mistakes. We didn't trust each other. Chase didn't want me to stay Kassie. I can't be Kassie and not have all that entails. But I know what I would do with the money."

"You don't feel that you can do that with Chase? I'm not advocating for him; I think you aren't facing your own feelings where he is concerned."

Kassie pulled her hair behind her ear. "Before all this happened, I asked Chase if we could talk and he was polite and professional. He said he wished me and Em the best. After that, he came into the hospital and begged me to open my eyes so he could apologize. All the time I stayed here before while they were putting the pieces together, he never told me he loved me. I never told him I loved him. After I was attacked, he felt sorry for me. I couldn't look him in the eyes without seeing the pity and guilt."

"Did he say he pitied you or is that how you felt?"

"It doesn't matter. I won't let him sacrifice himself to be with me out of obligation or guilt."

"Do you consider Chase a man that would spend his life with someone he didn't love?"

"Chase was engaged a long time ago. I've met her a few times. She's a bitch. She wasn't what Chase needed. She didn't have one single thought that didn't make it about herself. He needs someone that understands that his job will take him away sometimes. That his work is important to him and can help so many people that sacrificed for this country. This may have started as his dad's dream, but he'll make it a reality."

"Do you think Chase brought you back here as a job? Guilt?"

She sighed. "As a job, no. Guilt possibly. Obligation because he felt bad that we fought before I was taken and then because he didn't find me right away and I lost the baby."

Rollo walked in and sat down underneath Kassie's side of the window seat. She absently stroked his head.

"Do you feel you could talk to Chase about how you feel?"

She rolled her eyes. "If I start talking to him, he's going to want to know everything. I'm not ready for that. Believe me, I've gone over it. Right now, it's enough to say the words to you without wanting to scream and never stop. I don't want to give Roger that power over me. Even if it's from the grave."

"What are you ready to do?" Claire questioned.

"I want to start my life."

"Do you want to go back to Texas? Seattle? Or somewhere new?"

"I think I want to stay in Seattle. I'm scared to leave this mountain. I love the peace and security it offers, but I need to know I can function outside of this. Right now, I need to focus on getting Emma back into a routine, feeling safe, and knowing what happened that day wasn't her fault. I need to talk to my friends."

Claire nodded her head. "It sounds like you've given this some thought."

Nodding her agreement, she whispered, "Chase and I were put together because I was a job. Then when everything happened, words were said. I lost a child and my mind. I'm just not sure if circumstances were different, we'd still be together."

Claire shifted so her back leaned against the window. "I know you've been through the rape crisis training. I know deep down, you know what I'm going to ask. I don't think you give yourself enough credit. You may not have been raped, but Roger traumatized you. You survived, Kassie, and did what you had to do until you were rescued."

Claire shifted in the window, fully facing Kassie. "I don't think you're giving Chase credit. He didn't have to bring you here this time. Not only did he employ me, but he also orchestrated to have your family with you, made sure all your needs were taken care of, and put his dream on hold for you. Are those the actions of a man that thinks of you as an obligation?"

Shaking her head, she moved away from the window seat and placed her cup on the small side table next to a plush chair. "No. So much has happened, I'm scared he'll always feel guilty, and I don't want to get hurt again."

The blonde therapist bit her lip. "There are no guarantees in life. Running away from something to keep from getting hurt can sometimes damage you more. I know you. If I look in your journals, I'll probably find a list of things you need to do. If I ask you what you need to do right this minute, what comes to your mind?"

After mulling the question over a few minutes, Kassie lifted her face and looked at Claire. "I'd like to pack my things. It's time for me to take back my life."

Chapter Thirty-four

Chase looked irritably at Leo sitting next to his bed. The doctor felt he needed to be admitted and nothing he could say would get Leo to let him sign out AMA. He felt in his gut he needed to get back to the mountain. Cursing the tree that had hit him in the head, he worried about leaving Kassie that long.

"No use sending me shitty looks. If it was anyone from the team, you'd do the same. Claire is with her. I know you don't like it, but you getting injured jolted her. That's a step in the right direction, but she might need more help than you can give her right now. With that knock on the back of your head, you aren't in any position to think clearly either."

"Leaving Kass to her own devices for very long has always led to disaster. Especially in the state she's in. I just want to be there." Chase's arm hung over his head to stave off the pounding headache.

"I get it. But brother, you can't hold on to her if she's not ready to be held. If she's going to bolt, she will do it sooner or later. Plus, Cartwright's on her."

"Great." Unable to keep the aggravation from his voice at the mention of the man who seemed to be a pain in his ass every time he turned around. "I still don't understand why he's even here."

"I know. I was waiting on an opportunity to talk to you and Kassie. Let's just get through this. I understand there was a situation before this barn incident. Cartwright wanted me to tell you that he'll keep his distance, and maybe after this is all over with, you two need to have a beer. But he'll make sure she's safe."

Chase grunted from the bed.

Chase gripped his hair and laid his head on the pillow. Disappointment gripped him as he tried to remain calm. Fighting off the urge to completely lose his shit, his head pounded in retaliation for his effort. Leo gripped his shoulder as Chase said the words aloud.

"I've lost her."

"No. You didn't. She just needs time. Think about it, brother. That woman has been running for three years, then this awful thing happened to her. She's bound to have fears, anxiety, and second-guessing herself. You'll have to remind her of what you two had. We'll come up with a plan, brother." He tightened his hold on his buddy and let him have a moment of grief.

Tapping her shoe nervously on the front porch, Kassie waited at the door, hoping Samantha would be home. Missing her friend terribly, she needed someone to talk to about Chase.

A slightly disheveled Samantha opened the door. "I'm sorry I'm not open yet… Kassie!" She grabbed her friend by the hand and looked outside to spy Chase's truck in the drive. "Is Chase next door visiting Jake?" The worry in her voice was evident.

"No, I came to see you. I'm sorry you aren't open. I was wondering if I could get a haircut and talk?"

"You don't ever need to ask." Grabbing her friend, Samantha headed to the salon part of her home.

"Where's L.J.?" Kassie nervously wiped her hands on her leggings and smiled as the calming scents of Samantha's spa tickled her nose.

Samantha went to work grabbing bottles and jars off her shelf. Then she grabbed Kassie's long, limp ponytail and shook her head. "Liam's parents took him camping for the weekend. I swear he looks so much more like his father every day. I think his grandparents love every single moment reliving Liam's childhood with L.J. so he knows his dad."

Motioning for Kassie to sit, Sam grabbed a brush and began brushing out the mop of hair. Looking down at Kassie's hands and nails, she frowned. She shook her head as she then looked at the blue eyes staring at her in the mirror.

"First, you haven't been using conditioner or any of the products I sent. Second, I'm going to take care of this rat's nest, third, you aren't leaving until you get a mani/pedi. Do you literally eat your nails?" She shook her head, disgusted. "Now, tell me what you did with Chase and if I need to send someone to rescue him."

Her nose scrunched, and she held back the tears. "The storm caused a limb to hit him in the back of his head. Leo took him to the hospital. He's fine but he has a concussion and the doctor's admitting him for observation. I've talked to Claire and packed everything in his truck. Emma and I are headed to Seattle. I didn't think I could do this all today, but once I started thinking about her, I couldn't stop."

"Oh, honey. Are you sure you want to do this?" Samantha crouched down and gripped the arm of the chair to get a clear view of her friend.

"I love it here, but Emma needs me. I need time to figure all this out."

"First, you were *healing* and need to continue to do so." Her friend gave her a stern look. "I can't say we liked being shut out, Kass. But we didn't experience everything you did, but we understood." Quietly, she asked. "What about Chase?"

"I don't know." She softly answered. "I'm not the same person I was when he met me."

Brushing a strand of hair from her friend's face, Samantha spoke softly. "I know you're hurting, I just ask that you don't think I'm being selfish in asking that you remember we were in pain too. Watching you fight your way through the horror and nightmares was extremely difficult. By no means am I saying we suffered like you, but we hurt *for* you. So, when you are trying to make sense of everything, remember we're all on your side."

Confusion hit her in the face for a moment, but she knew that Samantha had her best interests at heart and after refusing to see or talk to her friends, Kassie felt the message Samantha was trying to convey.

She grabbed the hand that held hers and a sob escaped. "I'm scared. I remember bits and pieces of things. I know Roger can't hurt me anymore. I killed him. But I don't know if I could ever be like before… I might not be able to have kids. Chase wants a family…" She squeezed her eyes shut.

"That's when you ask for help. That's when you lean on friends. I'm not saying it's going to be a picnic. Chase loves you and no matter what doubts you have about that, it's solid. His love for you is just as strong as the love Liam and I had." Samantha swiped away the tears from her own face and then wiped her friend's. "You and Emma *are* his family. There are other ways to expand on that if you decide to. Talk to Chase. Tell him what you're scared of. This kind of love might change, it might grow, but it doesn't go away. Love can beat anything. You just have to believe."

She patted the hand that gripped hers for dear life. "Let's make you presentable for the world and show them that you didn't go through a storm. You *are* the storm."

Three hours later, Kassie's hair was perfectly styled. Her nails and feet were polished and smooth. She had on new clothes. Faded jeans and a light long-sleeved top with burgundy and pale pink flowers. Samantha was closing her shop while Kassie went to retrieve Em. Matthew followed at a distance.

Joe answered the door to the rental house they had been using since they had come into town. "Oh, Little Bit!" His voice cracked as he took her in his arms and held her lovingly. "Maddie told me you called, and I scarcely believed her! It's so good to see my girl."

Em's excited squeal could have been heard miles away. Running and jumping into her mama's arms, the little girl clung for dear life. Maddie surrounded them both and clung tightly to all that she held dear to the world.

Once inside she sat on the flowered chair next to the fireplace as Maddie placed a plate of cookies and tea in front of her. "You were supposed to come tomorrow! I don't know why I made these today, but something told me to make your cookies and here you are! I feel like I'm still dreaming that you've come back to us!"

"I've come to take Emma to Seattle with me," she stated quietly.

The couple shared concerned glances and private messages.

Joe spoke up first. "Little Bit, are you sure that's wise? You've had a rough time. Don't get me wrong, but are you up to caring for Em? What about Stanton? You still need security."

"She's my daughter, Joe. I know I've worried y'all and I don't blame you. We're just going to stay at a hotel in Seattle and I want you and Maddie to meet us in a couple of days. Emma and I have some catching up to do. Joe, I need you to set up a money transfer for Chase's hospital. The rest, I'll play by ear as I don't know what I'm doing from there. I would like you and Maddie to stay close. I'm not ready for you to return to Texas. If Leo is willing, we'll continue with the security until I can have him vet out a new security detail. Matthew's watching me now."

"Little Bit, you and Ladybug are family. We'll follow you anywhere. If this is what you need, we'll support you. But what about that young man?" Joe asked.

"I can only handle one step at a time. I'm working on it, Joe."

"There's my Sugar." Maddie smiled proudly. "You keep fighting, baby girl."

She smiled and went to help Em pack some clothes.

Samantha helped take her and Emma's bags into the hotel suite. Looking out the window, she could see the sprawling view of the sound and the early evening Seattle skyline. Although she loved the life she'd made with Em in Seattle, her heart lurched every time she thought of the mountain.

"Are you sure you don't mind watching Em?"

Samantha hugged her friend.

"Go see Chase. I'm sure he's worried himself sick by now. Emma and I will get settled."

Matthew drove Kassie to the hospital and stayed a respectable distance while she inquired about Chase's room number.

Chase's arm was slung over his head as Leo sat quietly in the corner. Upon seeing Kassie, Leo rose from his chair. The movement caused Chase to stir. His eyes widened at the sight of Kassie standing in the doorway.

"I'm going to make some calls out in the hallway." Leo excused himself.

Shyly, Kassie walked up to the hospital bed. Her fingers tentatively touched the bandages on his head as if reassuring herself he was okay.

"I talked to Claire." Kassie licked her lips.

"Good. I hope she helped you work through things." Chase was tense.

"That's why I'm here. I wanted to say thank you for bringing me to the mountain. For helping me to heal. I still have work to do. I spoke with Old Man Davis. He sold me the land, so you now own the mountain. You've put off your dream to help me. I know you don't approve of my decision to stay Kassie. It comes with a lot of money, and I was thinking that I could turn some of this bad into something good. I've talked to Joe and he's going to transfer money into an account, and I want you to build the hospital."

She placed the sketchbook on his lap. "Don't tell Claire but I used my journal to sketch out some ideas."

Chase was quiet as he flipped through the drawings and read her notes.

"You're leaving aren't you?" Chase couldn't hide his disappointment.

"Yes. I'm not running. Emma needs me and I need to figure out who

I am. I'm staying in Seattle and seeing Claire three days a week. I want to find José. Maddie and Joe are coming in a couple of days."

"Can I see you?" Chase asked.

"Emma and I would love that." Bending over the rail on the bed, Kassie placed a soft kiss on his lips. She smiled as she backed out of the hospital room, leaving Chase with his own thoughts.

Kassie put Em to bed and wandered around the suite. The lights of the city provided her with a pretty picture, yet she longed for the sound of cicadas and seeing the stars. Going around the huge suite with three bedrooms, she strategically placed nightlights and headed to the bedroom. Knowing she needed to stay strong for Em and focus on getting better, she formulated a plan. She pulled out her notebook with her lists. Feeling odd for putting herself first, she began to make a list for self-care. More appointments with Claire, getting Emma into preschool, arranging time for herself, and looking into whether she wanted to pursue going back to school.

Thoughts of Chase invaded her mind. When she'd packed her bags, she stole his sweatshirt. In desperate need to feel close to him, she pulled it out and inhaled his scent. Missing him, yet unsure what she was going to do, she placed her pad and pen on the bedside table and then lay down on the bed. Pulling the sweatshirt to her face, she closed her eyes while smelling Chase close to her. She realized that even with everything that occurred, he was her safe place. Now if only she could figure out how to stop running and find her way back home to him.

Chapter Thirty-five

Three days later, Maddie and Joe moved into the suite directly across the hall. The other two rooms in her suite were occupied by Leo and the team. Leaving Emma with the older couple so they could enjoy the day at the Seattle Aquarium, she made her way to the tiny apartment that Catherine and her mama rented.

Carol Reese opened the door with a huge smile on her face and welcomed Kassie with open arms. Catherine was next as she embraced her friend, talking at the same time. Catherine was the reason why she and Emma were no longer alone and running. She was still worried about Stanton trying to get Emma, but at least they weren't alone as they were before.

"Why don't you two get settled, I'll go grab us some tea while little Melody is taking a nap." Carol busied herself in the kitchen and Kassie couldn't help but wonder if Maddie and Carol would be great friends. Maddie had been her mama's best friend. When her mama died, Maddie's focus turned into helping her goddaughters get through their grief. Secretly plotting, Kassie decided to introduce the two women.

As Kassie and Catherine took a seat on the worn couch, Kassie looked around their apartment. Joe informed her that they refused his offer to help pay for. This was nothing compared to the cozy home they had shared all those months ago. Hopefully today, things would change for all of them.

"I'm so glad to see you, Kass. You look good." Catherine gave her friend a long appraisal before she smiled.

"Cat, I feel terrible for not contacting you before now. I wasn't processing things and ..."

"Water under the bridge. I'm just glad you are sitting with me right now. Your note said you wanted to talk to me?" Shuffling items on the coffee table to make room for the tea, Catherine easily dismissed her.

"I'd like to talk to both of you." Gripping the documents in her hand, Kassie was more determined than ever to help change the lives of her friend and mother as they had done for her and Em.

Carol brought in the tray of tea and cookies and sat down in a worn gold recliner. She grabbed up her knitting and started working on a scarf as she listened to the women chat over the food.

Slightly pausing, Kassie addressed her friend's mother.

"Carol. First, I'd like to say I'm sorry that you lost your home and all your belongings because of me. The reason I stayed away from you was that I knew what James was capable of. I got too comfortable, and never should've moved in."

Carol shook her head. "Nonsense. You had no control over what that man did. You put it out of your mind. I don't place one hair of fault on your head!" Carol's motherly protective voice reassured her.

"Same goes for me," Catherine spoke up.

She pulled out two manilla envelopes and held them in her hand for a moment before addressing them. "Catherine, if it wasn't for you, I'd still be running with Emma. Thank you for helping me find my way back to my family. A lot of things happened that we hadn't planned on, but I'm working on things. I'm grateful to you for taking care of my daughter for months while in hiding to protect both of us. You risked your life to come and stay with me. No amount of money could ever repay you. Carol, you gave my daughter a grandparent and she still thinks of you as one. She misses you and I can't wait to get the girls together."

Carol smiled as Catherine took Kassie's hand and gave it a slight squeeze.

"Carol, what is happening to the lot your house was on? Do you have plans to rebuild?"

Carol looked at Catherine. Her face masked the sadness that showed in her eyes. "You know how insurance is, they want to lowball you. I'm getting older and a two-story house just isn't good for the joints. Cat and Melody have their own lives. This is just temporary." The older woman gestured to the apartment around her.

"Mom, we already went over this!" Catherine's voice sounded exasperated.

"You don't need to have an old woman around all the time. You and

Melody need your own place. My sister offered me a place to stay in Florida with her. You can always visit me."

"How about I suggest a new plan?" Both women glanced at Kassie in confusion.

"I sent Chase my sketches of the hospital. He sent back a note and asked me if I had any ideas about nurses and someone to be in charge. It's forty-five minutes from here. You could commute or there is a little town close that you'll fall in love with. I've already had realtors looking at properties for rent until you decide. Catherine, I want you to help Chase interview and hire nurses. You'll know what to look for. There'll be a housing dorm for staff that prefer to stay on the mountain. Now as far as the lot you own here, Carol, I'd like to buy it. With your permission, I'd like to turn it into a community garden."

"Oh my! What a wonderful idea! What a perfect idea to help the community. I'll donate the land!"

"No" Kassie shook her head, "Please let me do this. Because of you, my daughter had a home, even for a little while. If you hadn't taken us in, I don't know if we'd be sitting here today."

She handed over the offer for the lot and the offer for Catherine's new job. "Don't say anything yet. Read over the offers and if you have any questions, call Joe. I'm not trying to buy back the last year of your lives, but I want to bring some good to all of this. Please let me help you as you begged me not so long ago." Kassie's eyes pleaded for her friend to accept.

"What are you going to be doing that you can't hire nurses yourself?" Catherine inquired suspiciously.

Kassie smiled. "I haven't made up my mind for sure, but I might be going back to school. Emma needs to be settled, and I still have some work to do. That's my goal right now."

Carol had opened her envelope and she gasped. "You can't be serious!"

"I assure you, Joe had the land appraised and that's the offer, plus extra to cover everything you lost. I'm not giving you anything that you wouldn't get if you chose to sell it. But you *will* have a house in Serenity, or if you choose to stay here in Seattle, that can be arranged. To be honest, Carol, I was hoping you could help with getting everything ready for the hospital. Maddie and Joe are helping and I'm sure the girls will have playdates while I'm getting everything handled."

Catherine mouthed "Thank you" to her friend. "And will you be staying at the mountain with Chase?"

"Emma and I are going to spend some time together before we make any further plans." Catherine's frown indicated that she didn't believe any of it, but she stayed silent. Kassie got up to leave.

"Oh! I almost forgot! Let's plan a playdate for the girls. How about a picnic in the park?"

Catherine agreed and the two made the necessary arrangements. Pulling her friend close, Catherine whispered in her ear, "I'm so happy to see you. If you need anything, will you promise to call?"

"I think you already helped by siccing Leo on me." She rolled her eyes.

Catherine let out a hearty laugh. "Imagine if I didn't like you?"

Kassie left the apartment building and headed for an appointment with Claire. She pressed her face against the window in the car and let the coolness soak into her skin. She wondered how Chase was doing. She knew he'd been released from the hospital and home on the mountain. Other than the note thanking her for the sketches, he hadn't contacted her in two weeks. She knew he was trying to give her some space. Shaking her head to change her thoughts from drifting to Chase, she mentally prepared herself for what was coming. Her meetings with Claire were getting more challenging.

Kassie faced Matthew Cartwright, her guard for the day. They hadn't addressed her outburst back at the cabin. Their relationship had changed. Matthew wasn't rude; he was coldly polite and quiet. For now, Kassie was leaving it as the status quo, needing time to determine how she was going to change Kassie Stanton. Reconciling herself that if she'd have to remain her sister, she was going to be Kassie 2.0.

"Matthew, I changed my mind. Could you take me to Pike's Place?"

"Sure." Matthew put the directions into his phone and pulled the car into traffic.

Kasie leaned back in the seat. If only everything had been as easy to fix as the morning had gone. Feeling guilty about missing her appointment with Claire, she sent a text apologizing. Right now, her head refused to be dissected. Kassie longed for the mountain and her window seat. She knew exactly where she wanted to go.

Chapter Thirty-six

Chase texted Leo as he placed a bouquet of wildflowers in his truck and headed to Seattle.

I'm on my way.

While he drove, he reflected on the days after he'd left the hospital. To say he was impressed with Kassie's designs was an understatement. Joe had contacted him the day he was discharged from the hospital to set up a meeting concerning the money. Chase refused, feeling it was hypocritical to take the same money that had been such a bone of contention between them. He'd find another way to fund her plans. The next morning Joe appeared at the cabin.

Letting Joe in and offering him a cup of coffee, Chase informed him of his decision.

Joe rubbed his forehead and shook his head. Exasperated, he pinned Chase with a stare. "Son, I know what you're thinking. I already gotta deal with the other hard head, you could give this ole man a break. Kassie knew that you'd refuse so she sent me with a note."

Relief had flooded him at getting any communication from her.

Chase,

Samantha told me that you can't change the past. You can still hold on to the pieces that you loved and move on. I've always loved your idea of the hospital since you told me about it the day at Pike's Market. Please use the money to make something terrible into something good. For me.

– Kassie

For her, he'd do anything. Instead of having a sterile building, Kassie made it a bigger version of a home. Spending hours, he smiled and nodded at some of her observations of his current plans. Of course, he was working with a limited amount of funds. Kassie was thinking on a larger scale.

He met Joe on the mountain, and they made plans. Joe knew how to get crews out for surveying and excavating the land. He contacted the first architect and went over all the changes. All that had been missing was Kassie by his side.

When Chase arrived at the area where Kassie was supposed to be, he texted Leo.

SITREP?

Walking toward the Ferris Wheel. Saints with her. Matthew's running some leads.

Chase read the reply as he parked his truck across the street and headed toward Kassie. Watching her hand the man operating the cars a stack of tickets, he approached the ticket booth. Slapping five twenties on the counter, he grabbed his tickets and flagged down the attendant. The man waved him up to get into the next car.

Chase shook his head and explained that he wanted to be in the car with the lady four cars over. The man looked at Chase and squinted his eyes, taking in his size and debating. Chase took out his wallet and handed him a fifty. "I know the lady. I want to surprise her." He showed the flowers he held in his hand.

"Okay, man, but if the lady indicates she ain't happy to see ya, you're outta there. Understand?"

"Absolutely." Chase agreed.

Purchasing enough tickets to stay on for the rest of the night, Kassie ignored the people exiting and entering the cars below and focused on the scenery before her. It had rained earlier, and the sky was still gray. But the evening was approaching, and she was waiting for the sunset. Just like the one Chase had shown her the first time on the wheel. Leaning against the glass, she waited as the wheel stopped to unload the passengers in front of her. When she felt the wheel move slightly, she expected it to bypass her and was surprised when the door opened and shut quickly as Chase entered the car.

Her eyes widened and her mouth parted slightly. The scent of oak and Chase assailed her.

"Hey, Princess." He quietly took her in.

"What…what are you doing here?" Kassie asked, astonished.

"I heard you missed an appointment and that was a deal breaker according to Claire." He grinned at her. Sighing, she placed her head back on the glass.

"May I sit next to you?" He waited to see her reaction and handed her the bouquet.

A smile appeared as she realized the flowers weren't from a florist but from the mountain. Bringing the blossoms up to her nose, Kassie inhaled the scent and let out an appreciative hum. "Thank you." Scooting over, she made room on the seat next to her.

Her heart sped up as his hip touched hers and he lightly put his arm around her.

"What are you doing up here?" He softly asked as she watched him take inventory of her, making sure she was okay.

"I just wanted to see the sunset. I wondered if I could see the mountain from the top."

"No, I'm afraid you'll have to come home for that. You know I have a spectacular sunset right there on the mountain." She smiled as she took in his scruff. His eyes looked tired.

"How's your head?" She leaned back and it was her turn to give him a physical run down.

"My head's fine. You did an amazing job stitching me up." He complimented her. "Which is a good thing for me."

She shook her head. "You didn't need me. Leo is trained."

He snorted. "If I wanted to look like Frankenstein, sure! Have you ever seen his idea of stitching? I believe Saint is an unhappy recipient of Leo's help in the field. You'll have to ask him to see it."

She giggled a little. Leo wasn't known for his patience. "Good thing he didn't have a stapler."

Chase chuckled along with her. Watching the sun go lower, he gently maneuvered Kassie, so her head rested on his chest.

She hadn't protested. It felt right.

"Tell me about the mountain. What've you and Joe got accomplished?"

"We are clearing the land for the hospital, the staff quarters, and I'm researching the service dog area. That was a good idea, Princess."

Unable to keep the smile from showing at his praise, she looked up at him. "I'm glad it helped. When will you start to break ground?"

"Probably in a couple of weeks. The contractors are getting materials delivered and Joe has been a huge help and knows how to get things moving. He and Jake have started having their meetings in the gazebo by the lake. I never thought Jake would go in there again after losing his wife, Bonnie. Knowing how important it was to my dad, Jake's excited about this project too." Chase leaned down and his nose tickled her ear. For a moment she thought he was smelling her.

"What are you doing in Seattle?" Her gaze continued to watch the sun go down as she leaned further back. God, she missed him.

"I came to find you. I've been thinking about what you said about us not knowing each other." Kassie started to rise to go to the other side of the car when he tenderly held her in place.

"Hear me out, Princess. As much as you think I don't know you, I'm convinced that I do. When we were on the mountain last time, I think we both learned that talking things out worked better than holding stuff in. I admit I wasn't such a great listener the day you left the mountain the first time and afterward. However, I listened to you when you told me how you ran from the dirty FBI agents. As upset as I was at you for keeping the truth from me about who you were, we handled it. I think we've forgotten how to communicate with each other, and it's left some huge misunderstandings. We also haven't addressed things that need to be talked about."

Kassie squirmed uncomfortably in the seat. Trapped in the small car, she wouldn't be able to end the conversation and she wasn't ready to discuss their relationship and everything that happened.

"Take a breath, Princess." She hadn't realized her breathing had become more rapid or the fact her hands had started to shake. Running his hand through her hair in a soothing gesture, he leaned close to her ear. Placing his hand gently on her chest and applying slight pressure, he nestled her further into him. Her body automatically started breathing along with the rise and fall of his chest. "Good job." He murmured as her eyes began to focus and the air got into her lungs. "I want to ask you out on a date. I was thinking maybe dinner and an outing of some sort."

Relieved, she gave herself a moment to collect herself before answering him. "What kind of outing?"

Chuckling at her curiosity, "I don't know, Princess. I thought I'd let you decide so you had a say in what we did and that you felt comfortable."

Thinking for a moment, her eyes lit up. "Can we go to Ty's for dinner, and then will you take me up the mountain so I can see the progress myself.?"

His eyebrows arched in surprise at her request. "I can't think of a better date than that. Shall I pick you up at say four o'clock? We can do the tour first and then dinner, so you see everything in the daylight."

"I'll be ready. I'll text you the address where I'm staying." She returned her gaze out the window just as the sun started to set over the horizon.

"Baby, I already know where you're at."

She should have known that. Knowing he knew where she was comforted her.

"I need to get back home. Emma and I have been working on a routine and it's going well. She misses you. On Sunday, I planned a playdate at the park with Catherine and Melody. Saint volunteered to cook hamburgers and hot dogs. The rest of the team will be there. Jake is bringing Samantha and LJ. I'm introducing Maddie and Joe to Carol Reese. Would you like to come?" Awkwardly, she waited to see if he would agree.

"Absolutely. I've missed Ladybug. Would you mind if I brought Rollo? He misses you. And Kassie, please reschedule your session with Claire."

Kassie smiled. She missed Rollo more than ever, especially at night when he used to hop on her bed. "I'd love for you to bring him. I promise I'll reschedule."

Silently they watched as the sun disappeared and enjoyed the peacefulness of just sitting together.

"Come on, Princess. Let me take you home."

Smiling, she clasped her hand into his as he waived to get the attendant's attention that they wanted off the wheel. Maybe, this wasn't going to be as hard as she thought.

Chapter Thirty-seven

On Saturday, Chase showed up at her door right on time. Wearing jeans and a dark green shirt that brought out the color of his eyes, she couldn't take her eyes off him. Stammering a greeting, she opened the door wider to allow him in.

Walking through the doorway, she felt his eyes travel down her body, causing her to tremble.

"You look beautiful, Princess."

Starting to reply, she was interrupted by the high-pitched squeal of Emma as she ran toward Chase with her arms outstretched.

"Hi, Dr. Chase! I've missed you! Where's Rollo? Did you bring him to play with me? Are you coming tomorrow? I painted him a picture! Mama bought him a huge bone for our picnic! Have you seen L.J.? Mama said we could have a playdate."

Laughing, Chase took it all in. "I've missed you, Ladybug. Slow down and I'll answer all your questions. Rollo is at home excited about the picnic tomorrow. L.J. and his mama are coming to join us, so you'll get to see him. I'm sure Rollo will want me to hang his painting on my fridge."

Watching, Kassie couldn't think of anything sexier than a man who could handle a child with such ease. The precocious four-year-old could talk off anyone's ear and it was like living with the Energizer Bunny, until seven-thirty at night and then it was like someone removed her batteries.

A slight knock at the door indicating that Maddie and Joe had arrived to pick up Emma interrupted Kassie's thoughts. As Chase placed his hand on the small of Kassie's back and led her out the door, she couldn't help but see the glee on the older couple's faces as they left for the evening.

Feeling excited about returning to Serenity, she hadn't realized how much she was looking forward to the trip back. Seattle had some of the best places to eat and living in a hotel with a small kitchenette, she and Emma had plenty of choices. Ty's was on a completely different level. It wasn't anything extremely fancy, the ambiance was relaxing and the patrons kept their conversations at a low level while they enjoyed their meals. Chase had taken Kassie there once before and her mouth had watered all afternoon thinking about the delicious food.

"You're awfully quiet over there, do you want to share your thoughts?" Chase broke into her daydreaming.

Laughing, she admitted, "I was thinking how much I was looking forward to today and about what Ty would have on his menu. You said he made his food with whatever was in season. Last year, we went at the end of October and it's only the beginning of April. Will it be different? Oh! I hope he still has that brownie with the strawberries and ice cream!"

Chase gave out a full belly laugh. "Princess, you sure know how to hurt a guy. I thought you were going to say you were looking forward to seeing me. Nothing prepared me for your admission that you're using me for food!"

"I'm sorry! I didn't mean it that way!" Kassie back peddled, laughing. "I skipped lunch so I would have enough room to enjoy all the food tonight!" The heat rushed to her cheeks in embarrassment; he must think she didn't want to see him.

A frown appeared as his eyebrows furrowed. "Kass, no skipping meals. You're still healing. I will take you to Ty's anytime you want, just promise me you'll eat."

The cab of his truck got quiet. "I promise. Can you do me a favor?" Kassie timidly asked as she gazed at him.

Glancing over at her, then turning his attention back to driving, he responded. "What is it, Princess?"

"You said we were going on a date to learn about each other. So just for tonight, can we pretend that all the rest of the stuff didn't happen? Can you not worry about how much I've eaten or if I can walk, or if I'm going to have another panic attack? I appreciate your concern and I'm trying. Claire and I are working on putting my needs first, she calls it self-care. I'm finding that it works tremendously with Em and I'm happier. Yes, I'm still having panic attacks and I've had a hard time sleeping. It's all part of the process. Just for tonight though, I'd like to just feel normal."

Taking her hand, he brought it to his lips and pressed a soft kiss on her knuckles. "I think that's a great idea."

Pulling up to the site where the hospital was being built, he came around the truck and helped her down. His hands clasped around her waist as he slid her body slowly down his. His cock jerked up in attention as if it recognized her body. He set Kassie back away from him in order to not startle her. Taking her hand, he pointed to various areas that had been taped off or marked with colored string. She occasionally asked questions or gave her opinion. Her nose scrunched and her eyes narrowed when he purposely proposed a problem they were having with the staff quarters.

Kassie stared at the area and walked around. Shaking her head, she turned around and faced the direction of his cabin. "No. I don't like this. The hospital is situated on the lake so your patients benefit from the peace and tranquility it offers and they get views of the mountains. From the cabin, you'll see the staff quarters. This needs to be down the hill farther and over to the left. That way the staff will get the mountain backdrop as well. More importantly, it keeps your cabin completely hidden. You won't see the lights from the hospital or the staff quarters at night. That way the cabin will keep its serenity."

Putting his arms around her, he kissed the top of her head. "It's like you know exactly how this place is supposed to be. I've had it in my mind for years as my dad planned it. I wish he could have met you. He would be so proud of what you've brought to this project."

He watched as Kassie's head ducked down and her face held a slight blush. "These mountains are magical. I might be biased, but this place holds some sort of protective healing power. No matter how hard you fight it, it has a way of seeping in and healing you."

"No, Kass. It isn't a protective healing power. It's love."

His hand brushed away a lock of hair from her face as the breeze whistled through the trees. She stepped up into his protective embrace. Kassie's hand slid upward on his chest. When their eyes met, she licked her lips and nervously moved up on her toes to reach his mouth. His hand slid behind her neck and up to the back of her head as he let her take the lead. Kassie refused to discuss what happened when Roger had held her captive and what Chase did know, she only admitted to him because she thought he was a dream. Still not knowing what all the bastard had done, he didn't want to scare her by taking control, as much as his body urged him to.

Kassie's lips softly met his and her hands moved to his shoulders. Chase could tell she was nervous as her hand trembled lightly. He pulled her body closer, molding her to him, encouraging her to go wherever she wanted to lead him. Kassie moaned into his mouth as hers opened slightly wider and her tongue met his. He could taste the mint toothpaste she used as she deepened the kiss. Allowing his hands to slide down her back slowly, he waited to see if she would retreat but she stayed where she was. Kassie's arms went around his neck.

"I've missed you. I've missed this mountain." Kassie sighed as she reluctantly let him go. Her chest rose and her eyes were a darker blue. The kiss had affected her as much as it had him.

"I've missed you too, Princess. How about we go have Ty feed you now?" He couldn't miss the big grin that spread across her face. He couldn't wait to see how she enjoyed her meal this time if it was anything like the last.

Walking into the restaurant, Chase placed a possessive hand along her back as they were led to the table in the corner that he had requested. It was the same table they sat at the first time he had brought her. Looking up at him, her eyes sparkled with delight as he held out her chair.

Taking the seat against the wall, he scanned the room. It was early yet, so the restaurant wasn't crowded.

Kassie's stomach growled in anticipation, and she giggled.

"I guess my stomach remembers this place too!"

Chase chuckled in response. Perusing the menu, he decided on a ribeye steak with sauteed mushrooms and a salad. Waiting for her to make her choice, he watched her from the top of his menu. The tip of her tongue swiped the top of her lip as she debated on her dinner choice. Her eyes would narrow as she read the description of a dish and briefly widen when she found something she liked. A waiter dropped off a loaf of warm, crusty bread with oil for dipping.

Kassie watched the waiter pouring the oil, completely entranced. Glancing up to see Chase's gaze upon her, she explained, "I remember the bread."

Shaking his head, he tore off a small piece and dipped it into the oil. She was already leaning in to eat it from his fingers. "Did you decide on what you wanted to eat?"

"Umm, yes. I think I'll have the broiled shrimp and scallops with a salad." Inwardly, Chase fist-bumped at how far she had come. Her confidence in her decision to choose her meal was significant.

"Would you like a side of Brussels sprouts with that?" He innocently inquired.

Kassie pretended to gag and shivered. "Ugh. Please tell me Ty doesn't serve those!" She glanced at the menu as if she was checking to see if it was offered as a side.

Chase laughed. "I don't know, but I think next time I see Ty, I'll ask him to make a side just for you."

"Chase Winters! Surely, you wouldn't do that to me?" She batted her eyes at him coquettishly.

There was no doubt in Chase's mind that the evening promised to be a good one. Kassie seemed relaxed and he enjoyed watching her enthusiasm at coming to Ty's. When she suggested coming to the restaurant and going to the mountain, he almost fell over. Ty was an amazing chef, and it was a hidden gem in the small little town. Out of all the choices that Kassie could have made, she chose to come home to the mountain and to the place where they had made such a great memory. Hope sprung up inside of him.

The rest of the meal had been delightful. Kassie tried a bite of his steak and her eyes rolled back in her head as she announced she would order that the next time he brought her. She almost finished her entire meal, and he didn't comment, respecting her wish for him not to worry about her food intake.

When the waiter came back with a bag and the bill, Kassie's face fell. "But what about dessert? I was hoping to get that fudgy brownie thingy."

"Come on, Princess. I've got something even better." Pulling out cash, he placed it in the folder and grabbed her hand. Her mouth formed a little pout. This woman was going to be the death of him yet.

He lifted her back into the truck and closed the door, then made it to his side of the truck. Sliding into his seat, he placed the bag between them and turned the truck toward the mountain. Kassie's fingers glided to the opening of the package.

"Uh, uh, uh, no touching," Chase reprimanded. Taking her hand, he held it all the way back up to his cabin.

Looking at him in confusion Kassie stared at the house. He just smiled at her as he grabbed the bag and helped her out of the truck.

"Aren't we going home?" Her voice held a wary tone to it.

"If you want to go home, Princess, just say the word." Still holding the truck door open, he waited. Chase wanted her to know she had a choice. "We had an early dinner and I thought you might want to watch the sunset from the back deck."

Chase wasn't prepared when she wrapped her arms around his waist. "Thank you for such a lovely meal and thinking of this. I didn't think I'd ever get to see it from here again." Her face turned into a slight grimace before she plastered on a smile for his benefit.

Turning her to face him, his fingers tilted her chin up to look at him. "You'll always be welcome here. You're a part of the mountain, now."

He closed the door and led her into the cabin. "Can you stay here for just a moment? I need to check on a couple of things."

She nodded her head, "Sure."

Going through the kitchen, he made sure everything he prepared earlier was ready. Walking back into the living room, he was surprised when Kassie wasn't there. Listening, he heard a noise come from his room. Finding her sitting in her reading nook with her knees drawn up, his heart lurched, thinking something was wrong.

Lowering his voice, to not startle her, Chase said, "Hey."

Kassie's head popped up. "I'm sorry, I should've asked before I came into your bedroom. That's so intrusive. I just wanted to sit in here for a minute. I didn't expect you back so quickly."

"How about we get out on the back deck or you're going to miss your favorite part of the day." Keeping his voice light, he held his hand out to her. Chase saw Kassie everywhere in the cabin. She belonged here. He was disappointed and hurt that she couldn't see it.

Accepting his hand, she let him lead her to the back deck. He opened the door and let her step out first. Kassie's mouth dropped open as she looked around her. Burgundy, silver, and white balloons were set around a cushioned patio sofa. A banner swung from the ledge saying happy birthday. Candles were lit around the balloons, the wicker table in front of the couch, and along the deck rail. The bag from Ty's sat in the middle of the table.

Tears came to her eyes as she whispered, "How did you know?"

Walking up to her, he took her face in the palm of his hands and gently wiped the tears away with his thumbs. "Because I *know* you," he murmured.

Kassie's hand flew to her mouth. Sobbing, she walked toward the decorations. Her fingers glided over the balloons and the sign. Looking back over her shoulder, she watched as he approached her.

"I'm sorry, Princess. I didn't mean to make you cry." Maybe he should have run this idea by Maddie and Joe.

Shaking her head, Kassie moved into his embrace. "Emma and I haven't had a birthday since we were on the run. I was afraid if I told her, she'd eventually let it slip as she got older. I don't recognize mine because of my sister. The day she died, Kaitlyn ceased to exist, and it didn't feel right. I told Maddie and Joe a month ago I didn't want to commemorate it. Claire made me see that I'm still alive and I should celebrate that. Then you asked me out for dinner, and I didn't want you to feel bad, so I didn't mention it. Thank you."

"We're celebrating your birthday from now on. We're missing just one thing." Chase let out a shrill whistle and a few minutes later Rollo ran onto the deck. Barking and whining at seeing Kassie, the dog greeted her with doggie kisses and leaned against her legs. Leading her to the couch as she giggled at Rollo's antics, Chase sat her down and pulled out her fudge brownie dessert with strawberries and ice cream.

Rollo finally settled at her feet. Chase lit a candle just as the sun started to set. "Happy Birthday, Princess. Make a wish."

Leaning in, she pulled the sides of her hair back from her face, closed her eyes, and made a wish. She blew out the candle then smiled as he pulled it out. Dipping a spoon into the treat, he alternated bites between them as they watched the sun go down. When the sun disappeared, and the dessert was gone, Kassie placed her head on his shoulder while her hand never left Rollo's head.

"In case I forget to tell you, this was the best birthday I ever had."

Chase stroked her jawline as he tugged a curl toward him, making her lean in. His tongue invaded hers. She tasted like strawberries and chocolate. Chase's grip tightened in her hair as she tilted her head to allow him access to her neck. A long moan escaped from her as she closed her eyes, and her hand caressed his scruff and lowered to his shoulder.

Instinctively, he knew she needed more time, and he didn't bring her to the cabin for a round of sex. Small pants came from Kassie as he continued his onslaught of kisses. Sitting in his lap, her hands roamed over the buttons of his shirt. Swallowing hard, Chase put his hand over hers.

"I think we need to get you back home, Princess."

A look of confusion and hurt crossed her face before she quickly masked it.

"Princess, don't go there. Don't hold back your feelings. If you're mad or hurt, I want you to tell me. I know by the look on your face right now, you're confused that I stopped. Here's the thing. I'm stopping because I don't want to make love to you for one night. I'm in this for the long haul and want to make love to you for a lifetime. Whether that's a week from now or a year from now, so be it. Princess, the next time I make love to you in our bed, you won't doubt that you're mine forever. You'll know that you're finally home."

Chapter Thirty-eight

Nodding at Julio's man at the door, Chase held the door for Kassie to enter. Maddie and Joe had texted that Emma had fallen asleep, so they had kept her in their room.

Kassie took off her shoes and set her purse on the table. "Would you like a beer or a glass of wine?"

"No, thank you. I'm meeting with the contractors first thing in the morning then I'll head to the picnic."

"Oh okay." Uncertainty filled her as she avoided his gaze. Looking down at the floor, she fidgeted with the back of the couch.

"Can I have a rain check?" Slowly moving in front of her, he tilted her head up to meet his eyes. Searching her gaze, he pulled her to him. "I can't wait to spend time with you and Em tomorrow."

"I reserved the shelter, it might rain. But I'm hoping it will hold out long enough that the kids have time to play outside." Biting her lip, she tried making small talk. Thinking about that kiss and the words Chase had uttered, shivers ran down her spine.

"I want to kiss you goodnight, Kassie. I want to take you to that bedroom and slowly strip those clothes off. I want to watch you come on my tongue and with my fingers. Then I want to bury myself so deep in you that you'll never doubt my intentions again."

Kassie inhaled deeply at his words, longing for everything that he'd described.

Chase wound her ginger locks around his hand, pulling her face closer to him. "Come here."

Melting into him, Kassie let Chase take control as he captured her mouth with his. Her nails dug into his sides as he left little room for doubts or insecurities when he was finished.

A wicked grin appeared across his face as he stepped away, never losing eye contact with her.

"Goodnight, Princess, I hope you have sweet dreams."

Kassie said nothing as she put her hand to her lips and watched him slip through the door.

Cutting up fruit for Emma's snack and starting a small grocery list, Kassie looked up when she heard a soft knock on her door. Smiling, she dropped the knife on the counter thinking Chase had returned. Turning the lock, knowing Julio's man would double-check anyone coming in, she opened the door.

"Chase, I thought you were—"

"Sorry to disappoint you, honey, Chase won't be coming back. Aren't you going to let me in?" Rachel's wide smile and confident stance threw Kassie for a loop. Nodding to Julio's man that it was alright to let her pass, Kassie allowed the woman to enter. Rachel smirked as she walked past her and headed for the couch in the living room.

Kassie fiddled with the edge of her sweatshirt feeling quite dowdy compared to the beautifully styled blonde. Not a single strand of hair was out of place. Diamond earrings dropped delicately from her ears and the designer pantsuit fit her body like a glove. As soon as Chase had left, Kassie pulled on a pair of leggings, piled her hair on top of her head, and slipped Chase's sweatshirt over her head. Now she wished she hadn't changed.

"What can I do for you, Rachel? And how did you know where I was staying?" Kassie's chin went up knowing that the woman's presence didn't bode well. Surprise and curiosity on why Rachel would visit her had compelled her to let Rachel in.

"Get me a glass of wine, darling. I think we should chat. I happened to be down the street when I saw you enter the hotel with Chase. I'm surprised he didn't stay longer." Rachel smiled at her like she was the cat that had just eaten the canary.

Pouring a glass of wine for Rachel and grabbing a bottle of water for herself, Kassie set them on the table in front of the couch. Sitting across from the well-dressed woman, she waited for her to speak.

Rachel took a long sip from the glass and made a sour face as if she had found the wine not to her liking. Toying with the drink and running her finger around the rim, she prolonged what she had to say as Kassie squirmed in her chair uncomfortably.

"So, I guess you're no longer the poor single mom that my Chase thought you were. You are *the* Kassie Stanton." Giving out a little laugh at her joke, Rachel pinned Kassie with a cold stare. "I wish I could've seen his face when he found out his sweet, innocent Kassie Smith was none other than the slut of Corpus Christi."

Kassie's eyes narrowed and she leaned back in her chair. "Not that I need to explain anything to you, Rachel. I was a victim of James and Phillip Stanton, I was never a whore."

Rachel's head tilted back as a deep, throaty laugh filled the room. Opening her purse, she pulled out her phone and started tapping on the keys. A few seconds later, she seemed satisfied by what she had found. She turned the screen so Kassie could see the pictures. Multiple shots of her sister wearing BDSM wear, naked, and tied in chains popped up. She was on her hands and knees in front of multiple men. In some pictures, she was naked as strangers were touching her. One picture showed her giving a blow job to a much older man.

Kassie's stomach rolled with nausea. Her pulse raced as her heart pounded in her ears. Clasping her shaking hands in front of her, she tried to hide the fact that Rachel had rattled her to her core. She knew some of the pictures were shown in court. With the kidnapping and her injuries, she hadn't spent much time surfing the web. She avoided it most of the time, not wanting to see any news about James Stanton. The last thing she needed was to set off triggers. Focusing on finding herself and making a life for her daughter was her priority. Kassie hadn't given much thought to the pictures being blasted all over the internet.

"What do you want, Rachel? I'm sure you didn't come to ask about my welfare, so what did I do to deserve this little visit of yours?" Kassie sat back in the chair stiffly.

"You know, I happened to come into Serenity a few weeks ago. I just love Samantha's spa products. I swear my skin's as soft as a baby's bottom!" Putting the glass up to her lips, Rachel took another sip of wine as she watched Kassie. "You probably didn't hear me come in when you were getting your hair cut. You remember that day, don't you? The one where you told Samantha that you couldn't give Chase any kids? What a shame! I mean, you must be heartbroken knowing how much Chase wants a family of his own."

Kassie's eyes widened and she swallowed down the bile that threatened to spill. Not wanting to confirm anything with Rachel, Kassie remained silent.

"Oh well. It's probably better that way. Can you just imagine how hard it's going to be when poor little Emma finds out about her perfect little mama? All those *nasty* pictures on the web! Good gracious, you must be horrified! I'm sure *some* people will believe you were a victim." Rachel paused for dramatic effect. "I just can't imagine Chase wanting to have kids with someone with that much…experience. Especially in that little town of his. Then there is that hospital project of his. Do you think reputable hospitals are going to want to do business with Chase, knowing what type of people he associates with? I'm just so worried about my poor Chase."

Finding her voice, Kassie finally spoke. "Last time I checked, Rachel, Chase and you were over a long time ago. Chase knows exactly what he wants, and he's made that quite clear."

Rachel stood, still holding her wine glass, walked to the window, and looked at the view of Seattle's lights.

"Do you think that while you were gone that Chase was a monk? Are you sure he's not with you out of guilt? I mean, really, you poor thing, all that you went through. By the way, next time you're at the cabin, could you look for my hat? It's cream-colored with a pom-pom on top. I lost it when I was there for a …visit."

"I think it's time for you to leave. I'll check for your hat next time I'm there and promptly send it back. Samantha wouldn't let me be caught dead in something so last season." Kassie stood and walked to the door.

Rachel grabbed her bag and slowly walked to the door. Handing Kassie the wine glass, she smirked. "I hope you enjoy your little outing. While you're there maybe you should think about what's best for Chase. He's been planning for a family and a future on that mountain for a long time. Are you willing to gamble his opportunities away just to be with him?"

Releasing the death grip on the delicate stem of the wine glass, Kassie opened the door, making it clear to Rachel that she was no longer welcome.

Chapter Thirty-nine

Kassie hadn't slept the entire night. Her face felt hot and blotchy from crying, and she sat in the chair in her bedroom looking out at the dismal rainy weather. Knowing she needed to get dressed before Emma bounded through the door, excited about having a playdate with her two best friends, Kassie dragged herself to the shower. Layering her clothes so she could put on or take off what she needed for a day of fun at the park, she set about getting Em's stuff ready.

Just as she packed another set of clothes in her bag, Emma bounced into the room.

"Hi, Mama! Are you ready for today? We'll get to see everybody! Are you sure Dr. Chase is bringing Rollo?"

"I'm sure he's going to be there. How about we get some breakfast in you and get dressed to go?" Kassie tried distracting Emma.

Kassie had finished stacking the breakfast dishes and wiping down the table when Shadow came in to escort them to the car. Casting a worried glance in her direction, Shadow asked if she was okay. Not wanting to ruin the day for anyone she quickly assured him she was fine. If Shadow noticed something was off with her, she needed to step up her game, because the rest of the team would be on her as well. Pasting a happy smile on her face, she laughed and joked with Emma all the way to the park.

The playground was still empty when they arrived and started setting up the shelter. Saint put up a tent over the grill just in case of more showers. Emma danced around the room, anxiously awaiting her friend's arrival.

Catherine and Carol walked into the shelter and the girls ran outside to play. Taco and Shadow followed closely behind, leaving Leo and Saint with Kassie.

Introducing Maddie to Carol, and talking with Catherine, Kassie neglected to notice when Chase walked in until he slipped his arm around her waist and placed a kiss on her cheek. Nodding a greeting to Catherine, Chase took Rollo off to find the girls. Catherine's eyebrows rose as she watched Kassie's face at Chase's familiarity.

"I take it things are going well with Chase these days? We live in the same city and I've hardly seen you since you've been back! A lunch date and a long gab session are on the agenda for us. Oh, let's ask Samantha to join us too when she arrives."

"Chase and I aren't together. We're just friends." Stacking the paper plates and pulling out the condiments, Kassie refused to look Catherine in the eyes. She had made her decision. Rachel was right. She had spent hours on the internet the night before scouring the web and finding pictures of her twin. Hell, there were even memes. Just the thought of what her sister had gone through made her sick. People on the internet made comments that were disgusting and degrading, adding to her misery.

"Hey, are you ok? You're looking a little peckish. Maybe you should sit down?" Catherine sat her down at one of the picnic tables and handed her a bottle of water and a cookie. "Eat and drink."

Noticing Catherine hovering over Kassie, Chase left Rollo running around the girls and chasing a ball. Leo intercepted him.

"Hey, how did everything go last night?"

Unable to hold the smile back, Chase glanced in Kassie's direction. "It went well. I wasn't sure how it was going to go, and we still have stuff that needs discussing but we're taking it slow."

Leo clasped Chase on the shoulder. "I'm happy for you, man. She's made a lot of progress since you brought her to the mountain."

Chase nodded as he watched Catherine and now Samantha animatedly talk to Kassie. She was shaking her head.

"Speaking of the mountain. I wanted to talk to you and Kass but can't seem to get both of you in the same room. I want to ask you a few questions. What do you plan on doing with all these veterans once they are healed? Do they just go back home? Do they look for jobs? What's the plan?"

"Once they heal, we'll help get them established. Help them locate jobs and housing," Chase replied, now completely focused on the women.

"What if you could do some of that right here? Would you and Kassie be willing to allow the team to have a training facility for soldiers that are unable to stay in the military but still want a job in that type of work? I have contracts that I can't take because I don't have enough men to cover the gaps. I still have Julio's team filling in for Kassie and the family. Julio's being very selective as to who's in that circle these days," Derrick explained.

"That's a good idea. Kass made suggestions last night that I need to address with the contractor. I gotta say it gives it a homier feel and less of a hospital setting. I can't wait to get it started. I've been recruiting a couple of docs and plan to have a twenty-four-hour team. I wish I could find another administrator that is as good as Elizabeth at Seattle Health."

"Did you ask her?" Leo's gaze followed Chase's and he watched as Samantha joined in on the lively discussion.

"No. Elizabeth already has a job. One that she seems happy with."

Leo's eyes rolled at Chase's response. "If you liked her so much, why not ask her? It couldn't hurt and she's the one that pushed for Seattle Health to take the VA overflow from the VA hospital. Sounds to me like she likes veterans. She might be ready for a change."

"It probably wouldn't hurt to ask. I hate all the paperwork and would be happy to get rid of that end. Joe is great with the business parts but doesn't know anything about hospital protocols and such."

"Why don't you go talk to the women instead of standing here wondering what they're talking about?" Leo joked as Chase's eyebrows drew down when Samantha sent him an exasperated look. Both men scanned the area as they walked toward the picnic table.

"Hello, ladies. It looks like the girls are having a great time." Kassie looked up to see Chase standing behind her.

"Emma's thrilled you made it, thank you for coming. We're getting ready to eat. Saint has generously offered to cook the burgers and hot dogs." Kassie smiled politely and went back to her discussion with the two other women.

Chase set down a bag filled with a jar of honey and a puzzle for Emma. Slightly surprised by Kassie's cool greeting, he sat across from her to observe her.

Joe ambled over to the table to join them.

"Kassie, Leo wanted to ask about setting up a training facility so they could train veterans to run operations for legitimate private contractors. I know we planned to provide training for other jobs, but I wanted to get your opinion. Do you have any thoughts?"

"I think those decisions should be left up to Chase. He's in charge of how the mountain runs." Kassie's answers sounded more diplomatic to how she offered her opinions to Chase the night before. Something churned in his gut.

"I appreciate the confidence in me, Princess. I was going to ask your opinion too." He regarded her stiff posture and refusal to look directly at him.

She paused. "Well, could we expand it a bit?" He looked at her as her nose began to scrunch and she reached for a paper plate. "Does anyone have a pen?"

Catherine handed her one from her bag. She began to sketch a large building and an outside training area, expanding it toward the back base of the mountain. She leaned in toward Chase to share the sketches she made.

"We should have thought of this before. You already have a training facility planned so they could find work, but being able to readily offer them jobs is even better. It needs to be closer to the base of the mountain. Maybe check on some sound barriers of some sort so the noise doesn't bother anyone with PTSD. Oh! Maybe expand it by also opening it up to jobs for veterans that want to help any of the troubled teens that might want to become active in the military. We could also hire maybe a dog handler from an outgoing military member to help with service dog training and offer other jobs to help with that too." Kassie was on a roll.

"That's a great idea. I think we need to concentrate on the hospital first. But I'm sure that we could figure it out. I love how you kept everything aesthetically pleasing with the mountain." Chase complimented Kassie.

Their heads almost touched, and the other two women silently excused themselves and walked to the jungle gym. Joe saw Jake arriving and went to greet his new friend. The couple hadn't even noticed.

"It's a place to heal. Not another institution. They need to feel the difference." Kassie's head bent in concentration as she placed different squares on the mountain with labels. "Does Leo plan to stay on the mountain?"

With a chin nod, he beckoned Leo to the table.

"Kassie has some really good ideas." They went through each one. The two of them bantered back and forth as Leo continued to watch them. "So, what do ya think?" Both turned to face him with serious expressions on their faces.

"I think it sounds great! So how much do I need to contribute to buy-in?"

Kassie bit her lip and glanced at Chase. He didn't know what she was thinking, but so far, she had hit the mark on all the planning stages of the facility, so he was eager to listen.

With his encouragement, she began to tell them. "I don't want you to buy in, Leo. I want you to set up a team in Texas and one in Seattle. I want Matthew to head the research and track down as many women, men, and children James Stanton and Mayor Thorton trafficked that you can. I've asked him to also find José and his mom."

Turning to Chase, she directed her statement to him. "I was going to ask you about it, but if we're going to discuss all this now, we might as well include this in the plan. Matthew needs a project. I'm not ready to give up my childhood home, but I thought we could use the house and the land as a halfway house of sorts, to help anyone recover. Maddie and Joe have already agreed. I haven't sold the mansion yet either, and it's gated with security. I was thinking we could use both."

Joe came up behind Kassie and placed his hands on her shoulders, then gave them a little squeeze.

"Your mama and daddy would be so proud of you, Little Bit. You're turning all this *gris-gris* into something special." Kassie didn't acknowledge Joe's phrase.

"I'll pay the payroll for whatever teams you hire to help with this. Maybe some of the newest graduates of the hospital will want to help. Do you have a name for your business?"

"D.S. Enterprises." Kassie rolled her eyes and punched him in the arm. "Real original, Derrick Strong. How about something like Serenity Security?"

"Sounds good to me. I'll start the paperwork immediately. I won't be able to start it until I get back into town in a couple of months. Chase and I'll be going on a mission in a few weeks. We'll be gone for about a month."

"Don't worry about all that, Joe has lawyers that can do it." Joe nodded his agreement. "I want you to get started on getting the best out there." Kassie grabbed water from the end of the picnic table. It seemed to Chase that she was hiding her face.

After a long draw of his water, Chase looked at Kassie. "Now that everyone has a job, what about you, Princess? What do you want to do?"

"I'm just a silent partner. I don't plan on having anything to do with it once it's done."

"It doesn't sound to me like you're very silent. You have Catherine looking for nursing staff and filling positions, and Joe working on contracts and contractors. Now you have Leo situated with his own company on the mountain and a training facility. Where do you fit into this picture?"

Kassie glanced uneasily at the other two men who promptly got up and headed toward the playground. She stood to leave when he grabbed her gently by the arm.

"Tell me, Kassie, do you see yourself on that mountain at all?" His voice had risen but not enough to create a scene. She looked around uneasily.

"Maybe we should talk about this later? The kids are getting ready to eat and—"

Out of nowhere a gust of wind started blowing the paper plates across the grass. A sudden downpour from the heavens struck without notice. The adults scrambled around ushering the kids into the shelter. Taco grabbed Rollo and headed in.

Running toward the walking trail, Kassie ran to gather the wayward plates with Chase on her heels. When they were far enough away from the shelter that they couldn't be heard, he asked, "Do you have any intention of letting me in, Kass? Or working on us? It seems like you've given everyone else's future a lot of thought but have nothing to say about where we stand. I'd thought I made my intentions clear last night and thought we were on the same page. Was I mistaken?"

"I don't want to talk about this!" Picking up the last plate, she turned to head back to the shelter, running straight into his chest.

Attempting to control his emotions, Chase gritted out, "I want to talk about it. You've been running the show for some time now, Kassie. I want to know what the hell is going on with us! You weren't the only one hurt. I'm by no means belittling what you went through, I'm trying to understand. Last night I thought you were letting me in. I want us to build a life together." His voice was controlled as he pulled the plastered hair from her face and took both her hands into his.

"You can't! I don't want you to! If I stay affiliated with your hospital, it could hurt you more than help you. Don't you get it? *I'm Kassie Stanton.* All my deeds have been blasted on the internet for all the world to see! You deserve better than that! There's so much between us, ever since Roger kidnapped me and I lost the baby. I see the pity in your eyes…How can I be sure that's not why you're with me? How can I trust you to be there when I need you? You didn't believe me when I said it wasn't about the money!"

Chase couldn't believe his ears. It was like they took one step forward and one hundred back.

"You don't have to see the pity in my eyes sweetheart, you're having a pity party all on your own!" Chase didn't bother to hold back his frustration.

Kassie hit his chest, letting the paper plates fly into the wind and rain. He grabbed her wrists, determined that she would talk to him. What had changed from last night until then?

Kassie screeched and tried to remove his hold on her wrists. "How dare you say that to me! You weren't there, you don't know what happened to me!" she choked out. "You don't know how scared I was that you weren't going to find me, or that I was going to die in that freezing, smelly room! You don't think I heard you guys all whispering about me when I lay in the hospital?"

Kassie laughed hysterically. "You don't know me! Who did you fall in love with? Kassie? You detest who I chose to be. This will always be between us, my choice and everything that it entails. The money, the reputation, the pictures, and constant worry of when James is going to go after Emma." She took a step back and he let go of her.

"Baby, *you* are who I fell in love with." The words were said softly but with conviction.

Kassie cried and shook her head. "Love me? Really? Or are you in love with the dead Kaitlyn? The stupid girl who got herself kidnapped because she trusted her sister. The same sister who stole ten million dollars and hid it somewhere. You want to know about Kaitlyn? She was tortured, Chase! All because I was an idiot. I can't make that mistake again. I trusted my sister and got hurt, and I trusted you and look what happened."

Chase stepped toward her to decrease the distance between them. She shook her head. He was reminded of a conversation he had with Leo concerning Kassie's ability to keep things bottled up until she exploded.

Leo had jokingly commented, "Your girl is fragile. Like a freaking bomb."

Maybe she needed to purge all of this out of her system. The park wasn't necessarily ideal but with the sudden rainstorm, no one was around to hear her confessions. He let her continue to let it all out.

Wracking sobs came out of her as he tried to pull her closer. This was what he'd been afraid of. She fought him but he refused to let her go.

"You can't love me! I can't give you what you need. You can't possibly understand. You weren't there all those months. I didn't talk because I screamed at all the horror in my head and hid from that monster in my mind. I was alone. Because of Roger, I can't have kids. Staying with me means you'll never have the family you've always dreamed of. I'm letting you go. I tried to find a way I could make this work. But things will never be the same. I can't do this anymore. Please, Let. Me. Go."

He heard the finality of her words and saw the misery in her eyes. Remembering his promise to Joe all those months ago that if he couldn't make her happy, he'd walk away. By refusing to let him in, she denied them the chance to heal the broken parts of their relationship.

Chase needed to let her go. He suddenly dropped his hold on her as the epiphany hit him.

"I can't do this anymore, Princess. I can't chase you. You won't let me in. You didn't trust me, and you still don't. I want you to be happy. I wish you and Emma the best." He cupped her neck, his thumb grazing her jaw, and pulled her slowly against him and kissed the top of her head. He whispered softly in her ear, "I love you."

Letting her go, he walked away, leaving her all alone.

Chapter Forty

Getting what she wished for hurt more than ever.

Every morning, Kassie showered, dressed, and started Emma in a preschool with Melody. Going through the motions of living when all she felt was a shell of her former herself.

Leo stopped by to tell her that Shadow would be staying with her while the rest of the team was gone. He didn't say it, but he wasn't very happy with her. With the team gone, Kassie missed them terribly. They had become part of her family.

Thunder rolled through the hotel suite as the doorbell rang. She had hired a realtor to find a home in Seattle for her and Emma. She was also trying to find one for Maddie and Joe close by. She didn't want them as close as they were now. Concerned about her welfare, the older couple had started to smother her. It was done out of love, but she had to learn to do this on her own. Just like she had to learn to adjust to Chase no longer being part of her life.

Once the realtor left and Shadow had vetoed all of her choices, an exasperated Kassie shot Shadow a menacing look.

"Tell me something, Shadow. Are there any houses in Seattle you would approve of?"

He smirked. "You and I know exactly where you should be. On top of that, when are you going to tell the grandparents that you don't want them right next door?"

Her nose scrunched up and she began shuffling all the paperwork from the realtor together. "I hope you don't plan on tattling on me, Shadow. You're not my babysitter."

Pulling the takeout menu for the pasta place down the street from the refrigerator door, Shadow faced her.

"I'm not your babysitter, but you're part of my family and that means I tell you things even when you don't want to hear them."

Kassie picked up the knife and began to chop the vegetables and fruit for snacks. Her face was full of sadness. "I know. You know, when I was on the run, all I dreamed of was getting back to Texas. Living in my childhood home and letting Emma grow up with Joe and Maddie. I love them and I know they love us. I feel suffocated. Joe asks me at least five times a day if I'm doing okay like I'm going to break. Maddie takes over every situation that she thinks will overwhelm me."

"The way I see it," Shadow got out storage bags and began to pack up the food. "Maybe you shouldn't act like you're so strong when you aren't, and you wouldn't look so fragile. You scared all of us. We thought we were going to lose you. We want to help you because we care." With that Shadow disappeared.

That evening, she placed the lasagna on the table with the bread. With everyone seated, Kassie began pouring drinks. Shadow's phone began to ring. He excused himself from the table as they said a prayer and began doling out the food.

Kassie wondered if it was Leo, but Shadow was tightlipped when he returned to the table. Maddie had taken over cutting up Em's lasagna and she let out a sigh.

Joe's eyes met hers.

"Are you okay, Little Bit?"

She wanted to pull her hair out. She glanced down at the end of the table where Shadow sat. His napkin covered his mouth as he pretended to cough. From the glimmer in his eyes, he was preparing to enjoy the show. Her eyes narrowed pointedly at him.

"I'm fine. Maddie, please allow Emma to try cutting her food before taking it over. I'm looking for a house for Emma and me. I don't mean to sound ungrateful. I love you both. I'd love to help you get a home in whatever part of the city that you decide to settle down in."

Joe placed his hand over Maddie's. Maddie looked at Kassie with wide eyes. She instantly regretted her spur-of-the-moment diarrhea of the mouth.

"Little Bit, we've been doing some thinking. It's time Maddie and I got on with our lives. We're moving back to Serenity. Jake has found us a lovely little home until we decide where we want to build. If you need us, we're only a short drive away."

She couldn't contain her shock. "Back to Serenity? You don't want to stay in Seattle?"

"We realize we've been a thorn in your side, Little Bit. You and Ladybug need your own lives. I'd like to resign as president of your daddy's company and allow the vice president to step in. He's a capable young man and I'll keep an eye on things. I've been having more fun building this hospital than anything I've done in ages, and I'd like to help guide it to its completion."

Maddie laughed. "Now you know good and well you want to get on all that big equipment and knock down trees. You and Jake are like two little boys."

The table erupted in laughter. Emma placed her fork on the table.

"Mama, can I ride the big tractors and push down trees?"

"No, honey, it's a construction site. It's not a place for children."

Emma's little nose scrunched up just like her mother's. "Dr. Chase will take me and keep me safe. He says girls can do anything boys can do and boys can do anything girls can do except have babies. That's a superpower for girls only."

"Yes, honey, you can do whatever you put your mind to, but we won't be going up to the construction site. Dr. Chase is away working with Uncle Leo. He doesn't have time to take you for rides on tractors right now."

Emma's eyebrows cast down in an angry slant. "Dr. Chase said I could come by and see his horses anytime. He already gave me *mission* to see them. He won't care if I'm there."

"Permission, sweetie. He gave you permission. Not now, Em. Now finish your dinner so you can get a bath and if we finish early, we can read two stories."

"I wanna go see Dr. Chase's hospital and ride on the big machines!"

"Emma. That's enough. We aren't going to Dr. Chase's house right now. Now eat."

"Just because you don't like Dr. Chase doesn't mean he doesn't love me!" She jumped out of her seat and ran toward her bedroom.

Kassie's face flushed at her daughter's outburst. "I'm sorry, Emma is more tired than I thought."

Maddie stood and grabbed Joe's hand, hauling him out of the chair. "Thank you for the meal, Sugar. We'll let you tend to that tantrum. Joe and I need to begin making plans to move to Serenity as soon as possible."

They walked right out the door. Kassie's mouth gaped open in surprise.

Shadow leaned over and grabbed another slice of bread and poured himself a healthy swig of wine.

"Dinner was great, Kass. Didn't realize we'd be getting dinner and a show."

She threw her bread at him while Shadow started laughing out loud.

Chapter Forty-one

It had been two weeks without a word from Leo or the team. She'd chewed her fingernails down until they were nothing but stubs. Emma had become a bear and was thankfully down for a nap. Maddie and Joe had made their move to Serenity. Julio's team kept their distance when Shadow was there. No one was hovering over her. No one was checking to see how she was doing. She was finally on her own. So why didn't she feel any better than she had before?

She was expecting the realtor to come with another set of houses to show her. Today, she was determined to find a house where she could make a life for herself and Em. The doorbell rang and she picked up her steps to get to the door before the bell woke Em. Swinging open the door, she found a slightly disheveled Leo in front of her.

"Leo!"

"What are you doing answering the door?" His eyebrows furrowed in anger, but his face was so full of exhaustion, that she didn't think he had the fight in him to really care.

"I was expecting someone. Emma's down for a nap, and I didn't want the noise to wake her. Julio's man is outside and Shadow's in the shower. When did you get back?" She tried to sound nonchalant, but she needed to know that everyone was safe, especially Chase.

"We've been back for a week now. I've been following leads and haven't had a chance to stop by. How have you been doing? I saw Maddie at the grocery store. She said they've moved back to Serenity."

She put down her cup, afraid that the shaking of her hand would betray her feelings. She nodded. "Yes, they seem to be happy there. Did everyone get back safely? Can I make you something to eat?"

He smirked, indicating he knew exactly what she was asking. "No

Kassie, I won't be staying. Just checking in on my clients and seeing if there is anything they needed."

Wincing at his choice of words at calling her a client and not using her new nickname indicated he was pissed, and she noticed he'd avoided answering her question. She glared at him but refused to repeat it.

"Taco's great with Em and she gets a kick out of saying she brings her own "Taco" on Tuesdays to class."

"I'm assigning a new guy to your security, his name is Jameson."

"That's fine."

Leo's businesslike demeanor let her know she wasn't off the hook.

Shadow came out of the bedroom with his phone in hand. He poured himself a cup of coffee and leaned against the counter.

"I've got some things to take care of and need to get going." Leo stood and gathered the files Shadow had left him on the table. "And Shadow?"

"Yeah, boss."

"She answers that door again without you present, you're fired."

"Got it, boss."

Kassie's eyes rounded. "You can't do that! He was in the shower!"

"That's correct. He can't afford to make mistakes. It could've hurt you or Emma. He knows he screwed up; he accepts responsibility. I know you don't believe in second chances." His eyebrows rose as he challenged her to say something.

Huffing, she got the message. He wasn't referring to just Shadow.

"I'll see you to the door."

Kassie opened it to find the realtor. Ushering her inside, she said a curt goodbye to Leo. "Thank you for stopping by, I'm glad you all made it home safely."

Leo hadn't answered. He just looked at her with steely eyes and disappointment covered his face. She glued a smile on her face as she closed the door and guided the realtor to the kitchen table. Why didn't she feel any excitement at any of the prospects?

The phone rang and startled her out of her thoughts. Samantha's name appeared on the screen, and she was relieved to see it was her friend. "Hi, Samantha!"

"Hi, lady! How are you holding up? I'm in between clients. I wanted to see if you, Catherine, and Elizabeth would be up to having a ladies' night in Seattle on Saturday. Maddie, my mom, Jake, and Joe have agreed to watch the kids. Leo said he will be in Seattle and could bring Emma over with him and Maddie and Joe can bring her home for Sunday dinner."

"That sounds great. What did you have in mind?"

"How about a quiet dinner and then do you think you could handle going to Sharkey's for a drink? You mentioned that you wanted to see him and thank him for everything he did for you and Em."

"Sure, that would be great. How about you call Catherine and I'll call Elizabeth?" Kassie suggested.

"Perfect, see you Saturday and before you argue, I'm coming in early to do your hair and makeup. The last two times I saw you, you looked like you had just climbed out of bed. No baggy sweatshirts and no grandma jeans!"

Kassie rolled her eyes. "I got it."

Saturday, she anxiously waited for Samantha to show up, knowing that she would have news about Chase and how things were going on the mountain. She told herself she wanted to ensure he was doing okay. They had spent months together, of course, she would care about his well-being.

Samantha, Catherine, and Elizabeth arrived together. After hugs went around, she opened a bottle of wine. Samantha sent her back to her bedroom three times before she came out with an outfit that they deemed appropriate for their evening out. Finally settling on a blue pantsuit with a jacket and low heels not to aggravate her leg, she was ready to go.

She'd made dinner reservations at a quiet upscale restaurant and then they would make their way to Sharkey's. Dinner was amazing. The food was good, and the company was exactly what she needed.

Kassie had been half listening to Samantha and Elizabeth talking until she heard Chase's name.

"You could have knocked me over with a feather when Chase came in and said, Elizabeth, I want you to run the hospital. He handed me a packet with the job description and pay. Kassie, did you have anything to do with this?" Elizabeth asked.

All three women turned their attention on her. Raising her glass and taking a big gulp of wine to calm her nerves, she responded. "No, Elizabeth. Chase makes all the decisions for the hospital. This is his dream."

Samantha had been the one to break the silence. "Are we ready to head over to Sharkey's? I've only been there a few times. Liam used to take me there with the team. It will be good to see Sharkey again."

The women began settling their checks to head over to the military bar. A movement out of the corner of her eye caught Kassie's attention. Chase walked in with Claire on his arm. As the waiter directed him to a table, Chase held the chair out for the pretty blonde woman. Claire turned her head and whispered something in his ear. Laughing at whatever she said, Chase took a seat across from her. The two continued to enjoy their conversation as the waiter dropped off drinks. Claire leaned over the table toward Chase. He smirked and said something back that caused Claire to laugh.

Watching the pair so engaged, Kassie realized she hadn't thought about what it would feel like if Chase moved on. Unable to drag her eyes away from the scene that was playing out before her, Kassie's heart tore in two.

The women at Kassie's table were suddenly quiet. Samantha's mouth was pursed in a firm line as Catherine reached over and took Kassie's hand. "Hey, let's get out of here."

Discreetly leaving, they headed out to the car. Shadow followed behind while Leo waited as the women climbed into the vehicle.

"I'm sorry, my migraine's getting worse. Do you think I could take a raincheck on going to the bar?" Nodding, the women all agreed as Leo navigated his way back to the hotel.

Leo glanced back at Kassie through the rearview mirror as she met his gaze. Tears pooled in her eyes as she turned to look out the window.

Dropping the women off at their prospective parking spots, Leo parked the vehicle. Shadow silently disappeared. When Kassie made no move to get out, Leo opened her door. Reaching in he handed her a tissue. As if a dam had broken, Kassie's body was wracked with heart-wrenching sobs. Gathering her in his arms, Leo let her cry it out.

When she finished, Kassie blew her nose and soft hiccups escaped as she tried to get herself under control. Leo wiped her face with a baby wipe from Emma's supply. Placing his hands on the roof of the vehicle, He peered in at her.

"Are you done?" His gruff voice caught her by surprise.

She nodded her head up and down but couldn't stop sobbing. "I'm done. Let's go up to the room, I'm ready for this night to be over."

"You let him go, but your feelings are hurt the first time you see him with another woman. You didn't think he was going to stay single forever, did you?"

"No. I didn't. I just got blindsided. That's all. I wasn't ready for it."

He handed her another tissue. No matter how hard she tried she couldn't shut off the waterworks. Leo ran his hand over his face in exasperation.

"You are the most stubborn twit I have ever had to deal with besides your friend Catherine. No wonder the two of you get along so well. For the love of God, Kassie. Honey. What the hell is wrong with you?"

"What? What's wrong with me? I don't know, Leo. I just spent a couple of years running from a hitman. My sister was planning on selling me to the highest bidder for a life she chose, and that I never wanted. I was kidnapped. My kid has turned into an absolute bear to deal with. I hurt Maddie and Joe. And…"

"Chase finally stopped chasing you?" Leo was direct and to the point and it stung.

Kassie nodded mutely. "I don't understand it. He wasn't there all that time I was going through this, but it felt like he was. Now I can't feel him at all. It's empty. Everything is just dark." She blew her nose once again.

"Why is that, Kass? You need to get your head out of your ass. I'm afraid if you don't soon, you're going to lose the one thing in your life that you need the most. Think hard about all that time I watched over you and when you first got home. You think you're getting your life together but you're falling apart because you aren't where you're supposed to be. Deep down, you know your sister was a bitch to put you through all that."

Kassie started to protest.

"Nope. You listen. She shoved her responsibilities on you, knowing you'd do it. Because of that, you ended up hurt and that asshole took something from you. Are you going to let that define you?"

They didn't speak as they walked through the lobby, walked into the elevator, and waited for it to stop on her floor. Opening the door, Leo gave her a slight shove inside.

"You need to get your heart straight with your head before you lose the one thing that is most important to you. I'm beginning to think Chase might be better off without you." He slammed the door shut.

Kassie splashed water on her face and got herself under control. She walked into the kitchen, then microwaved a cup of water for tea. Shadow and Taco barely looked in her direction as they walked to their room. It looked like she was in deep shit with the team. She thought about how possessive Chase looked as he had his hand on Claire. They looked like the perfect couple. His dark black hair and green eyes and her blonde hair and blue eyes.

Climbing into bed, she watched the clock change numbers as she willed herself to sleep. She shut her eyes and forced them to stay closed. Finally drifting off, she dreamed of the last moments in that room with Roger before all hell broke loose.

Roger leered at her as she lay there, unmoving. She needed water. He'd promised her. She could feel the blood sticky and wet between her legs and knew she'd lost the baby. Knowing she should feel more pain than she did, she knew she was close to the end. Her last thoughts were of Chase before she passed out.

Roger returned. This time with a gun. This was it. She was going to die. Hearing the gun go off, Kassie's body jerked at the sound. Someone was screaming. Chase was leaning over her and talking. She couldn't make out what he was saying…

The dream transported her to the rehab center.

Kassie's room was void of light. She couldn't handle being alone in the dark. Lying in the bed alone, her body was paralyzed in terror. Crying out in the blackness, her body shook in fear. The smell of oak and the mountain enveloped her. Again, Chase was there bringing her back to the light. She couldn't hear what he was whispering in her ear and desperately wanted to know…

Everything was just out of reach. *They had set her up in her old room. Emma was in the cottage with Leo. She was afraid that her nightmares might scare her daughter. But Leo was in her room at night, wasn't he? She was so confused…*

Shooting straight up in the bed, she placed her hand over her mouth to stifle the scream that threatened. Sweat ran down her back and her hair was plastered to her forehead.

Shedding her sweat-sodden clothes, she dressed in leggings and a T-shirt before padding to the kitchen and making popcorn. She turned on the tv and started watching an old movie. Shadow appeared out of nowhere.

Before he could ask, she answered the question she knew was coming. "Couldn't sleep."

He silently slipped his feet under her blanket and stole some popcorn from the bowl she'd made but hadn't touched it. Kassie continued to focus on the television, while her mind reached for what was missing in her dreams.

Chapter Forty-two

Maddie handed her a platter of cookies and Joe went over the counteroffer on the home she'd looked at. "Little Bit, if I'm not overstepping my bounds, I think I'd like to check this place out before you sign a contract. It's in an older neighborhood. I want to check it out to make sure you girls are going to be safe there."

Kassie bit back a giggle. He would've had a heart attack if he'd seen the small room she'd rented inside an industrial building. They had shared one bath with an entire floor.

Emma bounced into the room, excited after returning from Serenity and staying with Maddie and Joe. "Mama! Dr. Chase and I played cards, and he took me for a ride on his horses. He said that he saved them. One's name is Scarlett cause she gots red hair like you and the black one thinks he's so handsome, he named him Rhett."

She slowly placed her fork down and looked at the older couple while she answered her daughter.

"Wow, that's exciting! I bet you had lots of fun. What else did you do?"

Dr. Chase took me for a ride on the tractor and we knocked down huge trees! Melody and L.J. helped. Did you know that Dr. Chase is going to have lots of doggies like Rollo? He even let Rollo spend the night with me!"

"That was sweet of him," she murmured. Joe and Maddie showed no remorse for their decision to take her daughter to Chase's home.

"It sure was, Sugar. That man has a heart of gold. He was visiting Jake, and Emma spotted him. It was like a reunion with those two. Then Chase invited us up to see the hospital's progress. Joe's going to be handling it when Chase leaves with the team."

"Emma, if you're done with lunch, please take your plate to the garbage and pick out a story for a nap."

Emma slid out of her chair and dumped her plate. Pulling a book from her backpack, she exclaimed, "Look what Dr. Chase got me!" It was a book called *Ladybug Girl*. "He said it reminded him of me!"

Kassie pretended to show interest in the book. "Okay, go pick out your sleeping buddies, and then I'll be in to read to you."

She waited until Emma was out of hearing range. "I don't know what you two are doing, but Chase has moved on. I can't allow Emma to come to stay with you if you can't respect my boundaries."

Joe's mouth opened and closed. Maddie smiled sweetly. "Oh, Sugar, I didn't realize it would distress you so." She got up from the table. "All this upset isn't good for your stomach. Why don't you and I go for a walk on that lovely walking trail by the park? Joe can put Em down for a nap so we can catch a ray of this lovely weather!"

Following Maddie down the slightly muddy trail, Kassie stopped long enough to grab two water bottles from her pack. Handing one to Maddie, she broke the seal off hers and took a sip. Catching Maddie watching her drink aggravated her to no end. Due to the weather, the usually busy trail remained empty. Kassie leaned against a rock.

"I'm a nurse practitioner, ya know. I know exactly what you're doing."

"Good."

"No, it's not. It's irritating. I know what I'm doing!" Kassie leveled her voice. She wasn't going to yell at the woman who had been nothing but good to her.

"Do you?" Maddie snarked.

Kassie looked surprised that Maddie would speak to her that way. She was always as patient as a saint.

"Yes." Kassie bobbed her head up and down as if convincing herself the words were true.

"Then tell me. Because I've no idea, Sugar. You're trying to push Chase, a good man away. Leo has put himself and his men on hold to always make sure you're safe for his friend and I swear, you aren't grateful for any of it! How long is this gonna continue, baby girl? Your mama and I raised a fighter! Where are you? Why are you retreating now? Abigail would not stand for this at all!"

"I don't know. I'm sorry! I'm sorry, ok! I know I've disappointed you."

"Oh, Baby, you could never disappoint me. Tell me what you're chewing on. Good or bad, I'm right here, Sugar. It's time."

"Things aren't getting better. I don't know what I'm supposed to do anymore! Is that what you want to hear, Maddie? I'm mad that my sister put me in this position!"

"If that's the truth, yes. Kassie's actions put you in the circumstances you were in. But your behavior right now has put you in your current situation."

"Maddie, how can you say that?" Kassie stepped to the side, surprised that Maddie would speak to her in such a way.

"Because it's the truth. You're feeling mighty sorry for yourself."

"I want to go home." She shoved herself away from the rock and started to stalk away. Her leg didn't move as quickly so she stumbled and fell into the mud. Attempting to pull her shoe out of the sticky mess she stood to yank it out and promptly fell over again. She braced herself and attempted to rise again. Maddie shoved her back to the ground.

"What the hell did you do that for?" She was shocked that Maddie would shove her into the mud-ridden path. Her usual loving, patient Maddie was pissed!

"Ask me," Maddie's angry voice demanded.

"Ask you what?" Kassie sat on the wet ground completely confused at her godmother's actions.

"Ask for help!" Maddie commanded.

"All you do is help! I'm not going to ask you for more!" Kassie's flustered voice complained.

"How much help is too much help?" Maddie questioned her sternly. Her voice angrier than she had ever been with the young woman before her.

"What has gotten into you, Maddie?" Her voice went up an octave as she was trying to process if the older woman had lost her mind.

"Does our family have a limit on how much help we give each other?" Maddie's motherly voice demanded.

"Well, nooo?" Shame washed over her.

"Then why won't you let us help you? Why won't you talk to us? How many times did you lament about your sissy not asking us for help and look how that turned out!"

"Nobody can help me…I don't even know where to start."

"Let. It. All. Out, Sugar. We can't help if you won't let all that darkness out and let the light in!"

"I screwed up." Tears flowed down her face. "I chose to be Kassie to protect Emma. Now how do I tell her I'm not her mama? I lied to Catherine and almost got her family killed. I am now the famous Kassie Stanton in all the papers and all over the internet! I lied to Chase. I ran away and then I pushed him away. I may not be able to have children, Maddie. He wants kids. I can't be the reason his hospital fails, and he doesn't get the family he wants."

"Sugar. That's a lot on your shoulders. Let's start at the beginning. You will always be Kaitlyn Abigail Reynolds, no matter what name you answer to. That little girl back at that hotel has been yours from the day she was born. It takes more than giving birth to be a mama. Kassie loved that child, and she was put in a difficult situation. She entrusted her daughter to you because she knew you'd love her as your own. Now, Kassie Stanton is free to live her own life. She doesn't have to answer to anyone. Who says that people don't change after the experiences they went through? If you don't like what they're saying, then change the script, Sugar. You already started, just keep bringing good into this world."

Maddie's words were starting to sink in.

"Honey, Abigail, Nathan, Joe, and I, we've done you such a disservice. If you think that loving somebody means that you don't get hurt sometimes, baby, we've shielded you way too much. Joe and I've had some mighty rows. Abigail and Nathan fought as much as they loved. But you work it out. You say things you don't mean, and you apologize. You might yell and cry. You might have to walk away but you do so knowing that love is worth fighting for and coming back to each other. That man has been by your side from the day he pulled you off that helicopter. He's a good man. You've pushed him away cause you're running, because you love him, Sugar. You're terrified he won't accept you the way you are."

Maddie took a drink of her water. "Ask me how I know, Sugar. I lost a baby too and I couldn't give Joe the family we talked about having all those years ago. I've sat in your shoes, thinking I was denying the man I loved something he needed. That man showed me time and time again that I am what he needed. Then by some miracle, Joe met your parents, and Joe and I got you two girls to help raise. Life works in mysterious ways. Kassie, you've just got to trust in your love for one another. The only reason Chase would leave is because he thought you'd be happier without him." She pointed her finger at the wide-eyed Kassie sitting in the mud. "What are you gonna do about it?"

"I don't know!" Kassie yelled at Maddie. Frustration rolled over her as all the feelings she tried stuffing down were bubbling back to the surface.

"Then I suggest you figure it out."

Maddie left her sitting on the wet ground.

Chapter Forty-three

At precisely five minutes after ten her phone started ringing. The name Claire Meyers popped up on her cell phone. Kassie answered on the third ring.

"Hello?" Kassie coldly answered the phone.

"Hi, Kassie, It's Claire. I was wondering if you forgot we had an appointment today at nine forty-five. Do you need to reschedule?" Claire innocently inquired.

"Hello, Claire. Yes, I'm aware of the appointment. I won't be making it. No, I don't need to reschedule. Oh, and Claire?" Kassie paused.

"Yes?"

"You're fired." She hung up the phone. She wondered if Chase had felt the same feelings every time he saw her with Matthew. No wonder he'd jumped to conclusions. It cut like a knife.

She heard Shadow coughing behind her and turned to see if he was all right. His face was beet red, and his mouth was covered with a napkin but the crinkle around his eyes told her he'd overheard her conversation. Now she wished he was choking. She would have walked away without giving him the Heimlich maneuver. Okay, maybe she wouldn't have done it, but she'd crack a rib or two just to wipe that smirk off his face.

Later that day, Leo called and wanted to bring the new team by Wednesday as Taco and Shadow would be going with him on a mission. She knew Chase would be leaving too. Maddie and Leo's words kept playing like a recorder in her head.

Emma returned from preschool and settled in for a nap while Kassie and Joe met with the realtor at the property that she'd put an offer on. Joe was quiet as he walked around the rooms. Testing the windows, cabinets, and floors, he made notes.

Shadow stayed at the entryway, not once conveying his feelings about the place.

Forty minutes later, Joe walked over to the realtor. "Shadow will show you out. I need a minute with my goddaughter." The flabbergasted lady looked at Kassie, who shrugged and looked toward Joe.

When the door shut, she asked, "What's the matter, Joe? Don't you like it?"

"It doesn't matter whether I like it Little Bit. It matters whether you do. It's sound. The neighborhood is diverse and relatively safe. It has all the boxes checked."

"I don't understand. Why didn't you tell her that? Do you think I shouldn't offer more for it?" Kassie's eyebrows furrowed as she gave it some thought.

He stuffed his hands in his pocket and regarded his goddaughter. "When you think of your life, do you see yourself happy here, Little Bit? Close your eyes and tell me if this is where you belong."

Closing her eyes, she tried to imagine herself and Em making a life there. The first image she saw was the mountain. Emma fishing on the lake. Chase and her laughing as they watched her learn how to canoe. Walking through the trails. Sitting in her window seat watching the sunrise and Chase bringing her mint tea.

She opened her watery eyes. Joe nodded.

"That's what I thought." Joe inspected the ceiling one more time. "The boys are leaving in a couple of weeks. I've a feeling it's going to be an important mission. Don't take too long on deciding to come home, Kass." Joe exited the room.

She kissed Em goodnight and found herself wandering the suite. She ordered Chinese and the guys had taken theirs to their room, leaving her alone. She grabbed the book on her nightstand and tried to read. Her thoughts kept wandering back to Chase, feeling bad at how things ended. She realized that *she* was the one who had given up on them. After reading the same page for twenty minutes, she took something to help her sleep and laid back down. The dreams began again…

Staring out the window, Kassie paid no attention to the nurses that came and went. She refused to talk or take any medication. There was nothing they could give her that could take away the pain she felt.

Maddie kissed her cheek and turned off the light in her room. Laying in the darkness, Kassie felt her leg throbbing and her head pounding. Fear of being left in the dark shook her. Listening for any signs of anything coming for her in the blackness, she finally drifted off.

Roger had found his way inside the hospital. Scraping the bucket across the floor, he was looking for her! She cried out in pain as she imagined him dragging the knife down her leg and watching the blood pool on the floor.

The smell of oak and whiskey drifted into her dream. Strong familiar arms wrapped around her. It was then she heard the voice. *Go to sleep, Princess, I've given you something for the pain, and I'm watching over you. He's not coming back. He's gone…*

It seemed so real.

Kassie tried to wake herself up from the dream, but it held her prisoner, refusing to let her break the spell.

She was in her old room. A nightmare where Roger had broken her fingers made her scream out. Something warm massaged her hand and she confessed what Roger had done, whimpering at the hurt and how frightened she was. Chase's body lay on the bed next to her as he pulled her into his arms. This time the voice came out clearer. "Listen to me, Kassie. You were and will always be mine. No one will hurt you again. Come back to me. Come back to Emma. We need you, baby. I love you. Only you…"

Thunder boomed and shook the windows of the hotel suite, jarring her awake. His name ripped from her lips. Chase had been there with her the entire time and hadn't left her side! He was waiting for her to trust him and know he'd never leave her! What had she done?

The rain pelted the windows and thunder rolled, matching the feelings she held inside. She'd finally figured out who she was. She was the best of both herself and her twin. She now had the freedom to choose her life! Most importantly, she was Chase's and she wanted him by her side.

She grabbed jeans and a burgundy sweater. She threw on her tennis shoes. Shadow came to the doorway as she was brushing out her hair.

"Ugh. Kass? It's nearly midnight, are you going somewhere?"

"Yes! I'm going home." Realizing once and for all, she belonged on the mountain.

Shadow let out a big whoop and she heard Taco yell "Hell yeah, bout damn time!" from their room. She laughed a full laugh. She couldn't remember the last time she had felt so free.

"Well, is one of you going to drive me or can I drive myself? What if he doesn't want me? Maybe I waited too long?" Doubt hit her. What was she doing? She wouldn't get there until after one in the morning. He was going to think she was insane!

Shadow grabbed her by the shoulders and shook her. "No. Don't go there. Here's the keys to my truck. We'll follow you to the mountain to make sure you get there. Saint can stay with Em. From there you're on your own. And Kassie?"

"Yeah?" Kassie looked up at Shadow.

"Let's go home."

Hugging Shadow, she made her way to the door.

Chapter Forty-four

Kassie drove through the storm, anxious to make it to Serenity. Shadow called her twice to slow the hell down, but she had to get to Chase!

The phone rang again. It was Leo.

"PITA, if you don't slow your ass down, I'm going to be waiting in front of the cabin and I'm going to put you over my knee. I know you've finally come to your senses, but we don't need you ending up in an accident."

Her foot pressed slowly on the brake. She could see why he was a leader. The command in his voice rang through and she knew, without a doubt, he'd do exactly what he said.

"I'm scared, Leo." Kassie's voice wavered.

"I know, but one smart woman told him love was worth fighting for. It just took her a while to figure that out for herself. Now the guys better not wake me up again to tell you to slow down or you won't be sitting down for days. Am I clear?" Leo barked.

"Yes, sir!" she shouted, and he laughed as he hung up the phone. She carefully pulled into the drive and the boys turned around and headed back down. Gripping the steering wheel, she took a few breaths before getting out of the truck and making her way to the front door.

Chase took a draw of whiskey and swallowed it down. The storm matched his feelings. He couldn't sleep. He paced the house and even Rollo was restless. The last few days he resigned himself to Kassie giving up. Even the cabin felt the void of her absence. A deep ache hit his chest as he relived every moment of her with him in his cabin.

The doorbell rang and he frowned as he glanced at the clock. Thinking Leo was planning on leaving earlier than he planned, he rushed to the door.

Nothing could prepare Chase for the sight in front of him. A bedraggled, soaking-wet Kassie stood before him. Her sweater clung to her curves. Her hair hung sopping wet all around her. He couldn't tell if it was the rain or if she was crying. Her hands were balled up and she gripped the ends of her sweater sleeves.

"Kassie?" He blinked as if unsure he hadn't conjured her up in his dreams.

"You. Were. There. The whole time. I remembered. I pushed you away. You never left me. I'm so sorry, Chase. I forgot to fight for us." Kassie big round eyes met his as she shivered from the cold.

Chase stood there stunned. Leo had insisted that Chase tell Kassie he had never left her side. Chase refused. He wanted Kassie to come to him because she trusted him enough to know he never left her. This wasn't about guilt or obligation; it was about love. Fighting for the love they shared for each other, for their family, and for the mountain. It was all at stake. No matter how far his girl ran, he would always chase Kassie. She had forgotten their love could overcome anything. Now that she was standing at his door, he didn't need her to apologize. All he wanted to hear was that she loved him.

"Am I too late?" The hesitation in her voice sent him into action. He wasn't going to let her run again.

He shook his head. "No. Princess, you're right on time." He smiled at her as she jumped toward him and wrapped her arms around his neck.

"I love you, Chase Winters."

He pulled back a soaked strand of hair. "I love you."

He gently placed a kiss on her lips. He walked backward and closed the front door and locked it. "Kass, we need to get you out of these clothes. If you want to go grab a shower in my bathroom, I will find you some clothes to wear and we can talk."

She shook her head. "No. You once told me that the next time you made love to me in that bed, I would know that I was yours and I would know that I was home. I want to come home, Chase."

Her lips crushed his. He held her tight, refusing to let her go. Adjusting her more securely, he carried her into the bathroom and dried her hair with a towel. Grabbing the ends of her sweater, she pulled it over her head. Unclasping her bra, she let it fall to the floor.

Chase let out a throaty growl as Kassie hooked her thumbs through the top of her jeans and slowly peeled them off as her gaze locked onto his.

Licking her lips nervously, she looked down and winced. "I know the scars are ugly." Suddenly she seemed unsure of herself. There wasn't any way he was going to let her think she was anything but beautiful.

"No. Princess, those are battle scars. You won them fighting for yourself, for our child, and for us. You survived. Don't let me hear you say they're ugly again. Because of them, you're here with me tonight. I regret what happened to give you them, but I'm grateful that I can kiss every one of them and take all the pain away."

Bending down, he picked her up and carried her to the bed in his room. He turned on the fireplace, knowing she was still scared of the dark, then stood next to the bed. She sat up on her knees. Her hands roamed up his chest. Her head shot up to meet his eyes.

"I saw you at the restaurant the other night. You were with Claire. Are you dating her?" Her brows knitted together as she sucked in her bottom lip. Uncertainty showed in her eyes.

Stroking his fingers down her back, Chase looked her in the eyes.

"No, baby. I'm not with Claire. I recruited her to come join the hospital. She'd just accepted the proposal, and we went out to dinner to discuss the details. There's only one woman for me. You're it, Kassie. Make sure this is what you want because I'm not letting you go after I make love to you. We'll pack up your stuff in the morning and you and Emma are moving home."

"Okay. I need to apologize to Claire, I kinda fired her."

Expecting her to put up a fuss, Chase was surprised at her quick agreement. "Think about it, Princess. We can take this slow. I want you to be sure." Chuckling, he added, "I also want you to continue counseling after you talk to Claire."

Kassie's hand grazed the scruff along his jaw. "I love you, Chase. Instead of running away, I want to run toward something. This mountain is where I feel safe, and I can do the most good. I think I've known that all along when I was sketching in those journals. Most importantly, you're my home and I want a life with you."

Chase closed his eyes at her words. Suddenly remembering what his mom had told him about the woman that he should marry. Someone loyal, faithful, and willing to fight you as much as love you. Kassie was all those things. Cupping her face in his hands, he tenderly kissed her lips.

Kassie's fingers roamed down the buttons of his shirt, undoing them as she went along. Sliding the shirt from his shoulders, Kassie smiled as she saw the tattoo that covered his arm and shoulder. She'd missed how she traced the pattern as she fell asleep when they had been together the first time. Leaning in, she placed a kiss above his heart.

"I've missed you," she whispered, not wanting to break the spell.

Noticing that she wore the bracelet he had given her at the hospital, he toyed with the delicate charms as he kissed the inside of her wrist. Raising his eyes in question, he admitted, "I wasn't sure if you threw this away."

Shaking her head, Kassie looked at him. "No. I always carry it in my pocket. Every time I felt a panic attack, I would run my fingers over the charms and think of the meanings behind each one. When I first started, it took me until the Christmas tree before I could control it. Now, I only need to hold onto the mountain."

"We still need to talk about everything that happened. There were a lot of misunderstandings. Most of what I know you told me when you thought I was a dream."

Kassie began to interrupt.

"No, if we're going to jump into the deep end, we need to make sure all those doubts and insecurities you have are gone. Then we can pick up where we left off on Christmas Eve last year when I made love to you for the first time. The moment when you trusted me with everything. I'll never abuse that gift or question you again."

"I promise to talk to you about it, but in pieces and when I'm ready. Bits and pieces are missing, some I'm not sure are even real. For instance, I dreamed there was a woman with red hair in that room, and she looked like me. I thought at first it was my mama, but she spoke with an Irish accent. There was a man with her, they sent you to find me. But not tonight. Make love to me, Chase." Kassie leaned back on the bed as he removed his jeans and underwear.

Chase made a mental note to alert Leo of Kassie's revelation. There was no way she could have known about the young man that said he was sent to give them her location. Sitting on the bed, he pulled a condom from the drawer.

"We don't need those. I can't get pregnant." The sadness in her voice couldn't be missed.

"Princess, you've just recently told me about this, and there are many procedures and ways to have a baby. Since I haven't looked at your chart and we haven't seen a specialist, I want to use a condom. You and Emma are enough for me. I'd like to spend time with her before we decide to expand our family. Either way, you two are my world and we already have a family regardless of what the doctors say."

Sighing as he freed her from the burdens that she'd carried alone, she watched as he slid down her body and began to kiss every nick and scar along her leg. He nipped her hip, sending flutters running down her body. Flipping her on her stomach, he started his way down the other leg and up again. When he finished sealing all her wounds with his love, she turned back to him.

Placing tiny kisses down his chest, her hands roamed lower. Gripping his cock, she slowly began a rhythm. Chase's long moan let her know that he enjoyed it. The well-defined abs on his body were like a work of art and she couldn't resist running her tongue along them and upward and over his nipple.

He emitted a growl. Both of his hands found their way into the thick mass of hair as he pulled her up to meet his lips.

"You are mine. You are loved. You are safe. From this day forward we run toward our future. You and me, Kass. Say it. Say you're mine."

Straddling him, she placed his cock at her entrance. "From this day forward, I'm yours. You are mine. You are loved." Sliding down his cock, she smiled as a tear ran down her cheek.

Moving his hips, he pressed deeper into her and set the rhythm. Chase's hands cupped her breasts and he tugged at her nipples as she rode his cock. Watching Kassie with her hair falling below her shoulders, her mouth partly open and panting tiny breaths, he was sure he had never seen anything so beautiful.

Taking her with him as he rolled over, she giggled as he bit the side of her neck. Goosebumps instantly appeared, yet she tilted her head to give him better access. His mouth enclosed her nipple as he gently sucked. He alternated his rhythm; she'd start to peak and then he would slow. Kassie's nails clawed into his back as she fought to keep him deeper as she grew closer to the edge.

"Not yet, Princess. I want you to know there isn't any inch of you that I don't know. Not a section on this body that isn't loved and adored."

His cock slid between her silken wet folds, going deeper and then teasing her. Smelling her scent mingled with his own did something primal to him.

"Please, Chase, I need you," Kassie keened as her eyes locked onto his.

Picking up his pace, the slapping of their bodies, the crackling of the fire, and Kassie's moans almost sent him over the edge. Adjusting himself so he hit the spot that drove Kassie crazy, he moaned as her hands clutched his chest and dug into his shoulders.

"Ahhhh, Chaaaaaaase!" Kassie went over as she screamed his name. Just hearing his name come from her lips with such passion, Chase let the orgasm come over him, reveling in the fact that Kassie was now his.

Knowing that she hated it when he slid directly out of her, he propped his weight up with his shoulders in order not to crush her.

"I love you, Princess."

Her fingers traced his tattoo on his shoulder. Her eyes were glazed over, and a contented smile played on her lips.

"I love you."

Letting her up long enough to get ready for bed, Chase changed the wet sheets and placed a nightlight on Kassie's side of the bed. When she returned, he held back the covers to let her in. Kassie noticed his small gesture with the nightlight, smiled, and pulled it from the wall.

"Kass, I know you use several nightlights at the hotel. One step at a time."

Ignoring him, Kassie crawled into his arms and pulled the blankets over them. Laying her head on his shoulder, her hand stretched across his abs. She sleepily replied, "I don't need them now. I'm home. I'm safe, and I'm loved." The last words were whispered as she drifted off to sleep.

Chase kissed the top of her head. Laying there for several minutes, he gratefully counted his blessings. He had two weeks before he left with Leo and the team. Pulling Kassie tighter in his arms, he made a list of things he–no, *they*–needed to do before he left.

Chapter Forty-five

Kassie's and Emma's things had been moved to the cabin the next morning by the team. Maddie and Joe decided they wanted to tour their new home state before Chase left. They were taking Emma and Carol Reese and Melody were joining them. They would return the night before the team would leave so Chase could go over any last-minute instructions for the hospital with Joe. During the day, Chase worked with the contractors for the hospital. Excitement grew as structures started to go up.

The couple wasn't ignorant of the fact that the older couple was gifting them time alone. Taking advantage of every moment of it, Kassie and Chase made up for lost time. Knowing that Kassie was missing appointments with Claire, he urged her to either call Claire or talk to him.

Some nights, holding her close, they talked about the baby they'd lost.

They hiked to the top of the mountain to the family gravesite. Most of his family had opted to have their ashes spread so they could become part of the mountain they loved. An iron gate surrounded a circle of trees. Chase carried a small sapling and a shovel while Kassie carried the engraved stone plaque and a jug of water. He dug the hole for the tree, then placed the sapling in and Kassie poured the jug of water onto the roots before covering them. They cried and held each other as they said goodbye to the baby they'd lost.

In two days, Chase would be leaving. Before Kassie woke, he'd already visited Jake and had handed him a packet from his lawyer. After planning with Samantha, Chase headed back to his cabin with breakfast. Smiling, he hoped his parents were looking down on them and knew how happy he was. There was only one more thing to take care of and he'd feel like he had everything he could want.

Walking into their bedroom, he saw Kassie twined up in the blankets. She had stolen his pillow and held it to her chest. Leaning over, he kissed her shoulder, watching as her eyes fluttered open, the happiness evident in the sparkle of her blue eyes.

"Good morning."

"Good morning." She turned to fully face him. Pulling his head down, she kissed him. A mischievous smile played on her face as she pulled at the button on his jeans, her eyes darkening in desire. The sheet slid down to her waist as she sat up and slowly raised his shirt.

Sliding his hand through her hair, Chase moaned as he pulled her away from her nibbling on his abs.

"If you start, we'll end up spending the whole day in bed. Come on, Princess, I want to introduce you to Bear. He lives on the smaller mountain over there." Chase pointed through the window to the neighboring elevation.

Kassie's mouth formed a pout and her eyebrows slanted in confusion. "You don't want to make love to me because you want me to meet the guy that makes honey? I'm sure I can introduce myself to him while I'm waiting for you to get back."

Chase sat down on the edge of the bed. "Kass, we've talked a little bit about everything except me going on this mission. Tomorrow, Emma will be home and there'll be other things distracting us. We need to address this."

With a heavy sigh, Kassie looked out the window. "I know. I don't even want to think about us being separated. It seems like something always happens…"

"That's why we need to communicate. I don't plan on doing this once the hospital is up and running. Leo has done so much for us, I can't tell him no."

Curling up into his chest and wrapping her arms around his waist, she spoke into his shoulder. "I'm scared. What if something happens? I can't lose you again."

Feeling the wetness on his shirt, he pulled her slightly away from him and lifted her chin. "For the first time in my life, I have everything I've ever wanted. Don't ever doubt I'll walk through hell to get back to you, Kass. I'll do everything in my power to stay safe. Do you understand?"

Kassie nodded.

"You'll listen to Matthew and Jameson while I'm gone. Always keep the security alarm on. Bear and Ty will supply your basics as usual. I want you to meet Bear because we help each other. He and Jake will tend the horses until I'm back. Please, baby. I want to make sure I have you settled before I leave, it's for my peace of mind."

Knowing that taking care of her was Chase's biggest priority she quickly agreed. The last thing she wanted was for him to be preoccupied while on this mission they were involved in. Jumping up she took a shower while he made her hot tea to go with a muffin.

Pulling into Bear's property, Kassie was surprised. The man was a naturalist. She could see his beehives on a higher hill to the right of his property. His log cabin was just as big as Chase's and the property held more outbuildings. Chase helped her out of the truck when a man with an overgrown beard and brown hair approached the vehicle.

The two men clasped hands. "Bear, I want to introduce you to Kassie. As you know I'm leaving and Kass and Em are at the cabin. I've assured her that you'll be there to help while I'm gone."

Bear nodded to Kassie. Kassie approached with a smile as she looked around his property.

"Can I see your hives? How do you get the honey without getting stung? By the way, I'm hooked on it. So, is that the lake you get the fish from? How do you smoke the salmon to taste so good?"

Bear glanced at Chase with his eyebrows raised. Chase interceded. "Kass, Bear doesn't let—"

"You want a tour? I have different flavors of honey if you want to try them." Now it was Chase's turn to look at his friend.

For the next four hours, Bear showed Kassie how to get honey, his honey shed, and they tasted every flavor Bear made along with various meads he was experimenting with. The next shed contained every herb imaginable and flowers drying. Bear explained to Kassie what medicinal purpose each plant had. After lunch, Chase interrupted the two new friends as they discussed how he smoked the salmon as they did in Alaska.

"Kass, we have another appointment to get to."

Kassie hugged Bear, then took Chase's hand and let him help her into the truck.

"Where are we going?"

Keeping his eyes on the road, Chase told Kassie, "There's some errands I need to run. It will take me a couple of hours. Samantha is going to give you a spa day."

"I can do that when you're gone! Chase, I'd rather spend my time with you," Kassie complained.

"I know, Princess. But I have one more thing I need to handle and then I'm going to take you someplace very special to me. It's my secret hiding place, and I've never taken anyone there before. I want it to be our special place."

Sighing, Kassie agreed. "If it means that much to you." As she counted the hours they had left, she was disappointed he'd want to spend so much time apart.

When they got to Samantha's, he scooped her up in a huge kiss then left her standing next to Samantha as he sped away.

"Come on, we have a lot to do!" Samantha grabbed her hand and led her through the salon.

Leaving her in the spa room with instructions to strip, Samantha left no part of Kassie's body untouched. Kassie's complaints went unheard. She watched the clock tick by and couldn't relax as Samantha gave her a complete body scrub, a hair mask, and a facial, and started on a mani/pedi.

"Really, how much longer could he possibly be?"

Samantha smiled. "Be patient, Kass. The man is leaving you for the first time and going on a mission. They all have this primal need to make sure that their women are cared for. This is the first time I've never seen Chase this worked up, not even with Rachel. Let him do what he needs to do."

It started to turn into early evening when Samantha brought out an outfit for Kassie. The top was the same blue as her eyes and thick enough for chilly weather with an added thin thermal Samantha made her wear. The sleeves were flowy and romantic, and the material cinched on one side emphasizing her waist. The soft jeans formed to her body and a pair of hiking boots were added to the pile with a pair of warm socks.

Hearing the doorbell ring, Kassie practically ran to meet Chase at the door.

Seeing that he had changed as well into a dark blue shirt and cowboy boots, he helped her gallantly into the truck.

"You look stunning, Princess." Chase complimented her.

"You look pretty hot yourself." Kassie said with a cheeky grin.

On the way up the mountain, he seemed nervous. Fidgeting with her coat, she worried that something was wrong.

When they arrived home, he led her to the barn where Rhett was saddled and waiting. Getting her settled on the horse, he lifted himself behind her, encompassing her in his arms. Lying back against him, she watched the scenery of the mountain change the further up they went. The landscape changed to a small flat area. He got off the horse and held his arms out to lift her off. He tied Rhett to a tree then began to walk them down a small hidden trail. Up ahead, Kassie spied a flickering of light in the trees.

Just as they were almost at the entrance of the forest, Chase turned to Kassie. "Close your eyes."

She instantly complied. He hadn't said much, and she didn't want her anxiety to worry him.

Taking her hand, he slowly guided her into a small clearing at the center of the copse of trees. She could feel the heat from the fire along with hearing the crackling of the wood. The smell of the oak reminded her of him. He briefly let go of her hands and turned her away from the heat. She waited.

"Okay, Princess, open your eyes." Chase's voice sounded strange.

She opened her eyes to see the valley where the sun went down between the two mountains. It looked as if the sun was painted into the background, with oranges, yellows, pinks, and purples.

"Oh Chase, this is…special."

"Just like you." His voice held so much emotion that Kassie turned to look at him. Chase bent to the ground on one knee. Kassie's hands flew to her mouth.

"Princess, I once thought I knew what love was. I thought of it as an obligation, a duty to be carried out. You've taught me that love is something you give freely. The last two weeks have gone by so fast for me and I'll treasure every single moment of them for the rest of our lives. I told you that once I made love to you that you'd be home, and you are. We've had a few bad months, but I don't want to waste any more time to share my life with you. I promise to love you until the day I die. I'll be a great dad to Emma. Maddie and Joe can move into my mom and dad's cabin. I don't want to wait until I get home to know you'll be my wife. Will you marry me?"

"Yes. Yes. Yes." Kassie cupped his face and pulled him up from the ground. "I love you, Chase Winters. I'll always love you. You are my home." Kassie sobbed as she peppered his face in kisses.

Chase reached into his pocket and took out a ring. The blue sapphire in a princess cut surrounded by tiny diamonds sparkled in the firelight. The white gold band was made to look like leaves twined from the side and tiny sapphires and diamonds were nestled in each leaf. He slid it onto her finger.

"This belonged to my mother. But seeing it on your finger, I think it was also made for you."

Wiping away her tears, he led her to a blanket where heated bags from Ty's awaited them. Kassie tremulously smiled.

"Chase as much as I love Ty's food, I don't want to eat right now."

Laughing, he raised his head to the sky, "Thank God."

Grabbing another blanket from a tent set up on the other side of the fire, he set Kassie down on the blanket. Pulling off her sweater and thermal, he growled when he saw the sexy, lace bra underneath.

She lay down on the blanket and began kicking off her boots as she slid her jeans off. Chase's eyes roamed down her body and growled when he saw the matching lace panties.

Leaning on her elbows, she beckoned him close. He quickly discarded his clothes and lay beside her. His fingers traced her face as if memorizing it. She ran her fingers across his scruff. Pulling her forward he kissed her forehead.

"I want to go slow, Princess. I want to memorize every part of you to carry me through until I come home to you."

"Take all the time you need, I'll be here waiting for you. Always."

Sliding down the silken bra strap and undoing the clasp, he kissed her shoulder and nipped it with his teeth, causing her to quiver as he pulled it away from her body. Laying her flat, he took his time, slowly making his way down the valley between her breasts. Her hands roamed through his hair as he took a nipple in his mouth and lathed it with his tongue. She moaned and squirmed. His hand gripped her hip.

"Stay still, Princess. This is my time."

Lowering himself he pulled off the panties with his teeth, his fingers slid through her already-soaked folds. He again placed his body on top of hers letting his chest hair tease her sensitive nipples while his fingers stroked her leisurely. She let out a hum as he inserted a finger and then a second. Watching her face, he angled them upward as he stroked. When she got close to the edge, his mouth covered her clit and he gently sucked. Kassie immediately flew over the precipice. Her hips bucked as she moaned out her pleasure.

Rising, he crushed his mouth to hers as her frenzied hands began to explore his chest, moving downward until she grabbed his cock and squeezed. Setting a rhythm, he moved on top of her as she held onto him. Cupping her breast, he raised her nipple to his mouth and sucked, making her cry out.

Chase worshipped the love of his life. The firelight cast a glow around them as it crackled into the night air. The trees whispered in the wind. Grabbing a condom, Chase entered her leisurely, reveling in the feel of her as her sheath gripped around him. Sliding deep until their hip bones touched, Chase brushed the hair from her eyes and held her face as he set a painstakingly slow rhythm while staying fully inside her.

"I love you, Princess."

Kassie was lost in his eyes. As her hands clutched the back of his waist, her nails dug in. She couldn't tell where his body ended and hers began. It didn't matter; that was exactly where she wanted to be.

Their bodies were covered in sweat despite the chilly outdoor air. Chase's rhythm became faster and faster, he gripped Kassie's hands in his, and took her to the highest point and let her fly.

"Keep your eyes on me, Princess, I want to remember this moment forever."

Not daring to blink she flew and when she came down, he reveled in her slickness and closed his eyes as she took him with her.

The next morning, Chase woke up just as the sun began to rise. He smiled as he heated up water so Kassie could wash before they made the trek back home. Everyone would be arriving to congratulate them. Before Joe and Maddie had left, he'd asked their permission to marry Kassie. They had given their blessing. Jake, Samantha, Ty, and Bear had helped with setting up the proposal. It couldn't have been more perfect.

Kassie's arms came around his neck from behind. Taking the warm bowl of water, she quickly washed up and then grabbing another cloth, she bathed him. When he reached for his clothes, her hand shot out. Smiling, Kassie pushed him back on the blanket.

"It's my time to memorize you."

Chase grinned. They might be a little late getting home.

An hour later, mounting Rhett, Chase turned the horse homeward. As they rounded the lake, the sun came up between the two mountains and shined down on the water. Their cabin was mirrored on one side as the shadowed images of them and the sun were on the other, promising a new beginning. Leaning down in Kassie's ear, he whispered,

"Welcome home, Princess."

Chapter Forty-six

The following six weeks had been hard. Catherine seemed on edge. Elizabeth seemed preoccupied, and Samantha was constantly fighting with Matthew Cartwright. Kassie didn't care. Every day meant that Chase was coming back to her, and they were starting their lives together. She concentrated on the task list he had left her and talked to the colleges that Chase had recommended and added a few of her own to the list. She still hadn't decided on whether she was vested in becoming a doctor. She loved being an NP.

Kassie dropped Emma off at a new preschool. Chase had only been able to send one short text the entire time the team was gone.

I'm coming home, Princess. I love you.

She grabbed some groceries and headed up to the cabin. She and Emma would plan a special meal for him. Sure that he would be tired from the trip, she planned a dinner with the family, including the team, the next day. The men could stay on the mountain. The ride home was full of joy and she rolled the window down, taking in the crisp fall air. Winter was on the horizon, and she looked forward to having Christmas with everyone at the cabin.

Placing the bag of food on the counter, Kassie hurriedly put the items that needed to be refrigerated away. She wanted to shower and change before Chase returned. Already planning in her mind what lingerie she would wear underneath her clothes, she stopped short when a movement from the bed caught her attention.

Rachel lay sprawled on the bed in all her naked glory wearing Chase's Navy dress hat on her head. Her nails were painted bright red, her hair was full of waves and the red lipstick popped against her skin. Even Kassie admitted for a second, she was perfection personified before the anger of Rachel trespassing into her home hit her.

"What do you think you are doing here and how did you get in?" She shouted at the blonde.

Rachel raised her upper body off the bed, showcasing her breasts. "I got word that Chase was coming back into town tonight. I'm here to surprise him."

"I don't think Chase wants your kind of surprise."

"Don't you ever wonder what happened on the mountain while you were gone, my sweet, tragic Kassie? How many nights Chase pined for you and you refused him? How did he take the news when you told him you couldn't have kids?" Rachel smiled as Kassie's face started to falter.

"Get out." Kassie's voice was deadly quiet but her eyes spit fire. "Chase would never be with you. You have five seconds to put your clothes on. I don't know how you got up this mountain, but you better start walking."

Rachel laughed as if she knew that she had cast doubts in Kassie's mind. "Silly Kassie, I have a key and the security code. How else could I have gotten in?"

The sapphire and diamonds sparkled on Kassie's hand, reminding her that she was Chase's home. She wasn't ever doubting him again. Lunging toward Rachel, she grabbed a handful of hair and pulled the screaming woman to the cabin door. Chase's hat fell to the floor as Rachel twisted, trying to get away, yelling her outrage. Throwing the door open, she shoved the woman straight into the arms of Matthew. His mouth dropped open at seeing Kassie's nemesis thrown out the door completely naked.

"Sorry, Matthew, I'm just taking out some trash," Kassie said, almost out of breath. Matthew frowned, took off his shirt, and covered the naked Rachel. Placing the woman in the car, he yelled for Kassie to set the house alarm. Just as they headed down the drive, Jake's car pulled in. Kassie waited at the door, hoping he had news of when Chase would be home. Reminding herself to ask Chase to change the alarm code, she went through Rachel's pockets and found the key to the cabin.

It was then she noticed Maddie and Joe in the back. Their solemn faces greeted her. Joe reached her first.

"Little Bit, maybe we should go inside?" His hand gently prodded her through the door.

As they made their way into the kitchen, dread hit her stomach. They were too quiet.

"Did you hear when the team's arriving? I was thinking of having them stay here and have dinner with everyone tomorrow night."

Jake bent down and picked up Chase's uniform hat and lovingly stroked it. A tear fell down his face. "Honey, there's no easy way to say this. The team's helicopter crashed. There was a search, but no survivors have been found."

Kassie's heart stopped. "No. That can't be true. Chase promised he'd come home to me."

Maddie's eyes filled with tears. "The helicopter crashed into the ocean. They don't think they made it out."

Jake's face was crestfallen. Joe was trying to hold it all together but doing it poorly.

Maddie placed her arm around Kassie as she had twice before. "Come, Sugar. Why don't you sit down. Matthew will get Em from school."

Kassie backed away. "No. They are SEALS, maybe they escaped."

Jake's sad eyes looked up. "Honey, they most likely didn't have time. Or they were unconscious upon impact. We don't know if they were shot down or if it was a mechanical failure. It'll take months for an official report…"

Looking over their mountain, Kassie took a breath. "No. I'm going to believe in his promise. I don't know where Chase is, but if he's alive, he'll come home to me. Because love is worth fighting for . . ."

###

Excerpt from Keeping Kassie

Chapter One

Kassie Stanton sat in her favorite reading nook looking out the window at the view of Serenity Mountain and the lake below. The sun was just rising above the mountains leaving rays of gold and orange, as if giving her a message of faith and hope. Taking a sip of her mint tea with honey, Kassie thought over the recent events that happened in the last two weeks. Her fiancé, Chase Winters, and the retired SEAL team that had saved her life were involved in a helicopter crash. According to reports, there were no survivors. Kassie believed otherwise. In her heart she couldn't imagine Chase, Leo, Saint, Taco, and Shadow gone from this world. To her, they had been invincible. They were the man that saved her and never gave up on her for even a minute when she had wanted to. She had to believe they got out somehow. There had to be a way. Kassie wasn't ready to give up, unlike some of her friends and family.

A week after they were informed of the crash, Jake, Chase's Godfather came up to the cabin with a pile of yellow packets in hand.

"Kassie, I need you to sit down. I've a few things we need to discuss. Before the team left, they each left a sealed packet in case something happened to them. Chase didn't want to worry you about this, considering it was his first mission away from you and Emma. We need to face facts. There wasn't any way they survived that crash. I was only to give these to you if something unforeseeable happened."

Kassie shakily took the yellow packets from his hand and walked to the couch and sat down. She placed the envelopes on the coffee table. The first one was addressed to her. Noticing Chase's handwriting, her fingers slide over the ink as if willing this to all go away. Picking it up off the pile and opening the seal, she found a bunch of legal documents and a letter to her.

Princess,

If you are reading this, I didn't make it back home. Inside you'll find that I transferred the ownership of the mountain to you in hopes that you'll continue to build the hospital for me. Your vision for it has made me love you even more than I thought possible. As you've written to me before, make something good out of something so terrible.

I can't think of anything worse than being separated from you. No matter what sweetheart, I will always be with you on the mountain. I want you and Emma to be happy. Continue counseling with Claire and go on with your life. This is the hardest letter I've ever written because I know just how much I have to lose. My parents taught me about love and loyalty, but I didn't understand the difference until I met you. You are my life, Princess. I'll live through you. Make sure Ladybug knows how much I love her and was looking forward to being her daddy. Please keep an eye on Jake for me. He's been a second father to me, and I don't know what I would have done without him after my parents passed. He's going to need you, Kass. You and Emma will be all that he has.

I hope that you never have to see this letter. Leo insisted we all have our affairs in order. It's a good plan but I can't think of being without you for even a minute.

Don't ever forget how much I love you. You were everything I wanted and most importantly everything I needed. I'm so proud of you, baby. Don't let my death derail you from life. Find love, find joy, find yourself, and know that I'm watching over you. I love you, Princess.

Love,
Chase

Kassie set the letter down and placed all the legal documents back in the envelope. She swiped back the tears that threatened to fall after reading Chase's letter. Peering up at Jake, she knew he was struggling with Chase's death.

"I'm not ready to give up Jake. I promised Chase that I wouldn't give up on him. He'd walk through hell to get back to me." Kassie quietly informed the distraught man.

Jake shook his head. "I know it's hard to believe. Darling, no amount of wishful thinking is going to bring our Chase or the team back. Two of the teammate's families are holding funerals for them. I think we should attend."

Surprised that the families accepted their deaths so fast, Kassie furrowed her brows and shook her head.

"It's only been two weeks since we heard about the crash. We don't even know what happened! It's like pulling teeth to get any information. They could still be out there, Jake. Just waiting for us to help them. They could be hurt or hiding. I don't know. I just think if Chase was dead, I'd feel…something."

Jake sat next to Kassie "I understand that you feel that way. You haven't really lived the military life. We know this is a possibility. Every time someone goes out on deployment, this is always in the back of their family member's mind. In a way, we prepare emotionally for it. It still hurts, but we know we must accept it."

Kassie stood from the couch and walked to the floor to ceiling windows in the living room and looked out over the mountain.

"No. I don't have to, Jake. We have to do something. I'm not going to stop searching until there is some sort of evidence that proves without a doubt Chase and the team are gone."

"Taco and Shadow's families have set up funerals for next week." Jake quietly stated. Holding his hat, he looked down at the floor. "I'd like to have a memorial for Chase at the top of the mountain where his parents and your baby are memorialized. Chase would want that. We could do it the week after next. I'll take care of everything."

"What?" Kassie was flabbergasted. "Jake, how can you give up so easily? You raised him! You should know that if Chase is alive, he's going to fight his way back to us. I don't want to throw him a memorial. I'm not giving up!"

"The town wants to say their goodbyes. Chase wouldn't want you to struggle with his death after everything you've been through. We need closure, sweetheart. It will help us accept that he's gone." Jake gently persisted.

"I'm not doing it." Kassie pursed her lips. "I'll go to the other team member's funerals and pay my respects, but I'm not ready to give up yet. I'm certainly not planning Chase's memorial anytime soon."

They had only gotten word from Rebecca Rhodes that the helicopter had crashed over water. The pilot and the corpsman's bodies were found. A couple of personal items from the team were located but no bodies were located. It was assumed they were gone.

Jake frowned. "Instructions for each of the men are in those packets. They knew you would follow their wishes, so I'll let you get to it." Getting up from the couch he walked out the door.

Kassie's unclenched her hands that she had unconsciously balled into fists. Watching Jake walk out of the cabin, Kassie picked up the phone and called Matthew Cartwright. Matthew was left in charge by the SEAL team leader, Derrick "Leo" Strong, to watch over her and Emma with Jameson Parker, a new man on the team. Kassie didn't know too much about him and he didn't really talk.

"Hello, Kassie." Matthew's voice remained polite and professional.

"I know you're picking up Emma. When you arrive, could you come inside with Jameson? I think we need to have a meeting."

"I have Emma now. I'll be there in about ten minutes." Matthew hung up the phone.

Biting her thumb nail, Kassie dialed Michael, Chase's friend and the pediatrician that cared for Emma while she was chronically ill. Michael and Chase were saved by Leo's team and later Leo recruited the doctors with the intention of using Serenity Mountain as a base for his black ops.

"Hey Kassie, Is everything alright?" Michael was concerned about how Kassie and Emma, Kassie's daughter, were taking the news of Chase and the team.

Hesitating, Kassie bit off saying that nothing was going to be alright until Chase was back home.

"I was wondering if you were in Serenity. I'm meeting with Matthew and Jameson. If you have a few minutes, I'd like you to come."

"I took today off work. I can be there in half an hour. Will that work?"

"Yes, see you then." Kassie disconnected the call.

Kassie grabbed her notebook and pen and began to make a list. Emma would have to stay with Kassie's godparents, Joe and Maddie, while she attended the funerals. Security would be needed for both her and Emma. James Stanton, the man that killed her parents and hurt her sister, escaped prison. He was also Emma's real father. Kassie knew he wouldn't stop until he got what he wanted and the last time they met he was adamant he wanted Emma. Kassie drew a breath and wrote more ideas on the paper. Hopefully she could convince the three men not to give up and help her find the team that not only saved her but had become her family. Regardless of their decision, she knew she would never stop looking.

About the Author

Cassie Colton is a new and upcoming contemporary romance, military romance and suspense author. Always an avid book reader and storyteller,

she moved from Illinois to Florida to one of the happiest places on earth. It was there, she found her love for making magic and happily ever afters.

She lives in Virginia with her wonderful family and amazing Golden, Leia. She enjoys gardening, flowers, cooking, and learning about bee keeping.

Her first series, The Serenity Mountain Series, is the beginning of her author journey. Detailing the lives of former military men and women that have lost their way and have found their peace on Serenity Mountain. Like every story, her characters have to fight through their adversity to find their happily ever after.

Like life, Cassie writes about character struggles that sometimes become dark before they see the light, but she always provides a happy ending. She believes everyone deserves to find happiness and love, because it is the only thing worth fighting for.

Cassie Colton

https://www.cassiecoltonbooks.com/

Printed in the USA
CPSIA information can be obtained
at www.ICGtesting.com
LVHW021134130224
771711LV00003B/424

9 798988 600732